PRAISE FOR HANK SEARLS

"Searls has a fast, punchy style . . . neither slick nor predictable."

—*The New York Times*

"Searls is a writer who communicates urgency and tension."

—*San Francisco Chronicle*

"A formidable storyteller, Hank Searls creates characters who possess the stuff of life."

—*Buffalo News*, New York

THE

PENETRATORS

A NOVEL

HANK SEARLS

B
BERKLEY BOOKS, NEW YORK

THE PENETRATORS was originally
published under the pseudonym
Anthony Gray.

This Berkley Book contains the complete
text of the original hardcover edition.
It has been completely reset in a typeface
designed for easy reading and was printed
from new film.

THE PENETRATORS

A Berkley Book / published by arrangement with
the author

PRINTING HISTORY
G.P. Putnam's Sons edition published 1965
Berkley edition / December 1988

ISBN: 0-425-11258-6

A BERKLEY BOOK ® TM 757,375
Berkley Books are published by The Berkley Publishing Group,
200 Madison Avenue, New York, NY 10016.
The name "BERKLEY" and the "B" logo
are trademarks belonging to Berkley Publishing Corporation.

PRINTED IN THE UNITED STATES OF AMERICA

10 9 8 7 6 5 4 3 2 1

To my wife and kids,
who deserve to live

Foreword

REGARDLESS of personal consequences, the book had to be written. It had to be written because ICBM warfare will make the Black Death look like the caress of a kindly Deity, and the acts of Buchenwald and Hiroshima seem those of rational men. It had to be written because ICBM warfare will never be anything but racial suicide.

Mankind is not lemming-kind, though. Not quite. And the Communists know it. In ten years McNamara's present policies will have painted us into a nuclear corner. They will have reduced U. S. manned bomber forces to a few hundred obsolete hulks and the Western bet will be irrevocably laid on Communist fear of a thousand gleaming missiles straining at the leash. The missiles are a deterrent we must keep. But it will still be a U. S. President who must decide in a moment of crisis that mankind is better annihilated than violated. Perhaps we would not choose, for friend and foe alike, death before national dishonor. Or perhaps the Chinese or the Soviets will simply cease to believe that two-car families facing a choice between beginning worldwide nuclear catastrophe or surrendering would prefer to die on their feet than to live on their knees.

The manned bomber can be and is a nuclear weapon, but it need not always be. It presents at least a choice between nuclear and conventional warfare. The ICBM presents none. It is inherently inaccurate enough to be effective only when nuclear-tipped. Today the B-52s and B-58s hurtle into the SAC stratospheric pipeline, north to the Arctic Circle, along the northern rampart, back to Lake Charles or March Field or Omaha. The aircraft are already tiring. The men are graying; the younger ones groom Titans in the earth. Watchmen's footsteps echo in the bomber lines of Seattle and Burbank and Inglewood. The workers have found jobs elsewhere and their aircraft skills grow rusty. If aeronautical engineers and designers dusted their drawing boards and began today it would be six years before the first Mach 3 bomber joined its aging sisters in SAC. In fifteen years there will be no aging sisters to join.

Department of Defense civilians argue that ICBM warfare is statistically inevitable because manned bombers can no longer get through modern defenses. The Air Force and the Navy disagree with their bosses. It is not the military man but the young Defense Department computer expert who fails to see the solution to the approaching ultimatum of nuclear annihilation or no war at all. No computer has an imagination; none can visualize a thousand ICBMs as an archaic extension of the Maginot Line or foresee that Mach 3 bombers produced by countries which will soon put men on the moon need not be lumbering, high-flying monsters crammed with sacrificial airmen.

The first high-Mach bomber, whether produced by the USSR or the United States, may be so startling in action as to be practically invulnerable to the jabs of the nation which has forgotten to build it.

It will be flexible and returnable; virtually a thinking missile itself. It will screen itself electronically, streaking at low level from any direction over and around defenses to the most precise targets. Loaded for bear with what we jocularly call "nukes," it would perform the *coup de grâce* in an ICBM war if anyone remained to care. More important than that is its more likely contribution. Armed with conventional bombs it would be our only strategic hope should mankind, as usual permitting his instinct for survival to restrain him from complete self-elimination, nevertheless express in the next ten or fifteen years his inherent tribal urges in his characteristic way.

If the choice between suicidal retaliation and surrender is to be avoided it must be now, for since Khrushchev's downfall there is no lack of activity on the aircraft lines of Kiev or Minsk.

That is why the book, as fact or fiction, had to be written.

—HANK SEARLS

February, 1965

Had the attack been real, it would have wiped out several major American cities, including Los Angeles, Chicago, and New York.
—*London Herald*, January 7, 1963, alleging a successful penetration of U.S. defenses by foreign bombers.

There has been no substantiation of such over-flights and these have no basis in fact.
—NORTH AMERICAN AIR DEFENSE COMMAND

"It's inherent in . . . government's right . . . to lie to save itself. . . ."
—ARTHUR SYLVESTER, Pentagon News Chief, before the House Information Committee

"Cock the gun that is not loaded,
cook the frozen dynamite—
But oh, beware my Country, when
my Country grows polite!"

—Kipling

PART 1

"Cock the Gun That Is Not Loaded . . ."

Chapter One

HOPING that the sweat running down his side would not fog the lens of the camera hidden under his shirt, Group Captain Malcolm Scott, Royal Air Force, parked his sports car in the Lincoln, Nebraska, municipal airport. He opened his door and unfolded to surprising height. He stood for a moment gazing about in feigned indifference, but he did not notice the green station wagon which stopped quickly behind a row of cars at the entrance to the parking lot. He closed his door slowly.

He was a lean, rawboned man in civilian clothes who moved easily and unmilitarily despite twenty years of RAF camp life. He decried his casual bearing privately, as he sometimes did his damnable, Miniver-Cheevy imagination, but at forty-one he had accepted the fact that there was little he could do about disciplining body or mind into military channels.

He had a quick smile but a thoughtful face which bore marks in repose of recent sadness not yet overcome. His father had been pure Highland and his mother Gordon: there was no mistaking his Scottish features, although he had little trace any longer of Edinburgh in his speech except when his smile grew soft and he lilted Burns or Dunbar or Walter Scott.

Seeing or indeed suspecting no one, he strolled toward the airport terminal building.

From behind the wheel of his squeaking green station wagon Major Zachary Chandler, U.S. Air Force, watched his friend leave the sports car and move to the airport building. Then he drove across the lot himself and slid into an empty space next to the familiar little auto.

It was a cool spring day of Nebraska sunshine, with the memory of a snapping cold winter in the northeast wind. Leaves and gum wrappers and a mustard-smeared paper napkin took wing in a gust and flew between the two vehicles. Despite the chill the major was hot and flushed; his hands trembled on the wheel and when he set the brake with his foot his knee shook so badly that he had to try it twice. Then he removed a child's car-seat hanging next to him, tossed it to the rear, and slipped across to open the door.

He was a tanned young man in khakis with command pilot's wings on his tunic. He had a round face and sensitive mouth. His eyes were bloodshot; he seemed tired. He hesitated a moment, then moved to the sports car and rifled the glove compartment. He found nothing but a few local road maps, which he checked for marks and replaced carefully. His hands were still shaking. He searched the compartments in both flimsy doors as well. In one he found a cheap yellow dime-store diary. With a guilty glance toward the terminal, he opened the book and for some time studied its sparse pages. Suddenly he jammed the diary back into the door compartment. For an instant he sat rubbing his eyes. "Oh, God," he groaned.

Very quickly he returned to his own car. He backed from the space and drove to the exit. Here he braked uncertainly for a moment, looking at the terminal in his rearview mirror, as if he might change his mind and follow Scott into the building. Finally he jerked the car into gear, entered traffic, and sped back to Omaha.

In a small office leased by a flying-school off the airport waiting room, Group Captain Malcolm Scott towered uncomfortably before the desk of the beefy American flying-school operator. The American studied the half-filled first page of Scott's brand-new flight-log, he toyed with a chromed model of a shiny lightplane, he tapped it with a pen, he scratched his nose. Through the open door leading to the sleepy terminal, Malcolm Scott heard an unenthusiastic female announce the arrival of Frontier Airline Flight Something from Denver.

"I'll tell you, Scotty," the American began. "Dave says you've been a good student. There's no question in my mind but you might be safe to solo. On the other hand, you got to realize our position, insurance-wise. Five hours dual isn't much time . . ." He scratched his nose again, picked up a microphone on his desk. "Dave," he announced to the terminal, hangar, and flight line, "office please."

Malcolm Scott, who had not five hours in the air but close to ten thousand, grew tired of shuffling before the Cerberus guarding solo status and dropped into a chair to wait. A young instructor with whom he had bounced daily in an aging Cessna over the past week strolled in and flashed him a smile. The flying-school operator explained with tact that the student was overly impatient to solo. He tipped the scales heavily against Scott, but carefully, like a sly greengrocer, so that he would not take his fifteen dollars an hour elsewhere. "I been telling him, Dave, with maybe three or four more hours dual in the Cessna . . ."

"He doesn't need it," the young man said generously. "He's as safe as you or I."

The owner smiled patronizingly. "Well . . ."

"I mean it." The instructor turned to Malcolm Scott. "Scotty, how many hours have you got? Really?"

Malcolm Scott looked him dead in the eye. "Not worth mentioning," he murmured. "A little dual time during the war, cadet in the RAF. Then the flap was over."

"You're a natural, then," decided Dave. "You should have stayed in."

Malcolm Scott took a deep breath. His answer was ready, but he had never dissembled well. "The machine-tool industry held more promise," he said carefully.

It was a lucky reply and held a gratuitous dividend. The flying-school owner was all at once more convivial. He glanced at Malcolm Scott's enrollment form, at his new student's license, at his flight physical. "They don't mention what company you work for," he hinted.

"I represent a group of British tool firms throughout the Midwest," Malcolm Scott lied, suddenly seeing a wedge. The flying-school sold airplanes. "The reason I'm pressing is, I've had the idea of purchasing a small plane for business, an Apache or one of your Beech Bonanzas perhaps. Your own chaps are doing it: they're the competition, you know?"

In ten minutes he was alone at the controls of the rackety Cessna, taxiing as clumsily as he knew how to the runway at Lincoln Municipal Field.

Major Zach Chandler clipped a plastic identification badge unconsciously to the pocket of his tunic as he approached SAC Headquarters at Offutt Air Force Base near Omaha. The building itself was a great, rambling structure of tan brick facing an oval lawn on which towered a glittering Atlas Ballistic Missile; hidden under the building lay the SAC Command Post, a tightly guarded amphitheatre faced by a glassed balcony in which the SAC commander and his staff sat during alerts. From the airfield behind the headquarters, flying command posts duplicating the functions of the basement nerve center took off at eight-hour intervals, each with a general officer aboard who would circle endlessly within sight of the building, ready to take over from his airborne "Looking-Glass" station if SAC Headquarters disappeared in a mushroom of nuclear dust.

Zach Chandler entered the wide glass doors with a crowd of officers returning from lunch in the club across the lawn, took the stairs to the third floor. The thought of lunch—he had missed it himself, acting like a junior G-man—reminded him that Pixie had asked Malcolm Scott for barbecued steaks tonight with the Epsteins. The prospect so unnerved him that he almost missed his familiar office door. He retraced his steps, entering under a hanging sign: JOINT STRATEGIC TARGET PLANNING STAFF. *Northern European Section.*

To Zachary Chandler the brains of the SAC organism lay here, not in the basement Command Post or in the sky above. They lay in and around his own office, in the secret chambers of the Joint Strategic Target Planning Staff. Here he, as Group Captain Malcolm Scott's assistant, and some 200 other officers and enlisted men of the Army, Air Force, Navy, Marine Corps, RAF, RCAF, and even the minor NATO nations worked. They were bare offices. They were not dramatic like the Command Post amphitheatre below, beloved of newspaper and motion-picture photographers. No cameraman or reporter would ever be allowed here, but into these rooms flowed all of the bits and pieces of intelligence that made up what the free world knew of Russian and Chinese movements, military construction, and intentions. And from these rooms went daily the "SIOP"—the Single Integrated Operational Plan which told a carrier pilot off Saigon that today if the whistle blew his target was Shanghai and his time over it 17 minutes 20 seconds past H hour; informed the commander of a U-2 reconnaisance craft from Okinawa that his moment to assess the resultant Shanghai damage was 8 minutes later.

In the office he shared with Scott he moved past the desk at which their secretary Lennie sat, went to his own place by the window, next to Malcolm Scott's. He tried to relax, but he could not. He looked around the room. From almost every file cabinet hung the familiar red-for-secret cardboard "T" with, at this time of day, *Unlocked* emblazoned on it. He found himself studying Scott's empty desk, wondering what wealth of information had crossed it in the past two years, feeling fear and excitement churn higher and higher in his chest.

He forced calm on himself. He marshaled the silent arguments he had recruited for the past three days to quiet his suspicions; when he had them all in order his fears were somewhat stilled and he picked up the publication he had received in the morning courier-mail.

For a few minutes he toyed with it. It was a Rand Corporation study: "Evaluation of USSR Interceptor Approach Speeds Relative to RAF Vulcan Aircraft." He himself had inspired the report on a recent visit to Los Angeles. Not a dozen U. S. officers besides himself would ever read it from cover to cover; but as an interceptor-intelligence officer of the Target Planning Staff his own interest in it should be passionate. He should have been as elated as a child at Christmas. But now that he had it in his hands, now that all the hundreds of man-hours and thousands of dollars in computer time were spent, he found himself unable to concentrate on its figures and graphs.

"Zach?" Lennie was looking at him from across the room. She was a dark-eyed girl with a slender, trim-waisted figure. She was very pretty, almost beautiful, in a sturdy Midwestern way.

"Yes?"

She stood suddenly and moved across the office to a file cabinet. She found a pack of cigarettes, lit one with great attention to the lighter. "Zach," she said again, not looking at him. "When does he leave?"

"Tomorrow."

"How long will he be gone?"

He liked Lennie, but something in the question annoyed him. "A couple of weeks," he said, more sharply than he intended. "Why?"

She looked at him in some surprise. "I'm sorry," she said quite sincerely. "I didn't know there was anything secret about it."

There wasn't, and he could honestly not have said why the question bothered him. "He'll be back," he repeated, "in two weeks." He smiled to ease the tension. "I promise."

She nodded. She remembered something, moved to her desk, brought him a sheaf of papers. "His travel orders, Zach. Would you check them for him?"

He looked them over; it took years to learn the language of Air Force bureaucracy and Malcolm Scott refused to do it. He searched for the paragraph that would entitle Scott to per diem pay in Washington and London, found it. It scanned all right. He leaned back in his swivel chair, stretched his arms and yawned. He seemed unable to face work today.

Lennie said faintly, "Do you think it's possible..." She had returned to her desk, and now she sat facing her unfinished page. She seemed equally unable to concentrate. Her voice trailed off.

"What, Lennie?" She was acting more strangely by the minute.

She apparently gathered courage. "Do you think he plans

on staying? Do you think he knows something he hasn't mentioned? Is he being 'posted' somewhere else?"

Zach Chandler's pulse quickened. "Why do you think that?"

She shook her head. "I don't know. It's just a feeling I get. I wouldn't be at all surprised if he didn't come back at all." She tried to hide her distress with a smile.

"What *basis* have you got for that?" Zach Chandler demanded.

"I don't know. None."

"He's going on a goddamned inspection tour to try to figure out how to utilize a bunch of tired Vulcan bombers over the next five years," Zach Chandler said petulantly. "Then he's coming back to his same bloody desk, as he'd say. Why do you think there's anything more than that?" He was angry, he found, and he could not have told why. "I mean," he asked more softly, "do you have anything but a vague hunch?" It was very important that he know.

"No," she insisted.

Once again he turned back to the document he had instigated. It was no use. The roar of an aircraft taking off over the building became an affront; the ripple of Lennie's typewriter snapped the thread of his attention. He found that he was waiting for Malcolm Scott to appear, dreading it and wanting it at the same time. If he could only think of some excuse to confront him: "Scotty, understand you're buying flying lessons. I can get them for you wholesale, down at the flight line." Or: "Don't you trust our maintenance here?"

But then there was the question from Scott, the cold question, perhaps: "And how did you find out?" Unanswerable. "Prying." If he had brought it up in surprise, at the first hint, before his imagination had time to toy with the implications, then he could have carried it off. But to face Malcolm Scott as a busybody now, he knew, was simply beyond him.

After half an hour with the statistical report he could stand it no longer. He had to talk to his wife, to share the cancerous doubt that had grown in his mind for the last three days. He moved to the clipboard hanging by the door, signed out for home.

"I won't be back this afternoon," he told Lennie without

explanation. When she looked up from her typewriter he saw that her eyes were red. "What's the matter?"

"What do you mean?"

"Are you *crying?*"

She looked at him as if he were crazy. "Of course not. Hay fever. I always get it in the spring. It's the pollen."

Lennie had providentially distracted Malcolm Scott in the dismal days just after his wife's death when he had arrived in Omaha. She had always seemed to Zach Chandler to be leagues below Scott intellectually, but perhaps she made up for it through warmth and affection. Or perhaps she was simply good in the sack. He was halfway down the hall before it struck him that last spring she had had no hay fever. And as far as he knew pollen could not get into an air-conditioned building.

He wondered why she seemed so certain that Scott would not return. Intuition, perhaps, but not to be scoffed at; he respected his own wife's judgment too much to shrug off any woman's insight. Whatever it was that had triggered Lennie's alarm should not be ignored.

But there was no way to get at it.

Nebraska farmland stretched beneath Group Captain Malcolm Smith like a green-and-tan bed quilt spread to dry in the sunshine. To the west towered an ominous thunderhead, castellated on top with ramparts of black and white. The Cessna heaved gently through a thermal. A wing dropped; Scott, searching the earth a mile ahead and 8,000 feet below, caught it instinctively.

He loved to fly, even in so light a plane, enjoying the nostalgic sense of cushioned hazard the aircraft gave him, but there was no time to savor it today. He leveled off.

The Russian intercontinental ballistic missile sites over which he daily pored at work distinguished themselves to the trained photo-interpreter by hash-marked, parallel slashes on tundra or forest. At his darkened desk in the SAC Headquarters thirty miles away, Malcolm Scott had for weeks been shuffling paired aerial photographs of a new Soviet missile complex at Nordvik. He had watched in fascination day after day as successive flights of U. S. Midas satellites sent home evidence of the usual frantic and efficient camouflage. The Soviet experts had as always healed the fresh scars on the barren plain until this week there was no evidence that anything existed beneath grass or trees but the soil of Mother Russia.

His search today was easier than his chairborne mission. He knew precisely where the U. S. ballistic missile complex lay: it was the 551st Minuteman Squadron of the 818th Strategic Aerospace Division, headquartered at Lincoln Air Force Base, adjoining the civilian field from which he had just climbed. The Strategic Air Command quite often regarded efforts to hide an ICBM site as useless. Malcolm Scott's duties gave him access to the location of every military installation in the United States, but a few questions to local truck drivers or construction men would have led any pilot to the same target.

He had been instructed by the nervous flying-school owner not to stray from sight of Lincoln Municipal Airport. For all he knew, the man was watching him now on his first "solo" flight. So far he had not had to disobey the instructions in the least.

He looked around to get his bearings. A few miles behind him lay the ruler-straight streets of Lincoln, Nebraska, the golden dome of the State Capitol glittering in its geometric center. The municipal field was still in sight on the outskirts of town. He glanced down, found immediately the radial pattern of a U.S. ICBM site.

He trimmed up the flimsy aircraft, slipped his good, battered 35 mm camera from inside his shirt, checked the shutter speed and diaphragm opening. Then he dropped the nose, opened the window, waited until the slipstream howled above the beat of his tiny engine. He eased the controls into a steep *chandelle*. He steadied the stick with his knees, and, hanging at right angles to the earth, quickly put camera to eye and pressed the button. He took a series of photographs. He varied the exposure on each. He dropped to 3,000 feet, centered his viewfinder on the complex again, and took another series.

He worked thoroughly and methodically and precisely; it

had cost him $75 in quite useless flying lessons from his monthly pay of 200 pounds to hang suspended alone for five minutes in the air over the missile complex. He was too Caledonian not to be horrified at the thought that it would all be wasted if the pictures were poor.

"The question is not bombs versus missiles. We are all agreed it must be missiles."
—ROBERT S. MCNAMARA
Secretary of Defense

"I don't feel that you are going to ever get to the point where you will have the same confidence in the missile as you have in manned systems."
—GENERAL CURTIS LEMAY

Chapter Two

MAJOR ZACH CHANDLER opened the door of his house in the Bellevue suburb of Omaha and sensed immediately that Pixie was not home. She was probably shopping for tonight's steaks in the commissary. So far as discussing his problem went, he may as well have stayed at the office.

He walked disconsolately into the gleaming kitchen. As always it was shipshape. He moved to the refrigerator and found a can of beer. He poured a glass, wandered with it to a house trailer parked beside the garage. It was a relic of their childless days; they had actually lived in it in Texas during flight training. Now, air-conditioned, it afforded him a summer study, away from Skipper's noisiness and Jennie's nosiness. In it he had put a desk at which he did his UCLA correspondence courses. The kitchen counter he had made into a workbench. On the counter stood an almost-completed model of the three-masted bark *Danmark* he and Malcolm Scott were working on.

Moodily he regarded the ship model. Scott had bought it last summer in Denmark for Skipper. For a year now Zach and Skipper and the Britisher had crammed themselves almost nightly into the trailer, plank-steaming, cementing, ratline-tying. This ship was no plastic, do-it-in-one-night U. S. model; this craft had to be built as a real one was, keel, frame, and plank. To Zach Chandler the vessel had become an albatross around his neck, but Malcolm Scott never faltered. Zach would grow tired and head for TV or bed, but his boss was indefatigable. Quite often Zach would awaken to the sound of the little sports car finally pulling away and find the windows gray with dawn. The next morning there would be great leaps in construction.

"Because he likes you," Pixie decided finally. "Because he likes Skipper. Maybe because his wife was Danish and it's going to be a Danish ship."

"I wish he'd get interested in Lennie again," he complained. "Or booze, or something. I ought to give him the damn thing back and let him work on it in the BOQ."

Pixie had shaken her head. "It's a good excuse to have him here. For him, too. We're the only family he really knows."

"I think he's working on it just because he's too stubborn to quit."

Now Zach Chandler noted a loose brace on the mainsail, checked the blueprints for the proper belaying pin, touched a dab of model-cement to the threads. Holding it to dry, thinking of the hours he had spent here with Scott, his suspicion of his friend became monstrous.

And yet ... *Too stubborn to quit!* That was the key, the sudden switch in Scott's character that had prepared the soil for the seed of doubt. Too stubborn to quit, but he *had* quit, and on a matter much more important to him than a ship model.

He had never really understood Malcolm Scott, but one facet he thought he knew: a driving determination to finish whatever he started. That was a simple, basic quality of personality that seemed to go with his strength, his rank, his Scotchness. Who was it who had drawn determination from watching a spider spinning his web? Rob Roy, or Robert Bruce, or some other legendary Scotchman. It was supposed to be the national characteristic of a people tugging their living from barren soil.

Yet until a month ago, in the battle that was rocking the

NATO world, Scott had been totally dedicated to his own point of view: that if the U. S. abandoned the manned bomber it was dooming the free world to defeat or the whole world to nuclear destruction. Scott had been fighting for the manned bomber single-mindedly for two years. Now he had dropped into lethargy, as if he had done all he could. As if, in fact, he had come to some secret understanding with himself.

Why? Orders to retreat perhaps, from the British Air Ministry? But if Malcolm Scott felt deeply enough about the value of the manned bomber, he would be perfectly capable of disobeying such orders. He recalled the bitter, angry moods in which Scott had glowered for days after the staff meetings which sounded the first death knell of the U. S. B-70 program. He remembered the aggressiveness here in this trailer with which he attacked Zach's own view, as a fighter-pilot, that no bomber could get through modern defenses.

And yet, he was sure that if he brought up the controversy tonight Scott would only shrug. His surrender had bothered Zach Chandler long before he had found the logbook, the map, the damned, *double*-damned diary. . . .

What was frightening him now, because Scott was an unconventional officer, a maverick, was that all his arguments had been based on premises which seemed to rise above mere patriotism. Like Soviet propaganda! For a military man, Scott seemed too largely to dwell on the horrors of missile warfare, which he had seen in London; on nuclear destruction, which he had evaluated on a British bomb-assessment team in Hiroshima and Nagasaki.

Zach Chandler never thought of the next war in any but nuclear terms. The Air Force existed to prevent it, but if it came it would come in a blinding flash, not with the crunch of old-fashioned bombs. Apparently Malcolm Scott found nuclear war unthinkable and conventional war quite credible, or the alternative of surrender if the U. S. could not fight it.

He was certainly acting these days as if he had removed himself to an earlier age in history. Or . . . to Russia?

Ridiculous, of course. And yet . . . It was easier to see a frustrated Malcolm Scott cracking and defecting than in sound mind abandoning a course he had begun. It was inconceivable even if he contemplated defecting to consider him as an ordinary traitor or as a convert to Communism. He had learned to like many Russians in Moscow, Zach knew, and he hated the mold which had twisted them. But suppose, blind with anger at the failure to get his military views across in the U. S., he had developed some sort of Messiah complex? A sickening flash of insight into Scott's possible actions—for Scott would always act, not sit wailing—made Zach Chandler drop the thread of rigging he was holding. He picked it up, snipped off the end, and touched it with another dab of glue.

Scott, if he cared to sacrifice career, reputation, and future, might single-handedly force the U. S. into a change in military doctrine. All he must do, with his vast and detailed knowledge of western war plans and defense theory, was to defect. If the USSR had full knowledge of present U. S. deterrent forces, these forces would have to be changed, and immediately.

Certainly the location of some ICBM sites were known to the Soviets, but just as certainly many were not. The level of warning at which ICBMs were to be released was certainly not. The targets were not. The USSR knew the strength and disposition of the aging U. S. bomber forces now, but they did not know, could not be sure, that other aircraft were not on the drawing boards.

Zach Chandler tried to think of the reaction. If the Pentagon knew that Scott had divulged the location of secret ICBM sites, had convinced the Soviets that indeed there was to be no future American bomber force, the Pentagon would act, and quickly.

From Scott's point of view, if he cared to martyr himself, the results would be favorable. The Pentagon, forced into a new set of plans, might well activate a manned bomber program. Scott's motivation might be a sort of inverse patriotism, or it might be irrational anger, or it might be a genuine belief that no one could win a nuclear war anyway, but from the Britisher's point of view it *was* motivation, and it filled in the one great gap in Chandler's mind: how could a man like Scott defect? Zach Chandler let go of the tiny thread of rigging on the model. It held. He sat back. Now that he had faced the shadows which had haunted him for the past few days he felt less eccentric himself. He was not trying to play James Bond, after all; he was a normally astute U. S. Air Force officer who had stumbled upon puzzling, perhaps compromising, items in his superior's desk, had followed him on an unexplained errand, and was simply trying to satisfy his curiosity before embarrassing the superior, himself, and their own superiors with questions. And he had been right not to let their friendship interfere. Malcolm Scott had daily access to material so secret that proving his dependability became a mission to override any compunction.

He heard the garage door open. Pixie was back. From the noise, he knew that she must have picked up Skipper at school. He would not have time, probably, to discuss Scott with her until long after dinner when the Britisher had left. Unless, perhaps, he could get Scott and Skipper working out here on the model.

He went out to help her with the packages.

"We can't buy 10 billion dollars worth of nostalgia."
—LYNDON B. JOHNSON, of further
manned bomber procurement.

"I am not doing this from love and affection for the
bomber."
—GENERAL CURTIS LEMAY

Chapter Three

GROUP CAPTAIN MALCOLM SCOTT unloaded his camera in his
BOQ room across the street from SAC Headquarters. He held
the roll in his hand hesitantly. He had spent two years as
British Air Attaché in Moscow. The habit of hiding compromising film was deeply ingrained, although surely in his position he had nothing to fear in America. Nevertheless he
stuffed it in a corner of the half-packed suitcase on his bed
before he changed into uniform for the afternoon.

He left the BOQ. He crossed beneath the silvery Atlas
missile on the velvet lawn in front of SAC, glancing up at its
80-foot length in passing. It was presumably only a shell with
the workings removed; he had noticed before that the small
vernier rocket nozzles were covered with screens to bar nest-
ing birds. But disemboweled or not, the hollow weapon
seemed to mock him. A familiar anger throbbed again in his
chest.

He entered the glass doors and returned the salute of a
lanky air-policeman, resplendent in scarf, sparkling black
leather, and horn-handled, chrome-plated cowboy revolver.
Eleven thousand U. S. airmen worked in and around SAC

Headquarters; the smart air-policemen epitomized their dedication. The American might be casual at times, thought Malcolm Scott, but he seemed to keep his ICBMs and pistols polished, as if this were the answer to war.

"Afternoon, Mike," murmured Group Captain Malcolm Scott, as he could never have spoken to an RAF airman.

"Good afternoon, sir," smiled the boy. "Sir?"

Malcolm Scott paused. "Yes?"

The young man dropped his voice. "You going to London, sir?"

Malcolm Scott had marveled before at the inevitability with which truth trickled from the closely guarded aorta of the Joint Strategic Target Planning Staff into the tiniest capillaries of SAC Headquarters. He nodded. "Not just London, Mike. All over England. An inspection tour of the Bomber Command. For a week or two, at the most."

"Give my regards to Piccadilly," the young airman said. Malcolm Scott nodded as he pinned on his photo-badge. He hesitated, wishing there were some way he could say goodbye to the young man, whom he had grown to like and would probably never see again. He passed on through the door.

Lennie looked up as he entered his office. She was sitting motionless before her typewriter. As he caught her eyes he saw such misery in them that he stopped short. "What's wrong?" he asked her softly.

"Nothing. Hay fever," she said, then, as if to change the subject, "General Younger called. He'd like to see you before you go."

That was odd. He had met Hub Younger in the corridor this morning with his retinue of staff officers and orderlies. Hub had said nothing except, swiftly in passing: "Good trip, Scotty. See you in two weeks?"

"And there's another message," she said with suppressed excitement. "See?"

He moved to his desk and picked up a memo clipped into a walnut-and-brass oversized clothespin, part of the desk set she had given him for Christmas. He stared, looked back at Lennie. She was smiling at him faintly. "He called," she said casually, "just after you left for lunch. That is, his secretary did."

Malcolm Scott could hardly believe what he read on the slip of paper. It was a message to call Senator Brian Holiday. What purpose a presidentially oriented Colorado politician could have in calling an obscure group captain in the RAF was beyond him. He had a great desire to find out. But for Hub Younger, Commander in Chief of the Strategic Air Command and Chief of the Joint Target Planning Staff, even so famous a politician would have to wait.

As he left, he noticed that Lennie's eyes were misty. It was not from hay fever. "What's the matter, Lennie?" he asked again, dreading the answer.

She shook her head silently. "I don't know. I feel as if you're not coming back from England."

He could hardly bear to lie to her. He wondered why she had become suspicious. "It's in my orders," he said tensely. "You've read my orders."

"I *wrote* your orders," Lennie said. "What I want to know is whether they'll be followed out."

"What makes you ask that?" Malcolm Scott wanted to know, his pulse quickening.

She only shook her head. She removed a piece of lint from his lapel. "I just *wondered,* that's all."

He left to see the general.

There were two ways to enter General Hub Younger's office; the two doors were symbolic of his Janus-headed job. He was Commander in Chief of SAC: all of it, from the ballistic missile silos in Idaho and Maine to the bomber runways in Louisiana and Southern California. He was also Director of the Joint Strategic Target Planning Staff. An ordinary SAC officer entered the outer office, where a smiling secretary announced him on an intercom.

But one privy to the JSTPS passed the first entrance and continued down the hallway. At another door he flashed a special purple badge to an air-policeman, flashed it regardless of how often he entered; flashed it coming, and flashed it leaving. Passing the air-policeman, he doubled back through a long conference room with a door at the other end leading to the general's office. Malcolm Scott entered this way as a matter of habit to see the Single Integrated Operation Plan before he faced the general. Hub Younger was perfectly capable of quizzing one on any of its ramifications for that particular day, apparently unable to understand why the average intellect, unlike his own, could not absorb the whole ever-changing picture in a three-second glance.

In the center of the conference room was a rather impressive status-symbol—a long table finished in what Malcolm Scott had come to think of as "Air Force oak," light-colored and massive. Windows on one long side of the room overlooked the front lawn of SAC Headquarters. The ubiquitous Atlas missile rose outside, its nose cone at eye level. The other side of the room was covered with green, electrically operated double drapes. Malcolm Scott paused to press a button and the curtains parted dramatically.

A giant transparent polar projection of the U. S., the USSR, its satellites, and China appeared. For a glance at it a dedicated Russian agent would have given his life. This chart, so convincing in its glossy, manicured readiness, showed how it would be when the whistle blew. One had only to draw the thick green curtains aside, study the simple coding to know: red arrows for Titan ICBMs, blue arrows for Atlases, green for Minutemen; red-dashed lines for B-58 Hustler squadrons, green for B-52s, white for British Vulcans. This is how it would be within minutes after the first Russian ICBMs tripped the Ballistic Missile Early Warning radar line girding the Arctic Circle from Flyingdale Moors in England to Clear, Alaska.

The concept was one of total annihilation, and the effort of keeping it up to date daily consumed the time of the officers and men of the Target Planning Staff. The planning was evident even on the chart, the tight, minute-by-minute scheduling that sent the SAC bomber force hurtling into the air before its bases could dissolve in blinding flashes. The meticulous work was apparent in the bomber squadrons which would be unleashed after all the years of practice by one word from Washington, in the carefully chosen targets for each of the ballistic missile squadrons.

Updated within minutes at every change in NATO's strength or bit of new Communist Intelligence were the individual objectives on the National Strategic Target list. The bulk of free-world military power, all of its planes and missiles, rattlesnake response of NATO to a nuclear attack, were controlled by this map. The Plan was daily changed; the display of it in this room was so clear that a child could understand it instantly.

Malcolm Scott's job dealt with the ends of the brightly colored lines, the color-coded targets in Russia and China— red for first priority, yellow for second, green for third.

Scott thought of the SIOP, as the Single Integrated Operational Plan was called, as a living if dormant creature. Only one man, the President of the U. S., could awaken it; then, after a three-hour nuclear convulsion, it would be dead. It was a blueprint of the first hours of action, predictated on a sneak attack by the East. After the first flurry of hostility, it would be followed by other plans, to be sure; but SIOP slept here alone, waiting for the President's Emergency War Order to trigger its one-shot, lightning strike and immediate death, like a bee that expends a single stinger and expires.

Malcolm Scott moved closer to the wall map. His eyes found the site of the 551st U. S. Strategic Missile Squadron he had photographed two hours before. These missiles were Minutemen, targeted on Leningrad and nearby Kostroma. Their time-of-impact was 1,832 seconds past H-Hour; impact at Leningrad was to be followed in eighteen minutes by a 6th Fleet photo-recon plane from the carrier *Bon Homme Richard*. At Kostroma, where there were supposed to be military installations, a Norwegian fighter seven minutes later would skim the tundra for a series of low-level assessment photos of the aftermath of the nuclear blast.

Kostroma? All at once he was waiting with Karen for the Moscow express in the Kostroma railroad station, and they were watching a group of Russian schoolchildren see one of their number off, perhaps to a summer camp. The parents and *babushkas* stood in the background smiling; as always, the adults' clothes were dingy but the children's sparkled.

He moved impulsively to the button controlling the massive curtains. He jabbed it. The drapes closed with the gentle moan of smoothly functioning machinery, working perfectly. Like everything American.

He crossed to the private door of General Hub Younger's office.

General Hub Younger was more than Commander in Chief of the U. S. Strategic Air Command and thus automatically Director of the Joint Strategic Target Planning Staff: the magazines called him father of the U. S. ballistic missile. He was a very young father. He sat behind his desk, lean enough to seem taller than he was, handsome and tan. His crew-cut white hair was as thick as it had been in World War II in England, when he had served as U. S. liaison officer and occasional pilot in Malcolm Scott's bombing squadron.

"Afternoon, Scotty," the general said. His voice was Midwest, flat, emotionless. He looked at the clock on his desk. "Where've you been?"

"Sorry, Hub. I had a little business to attend to."

He deliberately let the statement hang nakedly, as bait. Younger was quite likely to ask even an RAF group captain why he had left during working hours, as he would a young lieutenant who had tarried too long over lunch at the club. The excuse was ready—a matter of picking up a uniform from the cleaner before tomorrow's trip. But Younger did not ask. Instead he flicked a dispatch across his desk. Malcolm Scott read it swiftly. It was an Air Force TWX, a teletype message, and its point of origin was the Pentagon. It requested—requested was a euphemism—that Group Captain Malcolm Alan Scott, Royal Air Force, report to Washington, D. C., on the following day.

Malcolm Scott stiffened. "I was going anyway. But how long would this keep me?"

General Hub Younger was regarding him with steel-gray eyes. "Why?"

"I've got a tight program."

"You didn't know about this?"

Malcolm Scott looked at him, puzzled. "How the hell should I know about it?"

"Did you notice who originated it?"

Scott looked at the code at the bottom of the teletype. It was Greek to him, like most military alphabet soup. He shook his head. "No, Hub. Who?"

"That's the Joint Chiefs of Staff."

"Oh," Malcolm Scott said slowly. "Oh, I see . . ."

"Somebody up there likes you?"

"Perhaps."

General Hub Younger nodded. "The Old Boy himself."

The Old Boy was General Halstead Norwood, ranking U.S. Air Force Officer and U.S.A.F. Chief of Staff, fighting a last-ditch battle for the Manned Bomber Force. He had sensed an ally in Scott, perhaps, more articulate than himself.

Hub Younger tossed a *NATO Journal* across the desk. It was a professional military publication for NATO officers. "It's that damn article you wrote."

"Two months ago?"

"It's just getting through to them. That's why Norwood wants you."

But it was too late for the power of the pen. Hub Younger here and his ballistic missile cohorts in the Pentagon were already well on the way to defeating the manned bomber. It did not seem to Malcolm Scott that any amount of article-writing or speechmaking would force the Defense Department to continue its shaky strategic bomber program. It only remained to wait six or seven years until the free world would be dependent on a few RAF bombers and their crews and whatever rusting hulks remained of the once-proud U. S. bomber fleet. And, of course, a thousand or so blind, glittering ICBMs with their smell of Pyrrhic victory.

"Isn't the blessed general a bit late?" Malcolm Scott asked bitterly.

"Not as late as you think," Hub Younger brooded. He demanded suddenly: "Anybody in Washington contact you in regard to testifying?"

Malcolm Scott remembered the message to call Senator Holiday. "Testifying?"

"Before the Senate Armed Services Committee, for instance."

It might explain the phone call from the senator. He shrank at the thought of being called before a Senate Committee for useless days of argument. And his program in Washington *would* be tight; every moment was already planned. He wondered if, as a foreign military officer, he could be forced to testify against his will.

"No, Hub," he said, not mentioning the senator. Strictly speaking, no one *had* contacted him. "Nobody's contacted me. At least not yet."

Hub Younger seemed to relax a little. "If you *were* called upon," he asked quietly, flicking the magazine pages, "would you be inclined to disavow this?"

"Disavow it? Why?"

Hub Younger shrugged. "In the last few weeks you've become less red-hot on the question. I just wondered, that's all."

"If I'd come to my senses?"

Hub Younger looked him squarely in the eye and nodded quite seriously. "That's exactly it."

" 'All the world is mad save thee and me,' " Malcolm Scott murmured. " 'and sometimes I wonder about thee.' Disavow? Recant is more precise, Hub."

Hub Younger put the magazine exactly in the middle of his wide oaken desk. "I think you should, Scotty."

"That's quite evident."

"This article puts me in a crummy position. It put the whole JSTPS in a crummy position."

"I'm just a group captain in the RAF," Malcolm Scott pointed out mildly. "Does what I say disturb anyone? For instance, would anyone notice what a U. S. Air Force colonel said? When they take no notice of your own man on the Joint Chiefs of Staff? They never listened to Billy Mitchell when he was a colonel! They didn't listen to that Army Chap—Colonel Nickerson! Why does the thought of a mere field officer testifying strike such terror into your heart?"

He said it lightly. He got no twinkle from Hub Younger's eyes. He ached at the thought of how far apart they had grown. Hub Younger was the only person in Omaha who had known Karen; even now, with the apparently insurmountable wall between them, there was comfort in his presence, as if she were not irrevocably gone.

"There's a difference between you and the ordinary colonel," Hub Younger said sharply. "There's a difference because you're not just a run-of-the-mill field officer. You're an intelligence man. You're an expert on Russia. You stand somewhat outside my control because you're RAF; therefore they don't expect to hear Air Force propaganda. You speak with a British accent, which for some damn reason, on military matters, impresses the Congressional mind. You've worked on the Target Planning Staff for two years. Christ, if they can't give credence to a man engaged in picking our targets, who can they?"

Malcolm Scott remained silent.

"As a matter of fact," Hub Younger continued, "if they feel there's no unanimity on the team that puts out the National Strategic Target List and the Single Integrated Operational Plan, how can they assume we've plugged all the holes to start with?"

"You feel I've stabbed you in the back," Malcolm Scott observed.

Hub Younger glanced at the magazine. "Why'd you do it, Scotty? Because we canceled Skybolt?"

The U. S. Department of Defense had pulled the rug out from under the RAF bomber command by canceling the program at the very start of its success. Malcolm Scott smiled. "No, Hub. That was simply proof that America, like other nations, is subject to Hegel's theorems."

"Like what?" Hug Younger grunted.

"Roughly, that the highest law governing the relation of one state to another is its own welfare. All nations are amoral, Hub. They act only in their own interest, or, in this case, what they consider to be their own interests. I don't expect altruism or even good faith from the U. S. Government, or any other government, when it conflicts with the nation's self-interest. No Britisher does. No people on the Continent do. Americans simply prefer to fool themselves about it."

"Do we?" Hub Younger asked tautly. "You might say we've acted against our own best interests a couple of times to get the British ass out of a sling. World War I, for instance."

"Remember the old squadron saying, Hub?" Malcolm Scott smiled. "'If bullshit—'"

"'If bullshit were music,'" Hub Younger said grimly, "'I'd be a bloody brass band?' I remember. But national interest is beside the point. NATO is a team. Foreign officer or not, you're a member of my staff. And you still wrote this!"

"Because I thought at the time it might save us a horrible mistake."

"All right. What do you think *now?*"

"I think it's too late," Malcolm Scott shrugged. "You ICBM people and the Pentagon have decided that the manned bomber is dead. You're in a position to advise those who vote the bloody funds. *Ergo* the manned bomber is dead. It's your pigeon."

"Has it ever occurred to you," Hub Younger demanded, "that *you* might be wrong? That maybe you and the Old Man could ride your goddamned bombers into the setting sun and never come back and it wouldn't have the slightest effect on a three-hour war fought ten years from now?"

Malcolm Scott sat back in the leather chair, regarding the general. "You know, Hub, even as a second lieutenant you were never a very good pilot."

Hub Younger flushed. For a moment Malcolm Scott thought he had gone too far. But Younger seldom lost his temper and never stood on rank. Now he smiled coolly. "Maybe not. But I survived twenty-one missions."

"That's right," Malcolm Scott said faintly. "Wave-level, treetop missions too, some of them. Nobody's questioning your courage, or luck, or mechanical ability, Hub." He leaned forward. "But do you remember Chaney?"

Chaney had been Hub Younger's cockney navigator. One day he had stepped from the plane, narrow-eyed, red-faced and grim. He had marched to the squadron commander's office, demanded that he be given another pilot. "That bloody American flies like he's got a ramrod up his arse. Everything's by numbers: airspeed, altitude, 'twelve-point three degree dive,' straight-out the book. He has *no* feeling for the bloody kite. He's going to cop it. I don't care to be along."

"I remember Chaney."

"He was right, you know," Malcolm Scott observed softly. "You never had the touch."

Hub Younger drummed his fingers on the desk for a long while. Finally he said: "I'll accept that. I've heard it before. But what's that got to do with it?"

"More than you think, maybe. You're not certain *you* could penetrate flying a B-52, so you think nobody else can."

"No, Scotty. I just recognize a revolution in warfare; whereas you? You love an obsolete weapon. The cavalryman's attitude. You and the Old Man were born twenty years too late."

"Or else," shrugged Malcolm Scott, "you and the Secretary of Defense have allowed the computers to delude you. There is a human element in this, and I don't mean just in the cockpit. You still have to find a President who'll wreck the world by pressing the button, you know."

Younger shook his head. "If the RAF wants to go ahead and build bombers in a ballistic missile age, you're welcome to it. But as far as U. S. military policy goes, you're wasting your time."

"U. S. military policy," Malcolm Scott reminded him, "is British military policy."

"I wish you'd tell them in London," Hub Younger growled.

"I have a prediction."

"What's that?"

"If you give the other NATO countries a few thumps as you did to us with Skybolt, and if you rattle those bloody Titans too loud, you may find yourself left alone with your toys and nobody on the whole bloody street to play with."

Hub Younger sat for a moment studying the back of his hands. Then he looked up. "Scotty," he said softly, "they aren't toys."

Malcolm Scott nodded. It had been a poor choice of words. They were certainly not toys. He had been in London when the V-bombs hit and in Hiroshima after the atom bomb. Crude as they were then, they were not toys and neither were the offspring of their mating. Whether any but madmen could conceivably espouse their use as the sole weapons to prevent war was another story, but they were not toys.

Hub Younger went on: "The RAF can spend the last British pound on bombers, but we're the ones that have to keep the Russians and Chinese too scared to move. And we intend to do it with ICBMs."

"'Peace is our profession,'" Malcolm Scott murmured bitterly.

"It's all academic." Younger looked deeply into his eyes.

"The manned bomber can no longer get through. It's finished."

It was a flat statement, and behind it, Malcolm Scott knew, lay U. S. confidence in its new radar, in the banks of computers at Rand Corporation in Los Angeles, in the opinions of young scientists and mathematicians, in the Defense Department in the statisticians, in the practical optimists of the North American Air Defense Command who were utterly convinced that a manned aerial attack against the U. S. was suicidal and by extension that a SAC bomber sent against the Soviet Union was equally doomed. Malcolm Scott smiled.

"They said the same thing in the squadron," he murmured, "about the Copenhagen Raid."

"You don't fight World War III with the weapons of World War II," Hub Younger growled.

"Not if you haven't got them," Malcolm Scott agreed.

"After Washington, how about coming back? I'd like to know the situation."

Scott looked at him sharply. "What about England? Don't you want me to go now?"

"I'm not sure it's necessary. I never was."

This was a complication. Scott could not simply leave, he needed orders. He had used as an excuse for the trip the desirability of discussing new Russian targets with the Embassy people in Washington and the Bomber Command at High Wycombe. It was perhaps a flimsy excuse, for everything was targeted from here regardless, but he was stuck with it. Hub Younger had signed the orders, but he could always cancel them, too.

"*I* think it's necessary, General," Scott said carefully.

There was a long, alarming pause. Then: "Okay," said Hub Younger. "Don't cut our throats, Scotty."

Scott smiled. He paused at the door, looking back. Hub Younger was looking out the window. He seemed lonely. Malcolm Scott felt a tug of nostalgia, almost of guilt. Karen had liked him.

"U. S. missile tests have set a very pathetic record. It is a mistake to abandon . . . the manned bombers of the Strategic Air Command."
—CHAIRMAN RICHARD B. RUSSELL
Senate Armed Services
Committee

Chapter Four

GENERAL HUB YOUNGER sat behind the big oaken desk after Malcolm Scott left. He had a strong urge to call him back, to somehow patch over the strain on their friendship, for it seemed that the older he grew the less friends he had. And he was depressed, too, and filled with a vague unease, as if Scott had departed without telling him the whole story.

And yet the whole story was on his desk. He leafed through the article. The editor's note in the box at the top: . . . *as a member of the Joint Strategic Target Planning Staff for the past two years, Group Captain Scott is eminently qualified to write on the historical impact of the U. S. decision to shift emphasis from manned bomber systems to the ICBM* . . .

And the article itself:

The note of danger is clear and loud. Our prospect is clouded with threat. It is the certain threat of weakness in what the Pentagon likes to call our "military posture." To abandon the manned bomber in favor of complete dependence on the ICBM is to face the prospect of battle with a desperate enemy in a closet, armed ourselves only with a grenade, with which to blow himself and us to bits, when he has his grenade as well, but still has had the foresight to have saved his dagger too.

In ten years, if we persist, our military posture will be that of a group of nations crouching behind an "ultimate" weapon. The accuracy of the weapon will never have been tested operationally, but accurate or inaccurate, it is an instrument of wholesale destruction, unlike the precise, proven manned bomber which is capable of the most minute adjustments in desired effect. One wonders what the advantage of the ICBM is over, say, germ warfare? The very *use* of the ICBM we may have to forego in battle simply because our society is more complex than Russia's or China's and the enemy's retaliation with the same weapon could destroy us more thoroughly than we can him. We must keep the ICBMs, of course, but to depend *solely* on the ICBM now is as if after World War I the allies, to save money, had disarmed all their troops except the gas-warfare experts to face Hitler with nothing but weapons of mass destruction. . . .

No U. S. officer on his staff could have written such a paper without risking professional disaster, General Hub Younger wondered suddenly whether Malcolm Scott had cleared it with anyone in the Air Ministry or the RAF Bomber Command. Well, if the Air Ministry had not already stumbled on the article, they would know of it soon if General Hal Norwood and Senator Brian Holiday dragged Scott before the committee.

The senator, with the present Air Force Chief of Staff, was a solid advocate of the manned bomber. The odd thing was that if he met Malcolm Scott now he would find, not the red-hot zeal that the article reflected, but a sort of I-warned-you attitude that might well disappoint him. It was very strange.

Hub Younger found that a shaft of late afternoon sunlight had fallen on his desk, bothering him with glare from a pile of unfinished correspondence stacked near his out-going basket. His secretary was typing rapidly in the outer office. He swiveled his chair, began to lower the Venetian blind behind him. The nose cone on the gutted Atlas outside glowed with ruddy brilliance in the Midwest sunset. He studied it for a while.

Even now it seemed to him incredible, when he read newspaper or magazine stories about himself, that he was as much responsible for its being there, for there being any Atlas missiles, or Minutemen, or Titans, as any man alive. The struggle to bring them into being had scribed tiny lines on his face; had almost cost him his wife; had torn him from his son's childhood as effectively as if he had been transferred to some inaccessible base for a decade.

But he and the scientists, engineers, and other officers he had led, those who had not cracked under the seven-day week, eighteen-hour day of the infant headquarters by Los Angeles Airport, had won in the end. The Atlas outside attested it.

He saw Malcolm Scott emerge from the entrance below, pause for a moment, looking up at the missile. He wondered what Scott was thinking, then lowered the blind, turned back to his desk. His gaze wandered across the room to the half-open closet door in which his tunic hung. Four bright silver stars winked at him from out of the gloom, reflected in a golden plane of sunlight through the slatted louvers behind him. He had earned the stars so quickly, in the last ten years during the birth-throes of the ICBM, that they made him feel a sham posing at the apex of 135,000 officers, many of whom he had started with twenty-five years before. The ICBM program had given him all four stars. Soon, barring quite incredible political reversal, they would give him one more.

It was all he asked. Some of the more ambitious scientists with whom he had worked had, through swift foresight, amassed fortunes by organizing research and production facilities for the military revolution they began. Other had become quite famous in academic circles. Regardless of how the rewards came, in money or prestige or rank, they and he had earned them. Together they had developed and put into silos a weapon which, so long as the world believed that the U. S. had the courage to use it, could eliminate war itself.

But what if, as Malcolm Scott said, no one would believe that the U. S. would use them first? What if the Russians held back and used only bombers? For a strange moment General Hub Younger sat in utter stillness, as the steady typing in his outer office stopped momentarily. Well, he thought wryly, they better believe it, or the ICBM would eliminate war the hard way, by eliminating the participants. It was a considered risk, like all wartime risks, hot war or cold.

Suddenly great sadness struck him. He had spent time in Spain on reflex alert as a SAC bomber pilot; the Spanish had a word for the feeling of vague loneliness, homesickness, trepidation, that bothered him now. *Nostalgico?* No. He could not remember it, and there was no English word for it. Only the emptiness itself.

He tried to hurry its passage by concentration on the daily addendum to the Single Integrated Operational Plan. He found that with the exception of reassigning as a target a supposed USSR Intercontinental Ballistic Missile site at Igarka in Siberia from a SAC objective to a U. S. Navy Polaris submarine, there were no changes for the day. He initialed it swiftly.

But the feeling had not passed. He shivered a little. He wondered if he was coming down with the 24-hour flu. Or was it fear that the hour of nuclear reckoning was approaching, fear that when it did he would be as responsible for it as the Russians or the Secretary of Defense?

Reluctantly he rolled his chair to his safe, twirled the dial, extracted a thin red-bordered memo. It was the CIA report of "Operation One-Two Punch," a nightmarish Moscow rumor so highly classified that not a dozen Americans knew of it. The memo was braced with bureaucratic hedgings and ambiguities, staid with governmental clichés, but to a professional military man who had bet his country's resources on ICBM warfare or none, it was a fearsome document. He had read it twice today and a dozen times the day before. Now he found himself studying it again, trying to evaluate it without prejudice.

It was built of widely scattered material. Part was diplomatic gossip and the suspicion of two U. S. military attachés, one in Moscow and the other in Taiwan. Through its structure ran the testimony of a young Chinese diplomatic defector in Washington. Part of its framework lay in the fact that in the past two weeks Fidel Castro seemed to have become a puppet in the hands of his brother. But when all the ambiguities and guesses were eliminated, it was supported on three concrete pillars of cold, unavoidable truth. The first was a Peiping peace delegation in Moscow, hard at work and swallowed ominously into the Kremlin for days at a time. The second was unprecedented Soviet bomber activity from Leningrad along the Arctic Circle to Petropavlosk on the Pacific—and this he could see for himself from reconnaissance satellite reports and U. S. Air Force Intelligence. The third pillar was a huge Chinese troop concentration on Hinan Island opposite Vietnam.

Khrushchev years ago had seen the SAC bomber forces as a weapon Russia could never match. He had bet on ICBMs and the U. S. had checkmated him here, too. But Khrushchev had hedged, perhaps under pressure of Marshal Sokolov, while the U. S. had gone all the way. The USSR bomber program might have slowed temporarily but now with Khrushchev gone and the marshal stronger than ever, Soviet bomber forces must be growing by the week.

Hub Younger wondered if he himself and the Defense Department had prepared their country for a war that could never be fought and neglected one that surely would. If there was any prospect of victory in an ICBM war it must go to the side which first pushed the button. The U. S. might never do so, but when all the verbiage was cleared away, U. S. defense policy rested after all on the hope that the Russians falsely feared that America would start a nuclear war.

If the Soviets had lost this fear, or if as Malcolm Scott said it had never really existed at all; if they had reached superiority in bomber forces and began conventional warfare—

Angrily he turned back to the safe, threw the memo inside. He whirled the dial. The report was secret not for any military purpose, since the Russians obviously knew what they were planning. It was secret because the Administration might be embarrassed by the thin ice on which its defense policy skated. As a military man Hub Younger disliked the prostitution of military security for political purposes. It seemed more common all the time.

He heard his secretary making preparations to leave, recognized the familiar rustle of her typewriter cover as she put the machine to bed for the night, the *rumble—clunk* of the secret file cabinets as she closed them, the snap of the iron bars dropping into their slots, the click of the padlock securing them.

Then he heard Emerson, the air-policeman, rattling the drawers to make sure that they were indeed locked. He decided to go home, swing a golf club in the back yard until it was time to get ready to go to dinner; he was entertaining the Mayor of Omaha and the Lieutenant Governor of Nebraska, and the relaxation would sharpen his wits.

He put on his coat, informed the Combat Operation Center that he was leaving the building and could be reached via car radio for the next five minutes. He locked his desk and left his office. Passing through the conference room he slid open the curtains on the wall to make sure the SIOP was up to date. It was, of course. He hesitated before closing the curtain, moved again by the vague apprehension of omission, or even guilt.

He shook it off. Damn it, all the cards were played. He hated to rely on a one-weapon system, an "ultimate" weapon, as much as anyone else. He fell back on the final truth with relief. No matter what arguments the manned bomber people pushed, statistics and war games proved that in the long run the manned bomber could not get through.

Group Captain Malcolm Scott surveyed the two piles of possessions on the bed of his room in the BOQ. One was large; the other small, for packing. To avoid suspicion he could take only what the ordinary officer leaving on two weeks' temporary duty would take; the rest he must leave. God knew what would become of it: the old RAF sword, the summer whites, the crazy bagpipes Zach and Pixie had given him at the last staff party.

He noticed a box of letters. Swiftly he went through them, found a few in Karen's precise Scandinavian hand, written to him eight years before, when he had first gone to Moscow to check on conditions before moving her and little Dee from London to their Embassy quarters. It had been three months —the longest separation in their first ten years. And now it was two years already, and would be forever, and all that remained were a few laughing photos and letters in the neat handwriting. Quickly he stuffed them into the bag he was taking. Then he repacked the remainder of the large pile into the bureaus. All of this he must leave behind. He wondered what would become of it, just how vindictive the Officer in Charge of the BOQ might be.

When he was through, there was only his suitcase and shaving kit and clean clothes for the next day. He felt under the shirts in the traveling bag. The small yellow diary with a detailed report of his espionage, his brand-new civilian log, and the exposed film were all where he had left them.

He glanced at his watch. It was time to leave for Zach and Pixie's.

> In minutes today's clear blue sky might become
> studded with the silhouettes of hostile bombers . . .
> bombers bent on unleashing a rain of nuclear de-
> struction across the country.
>
> —PRESS RELEASE
> U.S. Air
> Defense
> Command

Chapter Five

MAJOR ZACH CHANDLER slid his chair back. His barbecued
steak was only half eaten on his plate. Malcolm Scott, across
the table, let his eyelids drop in ecstasy. "Zach," he said,
"there's absolutely nothing like one of your steaks, from here
to the Argentine."

Captain Morris Epstein, balding at thirty and sallow from
too many hours in a football-shaped capsule 60 feet beneath
the Nebraska prairie, unsuccessfully hid an Arab belch of
gratitude. His wife Alice winced, arose to help Pixie Chandler
clear the dishes.

"Sorry," murmured Epstein to Zach Chandler and Malcolm
Scott. "Dyspepsia, or indigestion, or something. In the hole
we eat like pigs, you should pardon the expression. It's the
generator-whine or something gets on your nerves and makes
you hungry, and we never get any exercise, and . . . Christ,
what a way to make a living."

"He was an East Los Angeles social worker," explained
Zach Chandler to Malcolm Scott, "at about nine dollars a
month, and he never had it so good."

Zach noticed that Epstein's baby-blue eyes were on his,

strangely meditative. There was a moment of silence, and then Morris Epstein said, "Sometimes I wonder." He shrugged, called his wife, and arose. "Hate to eat and run," he told Zach, "but they're burying me again tomorrow. Some day the relief crew is going to get there and find me gone."

"With the tomb open," Zach suggested. "Maybe Easter?"

"Could be." Morris and Alice Epstein left, and Zach Chandler regarded his coffee distastefully. He had hardly eaten; whether reason or hysteria lay behind his suspicions of Malcolm Scott, the effect was certainly dietetic. Perhaps Morris Epstein would have welcomed his burden: Zach felt as if he were losing weight by the hour. Pixie darted from the kitchen to check Jennie's progress toward bed, her own cheeks red from the dishes, looking like a child herself. Zach had had no chance to talk to her about Malcolm Scott.

"Skipper," he suggested to his son, "have your Uncle Scotty out to the trailer and ask him to help you cut the rest of the halyards. I'll help your mother with the dishes."

Malcolm Scott looked at Zach quickly, as if he suspected that he was being railroaded. There were undercurrents between the two of them now that a week ago would have seemed ridiculous. Pixie sensed it. When she heard Zach come into the kitchen she asked without turning from the sink: "What is it, Zach?"

He put the dishes down, watching out the window until the lights in the trailer went on. In a few moments he could see Skipper's crew-cut head and Malcolm Scott's lean profile in silhouette as they bent over the model ship. He sat down at the kitchen table. "It's Scotty, Pixie."

"What about him?"

He found difficulty in admitting even to Pixie his fantasies of the past few days. And there was the damning admission to make, too, about the diary. He took a deep breath. "I haven't mentioned anything," he told her, "because I couldn't believe it *myself*. I mean, I couldn't believe that . . . that I'd be able to be so damn suspicious of a guy we like so well."

Sensing his seriousness, she sat facing him, her green eyes probing. "What is it, Zach?" she murmured.

He began reluctantly. It all seemed so trivial, and yet there was the golden mass of detail in the file cabinets; for precedent there was the British scientist Fuchs and the two defectors Burgess and McLean. It made him feel bigoted, small-town, Anglophobic, but there *was* precedent. "Last Monday we were working in the office. Lennie and Scotty were matching up prints—what you do is put them under a stereo viewfinder and if you have the right prints matched, everything's three-dimensional—a couple of old U-2 flights over the Ural Mountains, to check a batch of satellite photos that had just come in. Scotty asked me for our magnifying glass—we keep a big one in the office for detail work. I couldn't find it in *my* desk, so I moved over to *his,* and I was going through it when I noticed—it was at the bottom of his big drawer—this brand-new flightlog."

She was looking at him quizzically, as she might have looked at Skipper when he came up with one of his disjointed tales of the world of playground or Little League. He had better get to the point. "What shook me *is* odd, damn it. Pix, this was a regular civilian-type logbook, not one of ours. Not his own RAF logbook, either, which is a kind of sky-blue. This was one like a new civilian student would get at a flying-school, first thing."

"Maybe he ran out of room in his own log," she suggested. "Anyway what—"

"Maybe," he agreed. "But sticking from the ends of this thing, jammed into it, was a government form and a local flying map. Not a map he'd use when he flies the T-Birds here, either; not a jet map. A plain, old-fashioned low-altitude aeronautical chart. There was a square drawn on it, like you'd sketch out for a photo-recon pilot if you wanted an oblique shot of some target."

"But—"

"The center of the square," he went on, "was smack in the middle of the 551st Strategic Missile Squadron. OK. If he *wants* shots of our own missile sites, I guess he can take them. Well, I kept on looking for the magnifying glass, but then I got a good look at this government form."

He told her that it was an application to the U.S. Federal Aviation Agency for a Student's Flying License. The name filled in at the top was that of Malcolm Scott. "Now, what the hell, Pix? Why does he want a U. S. student's license? He must have a million hours in the air!"

She agreed that it was odd. Now he blurted out the real shocker. He had almost asked Malcolm Scott the question when his eye had fallen upon the address. He lived in the BOQ, but he had invented a civilian home. "You know what the address *was?*"

She shook her head. She had a half-amused, half-puzzled look; obviously, she did not yet share his alarm.

"The address was *our* address. Or, practically our address. Actually, it was two numbers down. On the opposite side of the street."

"Who lives there?" Pixie asked.

"Isn't that the Dopplers?" he wanted to know.

She nodded. "Why would he use that? He's never even met them."

He shrugged. "How many street names does he know here? I wish I'd asked him right there. I couldn't admit I'd read anything in the drawer. I should have, but I couldn't. You know what I mean?"

"I would have."

"Well," he continued, "I *didn't* mention it. I found the magnifying glass and I gave it to him and at lunchtime he took a long lunch. He'd been doing that for the last week, so I didn't think much of it. But I couldn't get it off my mind. You see, besides this, he's been acting real strangely."

"I hadn't noticed," Pixie said. "How?"

He told her of Scott's loss of interest in the manned bomber controversy. "He's like a kid who's been outvoted by the rest of the gang. The hell with them. He'll pick up his marbles and go home."

"What you're trying to say," Pixie said suddenly, "is that he won't be back from England?"

This was not exactly what he had been trying to say, but he had other things to tell her. "Maybe, in a way."

"He's *got* to come back," Pixie said with finality, "or it'll break Lennie's heart."

"That's another thing. I don't think she expects to see him back. But don't sweat *that*. I don't think he's taken her out once in the last month."

"Well, go on. Monday he was late coming back from lunch?"

He nodded. "By one o'clock it was driving me ape." He faltered, almost stopped. Then he went on: "I had to take a look at it."

"At what?"

"The drawer. The logbook. The map. The application."

"Why?"

He felt the blood mounting to his face. "Because, damn it, we're in the most sensitive office in the whole Western Hemisphere! Christ, Pixie—"

She was staring at him. "Do you mean," she murmured softly, "you've been worrying about his actual *loyalty?*"

"Wait. Not then, exactly. I was more curious than anything else. I mean, Pixie, honest-to-God! *Why* would a guy with Scotty's flight experience be applying for a student's license?"

"I don't know. What did you do?"

"I took another look through his drawer."

Pixie seemed to be repressing her amusement. "Oh, Zach! Not *you!*"

He was mortified even before Pixie; how could he have faced the security officer or the general?

"OK, Pixie. You know what I found?"

She shook her head.

"I found," he said dramatically, "exactly nothing. The logbook and the map were gone. Now, why were they gone? Why'd he take them?"

She shrugged. "You have to know why he had them in the first place."

"The reason they were gone was that he needed them over lunch hour. Why would he need them over lunch hour? It seemed to tie in with these long lunch hours he was taking."

"Oh, now, Zach! Not necessarily," said Pixie, but there was a hint of worry on her face.

"No?" He licked his lips. "Today—at lunch—I followed him."

"You followed him?" she gasped.

He nodded. "He left the office and went across to the BOQ and came out in civvies. Then he crammed himself into that little bug and I got in the Ford and—I almost lost him once, because I had to stay out of sight—anyway, he got on the highway to Lincoln—"

"I just can't see you doing it," Pixie exclaimed. "It's like a book by John Le Carré!"

"I did it," he grunted. "Anyway, he got on the highway to Lincoln. I saw him turn off at Lincoln Municipal Airport, and he went into the Terminal. There's a flying-school in there. While he was inside, I went through his car."

"Zach!"

"Well, I did. I ran across something else."

"What?" she murmured, in some dread.

He hesitated for a long moment. "A diary."

He had expected shock. But he looked into the broad, freckled face and found only understanding, and sympathy. "Zach," she smiled, "it's all right. You opened it. I'd have opened it too. Anybody would have, if they were that curious already."

"I'm sorry I did. But I did."

"What did you find?"

"It only started a few weeks ago. March 5th, as a matter of fact." He shoved his chair back from the table. "Just about the time he seemed to lose interest in everything: Lennie and the ICBM bomber brawl. Anyway, I looked through it."

"Was there anything bad?"

"I don't know. It was filled with things like . . . Well, roughly, I remember one entry: 'Unnecessary to prove citizenship in U. S. to obtain student license. Filled out form and mailed in this date . . .' and another one: 'From copy of *Aviation Week*, excerpted enclosed details of Atlas, Titan, and Minuteman sites.' *Enclosed!* Where's the diary going?"

"From *Aviation Week?*"

He nodded. "We don't try to *under*sell our capabilities. The whole theory of the ICBM as a deterrent is that if you want the Soviets to be afraid to start a war, you have to let them know what you have. But the diary reads like the record of a two-bit spy!"

He mentioned what he could remember of a few other sentences. " 'At Sheraton Hotel Bar, downtown Omaha, discussed location of 551st ICBM site with bartender. His name: Gerald "Jerry" R. Lister. He knows it is somewhere south of

Lincoln, Nebraska. Had a brother in the concrete trade who supplied the basic contractor.' And: 'Trucking concern at Dodge and 8th Streets delivered 80 thousand board feet of scaffolding to ICBM site on September 8, 1962.' And another day, something like this: 'In "Whiz-Kid" lunch counter, struck up acquaintance with Mr. Don Lerner, who indicated'—get this, Pixie—'indicated on a road map the location of the ICBM site, when I told him I was interested in setting up refreshment stands'—*refreshment stands*—'near airfields and army camps.'"

Pixie shook her head. "I didn't know that sort of information was available."

"It's available because you can't build an ICBM site without everything from a Country Building Permit to permission from Jimmy Hoffa. And the diary had more stuff, about flying lessons, innocent-sounding unless you realize that here's a guy who can already fly the crates they come in: 'Second flying lesson this noon . . . 1.1 hours.'"

"Are you sure it's *his* diary?" she asked practically.

"It's his handwriting."

"What did you do with it?"

"I put it back," he said.

She seemed surprised.

"I got shook," he admitted. "And what was I supposed to do, anyway? Keep it on suspicion and turn it in to Security and then have him explain it and never speak to me again?"

"Suppose he were a spy?" she conjectured thoughtfully. "Why go to all this trouble? Doesn't he have access to everything?"

"Everything! By just going through the files in his own office!"

"Do you suppose," Pixie suggested, "he's working on something you don't know about? For the Inspector General, or the CIA, or the Intelligence people, or somebody?"

He shook his head. "I hope so. Maybe the Inspector General's looking for information leaks. But why? These civilians . . . the bartender and the truck driver . . . are perfectly within their rights. Nobody told them they *couldn't* discuss ICBM locations. And it still doesn't explain the flight-log. And the map. With the square drawn on it. *With*, in the exact center, the 551st Squadron of the 818th Strategic Aerospace Division. Is he checking something out for British Intelligence?"

"I hope so."

"I do too. But still, why? They have access, too."

For a long moment the two sat quietly. The electric clock on the wall hummed. "You like him a lot," Pixie murmured.

"Yes. But he scares me, too. He's so busy seeing past the trees into the forest he makes you uncomfortable sometimes. He never figures anything quite the way other people do. And he's so smart—so *damn* smart."

"You don't really think he's doing a job for the Inspector General, do you?" she asked. "Do you, Zach?"

"No," he said finally.

"Or picking up something for British Intelligence?"

"All officers in foreign commands," he began hopefully, "do that sort of thing. *Especially* the British. It's not impossible . . ."

She was shaking her head. "But you don't really think so, do you, Zach?"

"No," he admitted in a hollow voice.

"What you're *really* worried about," she said softly, "is that he might be planning to defect."

Now that the word was out it seemed to echo in the kitchen. So she did not think it ridiculous. Perhaps he was not losing his mind after all. He knew that Malcolm Scott must have had the closest possible scrutiny before assignment to the JSTPS. But he knew that to have a man in a job so sensitive —and it was one of the four or five most critical in the Western Hemisphere—would be worth any extreme to the Communist world.

"Planning to defect . . ." he murmured thoughtfully. "Yes. I guess that's why I've been playing cops-and-robbers. That's it, all right."

"There's only one thing you can do."

"What's that?"

"Ask him to explain. Ask him about the things you found. Not as if you're suspicious. Just curious."

"I'm damned if I'll admit I looked into his diary!"

"Don't. Ask him about the flight-log. You couldn't help seeing it!"

"I will," he decided. "Tonight."

Malcolm Scott sat in the trailer inspecting the little ship. He ran his hand down the hull, smiling faintly. It was a good job, within a few hours of completion. He felt like a father: had it not been for him the little model would never have been created.

He had once seen the actual ship in Copenhagen; Karen's brother, a Danish naval reservist, had escorted them through the gates to the Copenhagen Navy Yard and aboard the vessel. She was not nearly as old a ship as she looked, really. She had been constructed in the 30's as a training craft for the Danish Merchant Service, but no three-masted bark could seem anything but a page from a history book. Karen had been fascinated by it too; they had marveled at the fine Scandinavian workmanship on the rails and the decks and the solid bulkheads. Stroking its tiny replica, he felt very close to her. The door opened and Zach Chandler climbed into the trailer and sent Skipper to bed.

"She's a credit to you both," Scott said.

"To you mostly." Zach Chandler seemed preoccupied. He stretched rather elaborately, as if something were on his mind. "I'm going to liberate her from Skipper and put her on the mantel."

Malcolm Scott's eyebrows shot up. It suddenly seemed very important to him that Skipper have the boat. "No. I want the boy to have her. After all, it was a present from me to him." There was a farewell sound to the demand that made him suddenly fear he had given himself away.

But Zach Chandler seemed not to have noticed. "By the time you come back," he said offhandedly, "he'll be on an airplane kick. In fact, when he is, you know what I'm thinking of doing?"

"What?"

"What do you think about buying him some flying lessons? I wonder if there's a minimum age limit? For a student's license?"

There was a curious emphasis on the last two words. Malcolm Scott's heart thumped. If he had been strapped to a lie detector the needle would be jumping. Swiftly, he tried to face the problem. Either Zach Chandler had brought up the subject by sheer coincidence or by design. Suppose he had stumbled upon something, was embarrassed to ask directly, and had simply taken this method of introducing it? It was an illogical, hurried gambit, for Skipper was obviously far too young to learn to fly.

"You know," Zach was stumbling onward, "their reflexes are so easy to train at his age. You know how well coordinated he is. What do you think of it?"

Malcolm Scott took the plunge. "It's strange that you should mention that subject. You know, I've been making a bit of a study on civilian flying."

"You have?" Zach Chandler asked sharply.

"Yes." Malcolm Scott nodded. "Did you know I'm thinking of retiring?"

Zach Chandler gaped. *"Retiring?"*

He had really thrown him a curve, as the American would have said. "That's right. I'm forty-one. I've been in twenty years. I can draw a thousand pounds a year for the rest of my life. That and what I have put away could start me in business. I'd be quite comfortable."

Zach Chandler was staring at him incredulously. "Scotty, for God's sake! Are you letting this manned bomber thing drive you out of the service? My God, it isn't the end of the world! Everybody has to take a licking once in a while!"

Scott decided to play the part to the hilt. He had been called a cavalryman so often that he might as well assume the role. "It isn't that, Zach," he went on with Colonel Blimp pomposity. "It's that I just don't see any future in a service which will one day ask nothing of me but the strength to lift a red telephone and the courage to press a button."

Zachary Chandler shook his head unbelievingly. "Which service are you talking about? The RAF isn't in the ballistic missile business! Hell, Scotty, even the U. S. will have manned bombers for the next ten years! We're not taking them out and burning them, you know!"

"You may well be, if things go on as they are."

"Balls!"

"I'm quite serious, Zach. Anyway, what the hell's the use of buggering about in the wild blue yonder in a weapons system everybody says is obsolete? Putting in your time, as you'd say. Not me. I'm a pilot and if our air forces are putting my machines out to pasture I'll find another way to use my skill."

Zachary Chandler could not seem to digest it. "You can't live on a thousand pounds a year! What's that?"

"In actual money?" Malcolm Scott asked dryly. "Almost three grand, as you'd say."

Zach shook his head: "It's not enough! You're too old to get an airline job! What the hell are you going to do?"

Malcolm Scott studied the backs of his hands. "You know, there's more money in Britain now than there ever was. Why not invest in a little flying-school? Probably near London, though quite possibly near Oxford. It'll bear looking into. That's been my idea."

Zach nibbled his lip. "I can't see you as a civilian."

"Can't you? Well, at any rate, I've done this much about it. Your chaps here are the old pros at this sort of thing. So I decided to get a student's-eye view of a typical American flying-school. Didn't tell them I'd flown—even gave them a civilian address. I had five or six hours dual. I think I learned a lot."

From the relief that burst over Zach Chandler's face Malcolm Scott knew that somehow, incredibly, the American had stumbled upon the facts. Perhaps he or someone else had seen him taxiing the little Cessna with his instructor. Or perhaps Lennie had glimpsed his logbook or license application before he thought better of it and began to keep it in his room at the BOQ. There was no doubt that Zach Chandler knew; his face was easy to read.

His approach was something to remember, too. For Zach had not brought it up in his usual straightforward manner; he had acted most obliquely. Scott, inconsistently, felt a tug of disappointment. The young man did not trust him, quite. The feeling was ridiculous in the light of what he was going to do, but he could not help it.

And there was another problem facing him. He had apparently underestimated Zach's curiosity. If the American had somehow stumbled across a clue that he was taking the flying lessons, he may have blundered onto something else. He hoped not; he thought not. There was no apparent relation between his trips to Lincoln Municipal Field and his meanderings in Omaha, posing as a British civilian trying to buy business properties. At any rate he must assume Zach's innocence, for there was no way to explain the latter anyway.

He would have to leave it as it was; once he was out of the United States, there was little possibility of his plan leaking out. He thought of the delay he faced in Washington, and felt a flare of irritation. He could have been in London in two days had it not been for the damned article. He stretched and stood up, taking a last look at the *Danmark*.

"Be sure she's finished when I get back," he said.

Zach Chandler's eyes were steady on his face. "Two weeks?" he wanted to know.

There was an undercurrent in his voice that alarmed Malcolm Scott even further. "That's right, two weeks. Why?"

Zach said slowly, "Lennie seemed to think you might be gone longer. She even seemed to think you might not be back at all."

"Why the hell should she think that?" Malcolm Scott asked with asperity.

"I don't' know, Scotty. You know how women are."

Malcolm Scott decided to shrug it off. "Well, two weeks is what my orders say. I'm not used to having them changed."

They flicked out the light in the trailer. Malcolm Scott said goodbye to Pixie with inward regret and to Skipper with real agony. He wished that he could take a last look at Jennie sleeping in the nursery, but it would only arouse more suspicion in Zach Chandler's mind. Then he was roaring down the winding residential street in vague discomfort. He wondered how good a spy he was making.

Zach Chandler sat on his bed. He was tired, but he was restless as well. He fought a temptation to raid the icebox and take his mind off the thoughts that were still troubling him. Pixie was in the bathroom, getting ready for bed.

"Anyway," he said to her through the half-open door, "I know why he's taking flying lessons."

Pixie appeared, wearing a lime-green nightgown that matched her eyes. He had been so troubled over the past few days by Malcolm Scott's mysterious activities that he had hardly touched her. Now he decided that he wanted her very badly.

"What about the diary?" she wanted to know.

"You know," Zach murmured thoughtfully, staring into space, "that might not mean anything. He's a bachelor, he had nothing to do but roll around town. Don't forget, to a Britisher the local pub is a clubhouse; he's used to that. He's just striking up conversations with people around town, and it amuses him to find out how much they know about the missile bases. He keeps a diary, so he writes down everything that happens to him."

She inspected a toenail, decided that it would do. She slipped into bed, turned out her bedside light.

"You're right, Zach," she said. "Let's forget it."

He got into bed himself. He let his finger outline the trace of her ear.

"What about the map with the square drawn on it?" she spoke from the darkness.

He was suddenly hit by inspiration. "You know what it is?"

"What?"

"It's the local flying area around Lincoln Municipal! Every flying-school has them! I'll bet his instructor out there made him draw it on a map, so when he soloed he wouldn't go far. The solo area just *happened* to include the damn missile site!" He was happy with the explanation, and he let his hand trace the curve of her cheek to her soft, warm mouth.

"Good," she said. He felt her fingers, gentle and tender, upon his own. "But Zach?"

"What?"

"Those lessons were expensive, weren't they?"

"They're an investment! If he's going to start a flying-school . . ."

"He wouldn't learn anything about the instructor's teaching techniques flying alone. Why would he solo? Why wouldn't he quit before he had to pay for a solo?"

He thought for a moment, suddenly had it. "He never *said* he soloed," he remembered triumphantly. "He specifically said 'five or six hours *dual!*' They had him draw the local area because he was *about* to solo, but he damn sure didn't solo!"

"Then maybe you can concentrate on something else," she suggested. "Just for a little while."

He reached out and turned out his light. "Just for a little while."

Malcolm Scott drove the little Triumph briskly through the dark streets. It was not yet midnight. On a sudden impulse he turned off the main street, moved through thin traffic across town, and pulled up alongside the home Lennie shared with her mother, a warm, intelligent woman who ran an Omaha beauty salon. There was a light in the living room of the frame house, and for a long while after he parked, Malcolm Scott sat indecisively, looking at it.

He would see Lennie tomorrow in the office before he left, but it was not the same. Two households had befriended him when first he came to Omaha. Zach and Pixie Chandler had taken him in as if he were an orphan, and Lennie and her mother had welcomed him as if he were a twenty-five-year-old suitor instead of a forty-year-old widower. And yet, in two years he had not brought himself to ask her to marry him. Although Karen would have blessed any marriage which could dull the ache, her own image was too bright still. Two months ago, when the Plan had been born, he had stopped seeing Lennie. It was hard at first, but it would have been unfair otherwise.

But it would be more unfair not to see her alone to say goodbye. He stepped from the car and crossed the street. Mrs. Norris answered the door and invited him in for a drink, which he refused, and a cup of coffee, which he took, sitting across from her while her plastic knitting needles danced in the light of the tiny fireplace.

Lennie was out on a date: "With a fellow from the University of Nebraska. Not a student, one of the new basketball coaches. They went to high school together, and he just showed up here last week—he'd been in the service—and they started going out."

Despite himself Malcolm Scott felt a twinge of jealousy. "I see."

"And how have *you* been?" The question was fraught with implications. *We haven't seen much of you lately, and why? And do you think you can leave a girl for two months and come back and find her waiting for you, you cad, and why, why, why, did you do it?*

"I've been fine, Mrs. Norris. Rather busy."

"That's nice. Scotty?"

"Yes?"

"What happened?"

Unanswerable. He wished he had not strayed from the road to the Base. It was a mistake to have come.

"Nothing happened, Mrs. Norris."

"Call me Barbara, still. Something did happen."

He took a deep breath. "I'm too old for her, Barbara."

"She didn't think so. She thought she didn't come up to your wife."

"She's wrong. They were two different people."

"I'm glad you realize that. Because you're throwing away —you threw away—a wonderful thing. I hope you knew what you were doing."

I hope so too, Malcolm Scott thought. *I hope so too*. He said good night to Lennie's mother and left.

Empty inside, he sat for a moment before turning the car key. An auto drew up opposite the house. Lennie, silhouetted against her own door light, sat in the passenger seat: a tall young man was driving. He leaned across the seat in swift familiarity and kissed her. Malcolm Scott saw her hand draw down his cheek. Angrily, hotly, he jammed his car into gear and pulled away. He was halfway to Offutt Air Force Base before his blood had cooled enough for him to face the fact that it was his own doing.

"I guess we considered ourselves a different breed
of cat, right in the beginning. We flew through the
air and other people walked on the ground. It was
as simple as that."

—GENERAL CARL SPAATZ

Chapter Six

ZACH CHANDLER awakened in the morning more rested than
he had been for days. For a long while he lay staring at the
gray light around the fringes of the window shade. He probed
his mental state as a man might feel himself physically after a
hard run. Apparently he was all right. The cold sheen of
morning illuminated his suspicions in their proper perspective,
as pure idiocy. He almost regretted that he had discussed them
with Pixie. Thank God he had dug no deeper into them with
Malcolm Scott himself.

When he heard Skipper's alarm go off he aroused him, for
the alarm clock never did, and helped him with some arithmetic he had put off until the last moment. He wandered back to
the bedroom. Pixie was still sleeping. He looked down at her
for a moment, marveling at how childlike she looked with her
broad button nose and her full cheeks, her stubby little hands
balled above the sheet like a baby's. He shaved and showered
and laid out a clean uniform. Pixie chatted cheerfully at
breakfast, apparently happy that together they had solved the
problem; her mood colored his and he found himself whistling

on the way to the Base, actually jaunty as he entered his office.

Lennie flashed him an odd shy smile, and then she showed him a ring. It was small but lovely; for a wild moment he thought that Malcolm Scott had surprised them all and proposed, that perhaps his odd behavior in the last couple of months had reflected a struggle to bury the image of his dead wife.

"Lennie! What happened?"

"His name's Cal—Cal Frisby."

His heart dropped. Of course it could not have been Scott. Last evening there had been not the slightest sign that he was a man getting ready to propose to a girl.

Lennie went on: "I've known him ever since grammar school, only he went away, and he's a physical instructor at the University. Isn't it a nice ring?"

He looked at it more closely. "It's the most beautiful ring I've ever seen!"

"Quit it, Zach." She giggled. "But he was so funny about it. First he told me what he makes, and then what he *will* make when he gets a professorship, and then he came out with the ring. It was all just so old-*fashioned*."

"I'm glad," he said. He warned her that athletes were poor lovers, that paunchy majors were the best; she denied it and his paunch too, but through it all his chest felt empty and his throat was tight and he realized how much he had hoped that Malcolm Scott would marry this girl. *Damn,* he thought. Scott would never find another like her.

She seemed to read his thoughts. "Zach?"

"Yes?"

"I think you ought to know that I didn't exactly jilt *him*. You *do* know that?"

"I know."

"Until last night, he hadn't been around to see me for almost two months." For a girl who was announcing her engagement, her voice was rather plaintive.

"Until last night?" he asked curiously.

"He came past last night and talked to Mother for a few minutes. He left just before I got home." She grinned, or tried to. "I was out. It wouldn't have made any difference, even if I had seen him. I love Cal."

He smiled at her paternally, feeling old, hiding his disappointment. The buoyancy he had felt was gone. Why, after two months, had Malcolm Scott found it necessary to go to see Lennie on the eve of his trip? Suddenly depressed, he sat down at Scott's desk. Last year Scott had taken him on this English tour. This year the office was one man short, and Zach would have a double job while Scott was gone: Scott's, which was to digest USSR Intelligence and incorporate changes into the basic Operational Plan for northern Europe; his own, which was to evaluate information on eastern block fighter defenses and make evasive changes to bomber routing.

He studied a chart of East German, Czechoslovakian, and Ural Mountain fighter-bases. He wondered whether a large interceptor complex near Posnan had yet received its new Sukhoi fighters. If so, the route of an RAF element launched from Southern Wales to a Ural oilfield should be diverted to the west or it would find itself clobbered over Poland. It had been weeks since a U. S. feint had scrambled fighters along the Iron Curtain. He thought for a moment, dictated a top-secret memo to Lennie, and thus initiated a fake foray from a U. S. airstrip in Bavaria. He hoped that by nightfall radar stations in West Berlin would be able to tell him whether the interceptors scrambled from the Posnan strip were fast enough to be the Sukhoi craft, or whether they were still making do with Migs.

He hoped it would work. U. S. planes never intentionally crossed the border; Russian confidence in their caution was becoming so solid that he was beginning to suspect that the feints were producing no true effect at all.

Well, there was nothing he could do about that. He worked for a few more minutes, but the problem of Malcolm Scott's actions tugged at his mind persistently. Why would he, after two months, bother to call on Lennie? Unless to say goodbye? And why would he bother to say goodbye if he were only going to England for two weeks?

Last night Zach had managed to stuff all the suspicions into a dark corner of his mind, but one fact refused to be confined. You simply could not rationalize the irrational, and it was beyond coincidence that the 551st Ballistic Missile Squadron site should appear encircled on Malcolm Scott's aeronautical map and located in his diary as well. His distrust returned. He could not walk away from the problem. The stakes were too high.

"Was Scotty in this morning before he left?"

"He picked up his orders. He's leaving this afternoon."

"Did you tell him you were engaged?"

Wordlessly, she nodded.

"What was his reaction?" he asked carefully.

Her eyes filled unexpectedly with tears. "Oh, Zach, I don't think he gave it a second's thought. For the last two months he's been so preoccupied, it's just as if he . . . Zach, I *know* he's not coming back! I don't know *why* I know it, I just know it, that's all!"

It was enough. The problem could be evaded no longer. Zach Chandler, with dismal foreboding, stood up. "Sign me out again, Lennie," he said dully. "I'm going down to Lincoln. I'll be back this afternoon."

He walked across the waiting room at Lincoln Municipal Airport, entered a door labeled NEBRASKA FLYING SCHOOL—BARTON COLBY. As a red-faced, heavyset man at a desk looked up Zach introduced himself and told him that he was interested in beginning flying lessons for his son.

It seemed that Skipper was officially too young—sixteen was the minimum age. "But look, Major," the operator urged, noting Zach's wings, "nobody can keep me from renting *you* a plane to take him up. Throw him a few lessons to keep him interested!"

They discussed costs. Zach promised to think it over. Leaving, he glanced at an aeronautical chart, framed and hung on the wall. "I'm not sure I'd like flying a lightplane so close to Lincoln Air Force traffic. Where *is* your local area?"

The flight instructor shrugged. "We don't have one, Major. We just keep the students the hell clear of the Air Force traffic pattern."

Zach Chandler chilled. So much for that theory. "I see," he murmured. He swallowed. "I have a friend who came here for lessons. Malcolm Scott. A Britisher?"

"That's right."

"He just started a week or so ago. I don't guess he's soloed yet?"

The instructor's face shone with pride. "Yesterday! You know how many hours he'd had?"

"How many hours?" Zach asked dully.

"Not quite six! Less than six hours, and he's over forty, and he soloed: Can you imagine that?"

"Amazing," Zach Chandler said.

"You cannot hit imprecisely defined targets with a missile. Manned systems can use judgment."
—GENERAL CURTIS LEMAY

Chapter Seven

MAJOR ZACH CHANDLER parked his station wagon some distance from the entrance to General Hub Younger's quarters, hiding it, really, because he was uncomfortable at being there uninvited. Besides, it needed a wash.

He had wrestled with his problem all afternoon. Once he had actually walked down the corridor to the Security Office of the Joint Strategic Target Planning Staff. The man was a superannuated colonel, an amiable, flaming-cheeked pilot who had lost flying status from high blood pressure. Zach had glimpsed him staring away into nothingness, obviously waiting for an opportunity to prove his worth. He had found himself unable to step into the colonel's sight. He must see the general.

He pressed the doorbell of the general's quarters, feeling as he had twenty years before, a chubby Army brat in the San Francisco Presidio, moving shyly from one quarters to another, soliciting magazine subscriptions for money to buy a motor scooter. He hoped, prayed, that General Younger's adolescent son would answer the door—anyone but the general's wife Louise, who would welcome him effusively and then take Pixie's aside at the next wives' luncheon and hint broadly at what an imposition his visit had been.

Louise Younger came to the door, looking quickly surprised and then bland. "Why, Major! What brings you here this afternoon?"

They had met several times since his official visit, but he was certain she did not remember his name. He smiled, feeling like an ingratiating idiot. "Major Chandler, Mrs. Younger. I hate to disturb the general, but I wonder if I might talk to him?"

"Now?" she asked mildly, as she might have asked a small child who wanted a piece of cake before dinner. "He just got home, Major. Of course, if it's necessary . . ."

It was necessary, he assured her. She disappeared for a moment, returned and led him into a small study lined with bookcases, mostly, he noticed, filled with engineering volumes. In a moment Hub Younger, wearing a bright red terry-cloth bathrobe, stepped from a bathroom adjoining the room, accompanied by a cloud of steam. He closed the door, smiled in a puzzled way, and moved behind his desk. He sat down.

"Yes, Major?"

Zach Chandler found suddenly that he was acting out a nightmare. He was here after all to inform the Commander in Chief of the Strategic Air Command that he had thumbed through a fellow officer's diary; a fellow officer who had been the general's squadron mate in the war; further, to suggest that the fellow officer might be a traitor. He took a deep breath.

"General," he said. "I don't know where to start."

The general shrugged. "The beginning, I imagine. What's on your mind, Major?"

"I wouldn't have come to you personally except—Well, I know you and Group Captain Scott were together in England, so I guess you're one of his oldest friends."

The general did not deign to help him. "Yes?"

"So I think you'll be able to evaluate what I have to say better than anybody in the command. Otherwise I'd have gone to Security."

"For God's sake, Major!" the general blurted. "What did he do? Leave a file cabinet open?"

"No sir."

The general sat stony-faced. Zach Chandler felt the sweat rising on his forehead, but he did not think it proper to rub it off. "Is there any possibility," he asked desperately, "that Group Captain Scott is doing some work for our Intelligence people? I have to ask that, General, to know whether what I have to say is . . . well, fair?"

For a long while the general only studied him. "Let's just say, for our discussion here," he said finally, "that yes, Group Captain Scott is an old friend of mine. To my knowledge he is *not* engaged in doing anything for Intelligence."

"Or the Inspector General?"

"He's a foreign officer. I doubt if the IG would try to enlist him as an agent. What are you getting at?"

Zach Chandler sighed and took the plunge. "General, the other day I ran across something that bothered me. Inadvertently. Something in his desk."

He told the general the whole story, finishing with his trip to Lincoln. For a long moment the general regarded him with his metallic gray eyes. "What you're hinting," he said softly, "is that you suspect this officer of *what?*"

"I don't really know, sir."

"Of what?" The general's voice lashed out more loudly. Zach Chandler had never seen him angry; no one ever had. He was said to be so disciplined that he never raised his voice, but he was coming very close.

"Well, sir," he said as firmly as he could, "at least I suspect him of not leveling with me as to why he's taking flying lessons."

"And what business is it of yours if he wants to take flying lessons? Is that any reason to follow him around as if you were a goddamned private detective? Is that any ground for looking into his diary? What *do* you suspect, Major?" The general got up, walked to the window, looked out, whirled back on Zach. Chandler forced his eyes to remain on the steel-gray ones. "You're hypothecating defection," the general spat. "Treason! On no grounds at all! Against a man who's spent his whole lifetime in the service of his country! Why would he?"

"I thought maybe, to force a change on the Defense Department . . ."

"Now you're hypothecating fanaticism! In Scott? That's pretty stupid, Major!"

"I *hope* it's stupid, sir," Zach Chandler said, his voice shaky. . . .

"You found a logbook. He admits he's taking private flying lessons. You found a map, which you consider to have had drawn on it an area for photographs. Why photographs? Jesus Christ, Major, if he wanted to take pictures of an ICBM site, why not check out an airplane from Offutt and do it? Or have it done by the 1237th Reccy? He's got access to anything he wants! Why in hell does he fall under suspicion simply because he takes up a lightplane?"

Zachary Chandler flushed. "That, plus the diary, sir. Which reads as if he were making a report to somebody."

"He's a lonely man since his wife died. Maybe he *feels* like talking to people. And maybe he feels like reliving the conversations in a diary! As I said before, Major, it's none of your goddamned business!" His eyes narrowed. "Have you discussed this with anybody else?"

"No sir. My wife. Nobody else."

"Don't." The general waved his hand. "You've unburdened yourself. Now you can go."

Face flaming, Zach Chandler moved toward the door.

"Major Chandler?" the general said, more softly.

"Yes sir?"

"Do you believe that you may have outlived your usefulness as his assistant?"

Zach Chandler's stomach sank. His doubts must be ridiculous, since the general thought so; he had acted idiotically; the consequences to his career might be staggering; and yet the thought that Malcolm Scott would learn of his suspicions was the worst of it all. "No sir. Unless he's told of this, of course. But he's one of the most intelligent and inspiring men I ever worked for. I'd rather leave the staff entirely and go back to the Air Defense Command if I can't work in his office."

"We just may arrange that," General Hub Younger said. "And you may find you'll be flying F-101s out of Thule, too."

"Yes sir."

He waited for a moment, but the general said nothing else. Cheeks hot with shame, Zach Chandler left the room.

General Hub Younger moved across the room and sat on the floor in front of the leather couch. He hooked his toes under it and began thoughtfully, automatically, to do his pre-dinner sit-ups. He counted under his breath as he did them— he owed himself twenty-five of them, morning and evening, to keep his stomach flat. He did them with particular vicious-ness, angry at the major but mostly angry at himself for hav-ing let slip his defenses in the shock and allowing himself to raise his voice.

Chandler had angered him, he had showed it, but it was done now. Next, quite simply, he had to decide what to do about the young man. The JSTPS was certainly no place for an eccentric, or even a nervous old woman. Very likely the decision was a simple one; he could simply divorce the major from his staff, although already he had cooled enough to dis-card the idea of maneuvering him to an Air Force Squadron in Greenland.

For Chandler had, after all, despite an excess of zeal, acted from proper motives. The overzealousness was unfortunate, because what little he knew of Chandler he liked; he had always thought of him as solid and dependable. In fact, the former impression had lent a taint of credence to even the suspicions that he had aired tonight, which may have been the reason for his own shock and anger.

During Hub Younger's sit-ups, his eyes came on a level again and again with a picture of himself and Louise taken at the very beginning of the ten years which had changed his life. They were on what had turned out to be their last vaca-tion, stretched on the foredeck of the *Happy Hour,* company yacht of the president of Norco Aviation. They were bound for Catalina. Hub Younger had been thirty-three at the time, a full colonel stationed at Cal Tech for his doctorate in astrophysics. The face in the picture was unlined, the hair jet-black, and he looked at the time even more youthful than his age. There had been on that day nothing on his future horizon but a slow climb through the Strategic Air Command to general rank, someday a division, perhaps eventually command of the Second or Eighth Air Force.

But while they were on the Catalina trip a Hungarian-born U. S. scientist named John von Neumann had announced that nuclear weapons could be wrapped in packages small enough to hurl into space. The Russians exploded an H-bomb in Siberia. Sputnik was soon to hurtle overhead. No one believed in the concept of the ICBM, but a few cards had dropped from Air Force personnel computers in Washington. Hub Younger found himself an ICBM expert assigned to the Air Research and Development Command in a day when the thought of a weapon hurtling from continent to continent through space was a long-hair's dream, a science-fiction trap for a military officer.

He had braved the trap, had sustained the mighty pressures of the Western Development Division as it strained to narrow the missile gap. His command burst through the walls of an abandoned Los Angeles parochial schoolhouse, mushroomed into the rambling rock-faced buildings of the Ramo-Woolridge Corporation, which managed the Atlas and Thor projects, and spread tentacles to the sands of Cape Canaveral and Vandenburg. It absorbed three quarters of a million engineers, scientists, and military men in the greatest weapons-effort that the peacetime world had ever known.

The political battles with the Army and Navy, the task of teaming technologists, aircraft contractors, military officers, and politicians, had not bowed him. In ten years he had helped forge for his country a group of weapons that hung like swords over Russia and China as Russian weapons had threatened America during the critical days when the Soviet had ICBMs and the free world none. He believed quite sincerely, if incredulously, that he and the men who had worked with him and saved the Western World in their days of the hurried luncheon sandwich, the darkened conference, the unrelenting Russian presence poised to strike.

He had gone to Kelly Field as an Iowa-born youth in World War II with an image of clear-eyed Texan girls crowding around him in an Air Force club, of last cigarettes before the predawn strike, of raucous leaves in London. In England during the war there had indeed been some of that, as advertised:

he had welcomed it because he was human and needed it to dull the fear that rode in the cockpit. But those days, for him or for the new young men, were gone forever. Now, if it ever came again, it would come in a cataclysmic roar of unleashed LOX and rocket fuel, and in a few hours it would all be over. Remembering the CIA report on the Chinese-Russian truce and the imminent one-two blow in the Far East and Cuba, he shivered. It might be closer than anyone thought, though the manned bomber diehards would be the last to realize it.

He finished his sitting exercises, rolled over and began push-ups. When he was through he moved to his desk. It was almost time for his pre-dinner cocktail. In these less hurried days he liked for the sake of domestic tranquillity to stick to Louise's dinner schedule as they never could in California. But there was the matter of the suspicious major.

He had always been more engineer than military officer, even in the impossible RAF raids against the low countries. He had always found personnel matters more difficult than technical ones. The necessity to decide what to do about Major Chandler made him uncomfortable. But a problem was a problem. The brain was after all a muscle. Some people had better brains than others, of course, but it was quite obvious that anyone who kept up its tone by exercise could approach its capability more closely than someone who let it atrophy. He took a clean sheet of paper, slashed a line down the center. He had evolved a method of handling personnel problems—a mere matter of weighing the factors on each side of the equation.

The phone rang. It rang not only on his desk but in the back yard, where he often grilled hamburgers. It rang on an extension in the bathroom, although there was another extension not ten feet away in the bedroom, and in eight other places in the four-bedroom house. If he had not turned off his pocket receiver-transmitter before he laid it down, it would be buzzing for him too. He picked up the receiver with a chill, as always he must.

"Would you hold the phone, sir?" the Command Operations Center Duty Officer said. "Secretary of Defense."

And then Charles Van Ness was speaking to him, his voice pleasant but staccato, clear, and very precise. The essence of the conversation was plain. The Secretary realized that no one on the Joint Strategic Target Planning Staff, or SAC Headquarters, or any place below the British Air Ministry could conceivably have prevented Group Captain Malcolm Scott from having written the article in the *NATO Journal,* but military Washington and the Senate Armed Services Committee were shaken over it, the Britisher was coming to town, and someone would have to turn up to blunt his attack.

Who better, suggested the Secretary of Defense, than the group captain's boss himself?

Hub Younger expressed reluctance to testify before a Senate committee without more preparation. "Hub," answered the Secretary, "I wouldn't ask you if I didn't think you'd make your usual impression." With some irony, the Secretary added: "They tell me you've known this son of a bitch for twenty years. How'd you let him sneak into our staff?"

"I *asked* for him," Hub Younger said coolly. "He's the foremost Russian targeting expert in the RAF Bomber Command. He also happens to be a hell of a good Operational Plans man, and he's got more imagination than any dozen officers on the Joint Strategic Target Planning Staff, including me. That's why I picked him."

"I'd think," the Secretary said, "that in two years you could have indoctrinated him into our thinking."

"It's a funny thing, Van," Hub Younger said. "But maybe we have."

"You think so?" The Secretary sounded hopeful. "Tomorrow morning we're going to have a little battle conference back here. I'm inviting Alf Karman to give us the Air Defense Command picture. You know what?"

"What?"

"I'd like to invite your pesky Englishman, too. Do you agree?"

"He's just taken off for Washington now, commercial air. I don't know where I'd get hold of him," Hub Younger said, not liking the idea of Scott meeting the Secretary at all.

"General Norwood will," Charles Van Ness said wryly. "And I guess the general still works for me. Will you come to Washington too? By, say Tuesday?"

"Yes sir," Hub Younger said. "Van?"

"Yes?"

"Anything new on the other?"

There was a heartbeat's pause. "Nothing's changed. Raoul's still got the ball, Fidel's on 'vacation' in the Sierra Maestra. Nothing the CIA can put their finger on. Wait. Yes, there's one other thing. The *Red Star* ran a speech by Marshal Sokolov today. Nuclear weapons are passé. No further ICBM procurement. Tanks, bombers, and conventional bombs, now. So they have their own problem child, you see?"

"Their problem child is running the show," Hub Younger observed.

"So what?" demanded the Secretary. "He's wrong."

"We hope."

He sensed the Secretary's irritation: "Listen, Hub. If you're haunted by the ghost of manned bombers, forget it. The Sky Blue Yonder boys can still pluck at your heartstrings, because you were one of them. I'm not, and never was. Up here, the view's clearer. The manned bomber is a sitting duck."

"OK, Mr. Secretary," Hub Younger said wryly. "It's a little late to build a Mach three bomber this week, anyway."

"Yes," agreed Charles Van Ness. "It is. Goodbye, Hub."

Hub Younger held his finger on the phone, got the SAC operator back, and in a moment was talking to his deputy, General Hank Schwartz. He told him to increase the Minuteman and Titan practice launches from two to four in a 24-hour period, and to double the communications checks. He replaced the phone and sat staring for a moment into space. Above his desk hung a group picture of an RAF squadron, lined up beneath the wing of a Mosquito bomber. There were two or three U. S. Army caps at one end of the second row of pilots. One of them rested on his own callow head at a sickeningly rakish angle. He noticed with distaste that he was smoking a cigar. Next to him stood Malcolm Scott, wearing the Scotch fore-and-aft plaid cap he affected instead of the RAF visored one. Non-reg, even then. Out-of-step. Stubborn. Brilliant, sometimes dangerous. A fanatic anti-Nazi, then, and like all British, a quiet, fervent patriot.

To suspect him of treason was fantastic, and yet . . . A man could change in twenty years; a man could change in months. He began to write on the sheet he had divided, but now he found that he was evaluating not the major but Malcolm Scott. In the left-hand column he put down those facts which the major had presented: the logbook, the local map, the detailed diary. After each item, because the major could not produce them and might even have imagined them or lied about them, he put a question mark. Beneath the facts he wrote: *Strange recent behavior; unhinged by Karen's death?* Then: *Cracked up over bomber missile decision? Attempt to force change on U. S. policy?*

He paused for a moment, digging for further possibilities. There were others, even more nebulous. He put them down: *Saw buzz-bomb attacks on London. Member British damage assessment group, Hiroshima.*

Finally, with a sinking heart, he put down: *Duty in Moscow . . . Sees USSR objectively.* Then, slowly, he crossed out "objectively," and put "sympathetically." Finally he added: *If so, Operation One-Two Punch appropriate time to defect.*

There were items for the right-hand column too, undoubtedly outweighing the circumstantial evidence of the map and the diary and the logbook and Malcolm Scott's sometimes irritating habit of praising Russian society where he felt it was being unfairly maligned.

But after he had listed them—*Over twenty years in RAF. Cleared top-secret*—there was nothing to balance the black certainty that if Malcolm Scott defected the very foundations of NATO would shake. The man was an encyclopedia of western war-plans; the free world could recover more quickly if a Communist agent turned up on the U. S. Joint Chiefs of Staff.

"Oh, Christ," he murmured.

His wife called him to dinner. He started to his feet. Then he sat down again and picked up the phone.

Major Zach Chandler tugged the telephone from his daughter before she confused the caller irremediably. He spoke for a moment, replaced the receiver and returned to his living room. Pixie watched him closely over her sewing.

"Pixie," he murmured shakily, "that was the general! Hub Younger!"

"The hell with him," she said. "Did he apologize?"

"No."

"Thule or Alaska?" she asked, smiling weakly.

"Neither one," he muttered.

"Then *what?*" she demanded.

"He wanted me," he said, "to write down what I remembered of Scott's diary."

"And do *what* with it?"

"Lock it up. Just lock it up." He sat down, scowling into the drink he had left.

She put down her work and moved to him across the room. "Zach?"

"Yeah?"

"Zach, that's *good*. He *doesn't* think you've flipped."

"I wish to hell he did."

Chapter Eight

CAPTAIN MORRIS EPSTEIN, clad in antiseptically white coveralls with a blue scarf, sat in his lushly padded chair 20 yards beneath the soil of Nebraska and craned down the length of his green-tinted cell. He had swiveled the seat around from his control panel to watch the arrival of the cooks, as security demanded. He peered through horn-rimmed glasses past an iron cot facing a second panel and chair at the other man in the vault, his deputy Dan Frost, a bus-length away.

Frost had pumped the locking pins in the 10-ton blast door free. Now he yelled "stand clear" at the cooks behind four feet of steel and leaned against the door. He did not push. He never expended unnecessary effort, Morris Epstein thought enviously. Frost laughed at exercise, and yet his .38 pistol hung low on his lean hip like a cowboy star's. His own armament, no matter how he worked-out or how much he loosened the belt, cut constantly into his midriff to remind him that he no longer served man but Mars.

The door began to swing silently, its six monstrous locking-pins glinting for a moment in the light from the outer passageway. Outside stood two cooks with a gleaming dinner cart. They stooped low through the entrance and wheeled it in. Epstein watched them leave together. Despite the fact that at ground level above them stood a barracks full of air police, and that he and Frost at any rate could cover the entrance passageway without moving from their seats, it was a "no lone zone," never to be occupied except with a companion of equal skill: a precaution against sudden madness or, Epstein had decided, simply against an overwhelming desire to throw a switch to see what happened.

"Closed and locked," Captain Dan Frost reported automatically. With the door shut, in their steel womb cushioned against nuclear blast by four giant shock absorbers, no outside sound could reach them and the high-pitched screech of electrical equipment became bothersome again. Morris Epstein looked up at the clock. 2300 hours in Greenwich, England, and here in the capsule; 5 P.M. in the world above. Fifteen more hours to freedom. His impulse was to move to the dinner cart and distract himself with food, but Dan would order a midnight snack and if he could restrain himself for a while now, he might not be tempted to join in later.

With a sinking heart, he saw that Frost, as always, was already at the cart. "Creamed chipped-beef, on a shingle and crummy," said his deputy kindly. "Yesterday's roast beef warmed up, I bet. Cold potatoes. Rolls like rocks. Butter looks like oleo. You don't want any?"

"No, Danny," Morris Epstein said, trying to keep the irritation from his voice and the saliva in his mouth.

"I didn't think so," Danny agreed comfortably. "I'll just have a bit."

A year ago Morris Epstein had almost requested another partner because Danny had bribed the cooks to make cheese blintzes on the night he was starting another of his endless diets. The two had talked it over, fortunately, and Danny seemed all at once to realize that Epstein's concern was real. Now Dan discouraged his eating, or seemed to try, but food seemed interminably to be a subject and sometimes there was a gleam in his eye that made Morris Epstein wonder if down deep he was not as amused as ever.

They were as diverse as two men could be, and yet they got along well, as Epstein had always managed to get along well with those—policemen, juvenile delinquents, court referees—a little harder, surer, less introspective than himself. Danny was that: quick and certain on the console, beyond mistakes in place where a mistake could be catastrophic.

Morris Epstein became suddenly very conscious of the key, as innocent as the one to his house, hanging around his neck. He felt the familiar dread starting deep in his subconscious, and he fought it in the only way he knew. He stood outside himself and observed a pudgy, sincere human being, a sociologist by profession, putting in four years in the Air Force to finance his doctorate. If at times he felt dishonest in allowing the Air Force to pick up the tab in the mistaken belief that he would spend the next twenty years in it, there were plenty of others like him. And he had mastered the technology of death, as they had asked him; they owed him something for that.

He had no apologies to make to the Air Force. He had rented them a good brain and an utterly stable personality— both he and Dan Frost were checked once a year by a flight surgeon for cracks in their mental fissure. Even their wives were watched. When his four-year missile tour was over, when the doctorate was earned, he could resign without apologies. Socially, he had no apologies to make either. Peace was after all his profession, they kept telling him; international peace under the sword of Damocles was just as important as sociological peace in the playgrounds of East Los Angeles.

He was a small cog in a great machine, and he need not dread the turning of the key, for his very presence in the tomb, the very existence of a hundred vaults like his own, would prevent the keys from ever having to be turned.

So, then . . . the nightmare, the turning of the key, was all academic. It could never be turned, simply because he existed and both sides knew it. Somewhere under the Russian steppes sat a man very much like himself and so long as they sat thus, balanced like children on a seasaw, neither would get hurt.

Dan Frost lounged three feet away, chewing meditatively. His own key hung glittering in the harsh light as he leaned over to inspect the dessert. Morris Epstein envied his outlook; there was not the slightest chance that Frost was plagued with doubt. If the time ever came, his key would click firmly. The only thing that seemed to trouble Frost was the fact that neither knew where the ten missiles of their complex were targeted. Morris agreed with SAC policy vehemently; he was certain if he could visualize a hundred thousand men, women, and children in Moscow or Leningrad or Murmansk consumed in a flash he could not so much as enter the capsule. For all he knew, and this he hoped and sometimes almost believed, their own particular complex was trained on a Soviet ICBM site. Dan Frost speculated that their ground zero was a city; he longed to know which, and he admitted it.

Now his lean lantern-jaw was wrinkling in feigned disgust, presumably for Epstein's benefit, as he spooned more chipped beef onto a slab of toast. Why in hell, Epstein wondered, creamed chipped beef? For men imprisoned without exercise or other distraction than eating? If it kept up, the whine and the boredom and Frost's ectomorphic, unpunished gluttony, some day they would have to widen the blast door to get him out.

Danny Frost chewed onward, his cool gray eyes crinkled in revulsion. "Awful, Morrie. The worst yet. I got a good mind to send it back up."

"Eat, you bastard," said Morris Epstein. For a moment he wondered if Danny had reformed at all, or simply had chosen another tack because it would look bad on his record to have been rejected by a crew commander so early in his missile career. No, he decided; Danny was trying to help him diet, his distrust was a facet of his own gnawing hunger. The delicate, steamy odor of mashed potatoes overcame the smell of electrical discharge. A berg of butter floated on a yellow inland sea on Danny's plate. "It's really bad?"

"Um," mumbled Danny. "You're not missing a thing."

Morris Epstein had a quick vision of Danny Frost standing with Alice at the side of a glutton's early grave, shaking his head. *Poor little Jew-boy,* Danny mourned. *Might say he gave his life for his country, in a way. Let me take you somewhere and buy you a drink . . .*

"Oh, Christ," moaned Morris Epstein, lurching toward the cart. Danny looked up at him, his face a mask of sympathy. "Now look, Morrie, let me call them and tell them to take it up . . ." Morrie Epstein shook his head. Ravenous, he was spooning chipped beef onto his plate when a quick, sharp buzzer sounded. He whirled and leaped for his seat, hearing the dinner cart roll across the floor as Danny Frost jumped for his own. He looked at his line of lights: OUTER SECURITY VIOLATION. Number four was blinking. He picked up a phone and called the Wing Command Post at Lincoln. "This is Minute Kilo. I got a Seven High at Kilo Four. We're sending a strike team out."

He heard Frost talking to the ground above, ordering an air police strike team to number four silo of the complex they controlled. A jackrabbit, perhaps, had triggered the alarm system near the bird. But Kilo Four was six miles away; his food would get cold while he waited. He sighed. In ten minutes the report was back. It had indeed been an animal, a grazing cow. But just as they were turning back to the dinner cart a familiar high warble filled the capsule. Morris Epstein swung his chair back to the panel, tensing involuntarily. "Gravel Gertie," a man's voice broke in: "This is Hangdog, with a message for the Primary Alert System." The voice began to recite phonetic letters in a toneless, grating chant: "Yoke Tango Lima Alfa, Break . . . November Alfa Zulu Mike . . ." Quickly, as if performing for their six-month Standardization Board, the two decoded the message from SAC Headquarters. It was a practice launch. Quickly, automatically, they strapped themselves into their seats.

"Arming switches," Epstein said. He heard Frost, behind him at his console, begin to click the switches in sequence: "Two, armed. Three, four, five, six, seven, eight, nine . . ."

Morris Epstein pretended to open the plastic cover of his Launch Control panel. He left it closed, though, as a precaution, then, reluctantly, pulled the chain with his key on it over his head. He kept it in his hand; once in the panel, it could not be removed. But procedure demanded that he pretend to insert it, so he did; he knew that Dan Frost, six feet away at his own console, was pretending to insert his own.

"Conference call," Epstein said without looking up.

He heard Frost pick up a phone. "Kilo One, ready to launch . . . Kilo Two, ready . . ."

When all ten silos had reported ready, Epstein called Wing. "Launch on your count," said Wing Command Post.

Morrie Epstein stretched his hand for the lock, key between his fingers. "Rotate key on two," he told Frost. "Release on four."

"Roger," said Dan Frost.

"One, *two* . . ." began Epstein, twisting the key in the air. "Three, *four*." He turned his hand back. In 15 seconds they repeated the procedure. If the keys had been inserted, and if a "second vote" had been received through the same operation from another capsule in the Wing, the die would have been cast. Once the two sets of keys had turned, there would be nothing to do but sit and wait. Inevitably, irreversibly, the computers would grind and whirr; in thirty seconds ten 86-ton lids would be hurled explosively from ten silos across the Nebraska plain, 44,000 pounds of fuel would cook for a moment in the holes, and in seconds ten birds would slam from their burrows into the Midwest sunset, each riding a lance of flame to the north, and disappear.

And in thirty minutes a hundred thousand, a half-million, a million human lives would cease in a heartbeat, and the key was in Morris Epstein's hand.

Fingers trembling, he put it back around his neck.

> NORAD must maintain a weapons fence 15,000
> miles long around 10 million square miles of land.
>
> —PRESS RELEASE
> U. S. Air
> Defense
> Command

Chapter Nine

MALCOLM SCOTT lounged in the satin-quiet DC-8 next to a
well-dressed Negro who had instantly emersed himself in
work from a briefcase. He looked down at the billiard-table
pastures of Iowa, Illinois, or perhaps Indiana.

The vastness of the U. S. always overwhelmed him, as it
usually did Britishers. The greater spaces of the USSR had
staggered him as well, but over Russia one felt that the riches
were beneath the soil, untouched yet by those who plowed its
meadows and crowded its streets.

He remembered his first flight over the USSR from London to Moscow. It was winter. He was riding an Aeroflot jet,
bathed in an aura of excitement. He had never been to Russia
before. The two years he was to spend here as attaché was the
climax of study, career-management, political maneuvering,
and everyday stubbornness. He had looked down at towns and
woods and frozen lakes. Each tiny village was a row of
houses facing a single street like soldiers lying on a firing line
guarding the fenced enclosures in back, overwhelmed by the
huge farms surrounding the lot of them. Long cooperative
livestock buildings, presumably where animals were kept dur-

ing the winter, basked in the northern sunlight. From the jet's altitude there was no visible sign of human life, of course, since there was little transport below. He wondered what the peasants were doing; apparently, they spent the long Russian winters inside, as they had always done. Perhaps those who ascribed the moody, hilarious personality of the stock Russian to the imprisonment of winter were right after all.

It was all very neat and Christmasy, and one could almost imagine the tiny dot below as a troika jingling across the steppe, horses breathing steam and harness creaking, lashed by a bearded alcoholic with a gleam in his eye and a shout in his throat. Of course, he had found it later to be not quite so, but the Russian innocence and love of life was there in the country nevertheless. It thinned, he found eventually, as one approached the cities over the big estates, now museums, past the steaming factories into the bustle and haze of Moscow or Leningrad or Minsk. It was easy to see why the soil exerted so strong a pull on the Muskovite; apparent on that first flight in; easier yet as he grew to know the people.

He had a sudden vivid memory of a trip into the country with Karen. They had driven on an icy road through a little village near the Archangel Estate. They had asked the driver to stop, left him in the car, retraced the route along a street of long cabins with brightly carved wooden fronts. It was all very storybook-like until they had stumbled upon an open garage with a car in it.

The recollection of Karen's hand in his in the snapping-cold Russian winter started a dismal ache. He deliberately put the memory from his mind and looked out the window of the DC-8 at the fields of Ohio.

From 30,000 feet, to the trained eye, minute flecks of red and yellow meant farm machinery working the fields. Passing near Columbus, he could see the tentacles of the American turnpike system, crawling with tiny specks of ebony and chrome that meant speeding autos. Somewhere below, converters in the steel plants were showering sparks; the Detroit lines just past his northern horizon were moving in ponderous precision as they had for fifty years; the wealth of America, from her lush prairies to her half-gutted mountains of iron, was in plain sight for anyone to see.

He wondered if he would look down from a more lethal aircraft on another day and see this flat, lush country again. He glanced at his watch. In an hour, despite the vast distance, he would be in Washington, where General Norwood and Senator Holiday would try to lift him above their lonely parapet as another target for the Pentagon. He did not care. Soon, his actions would speak for him.

He was tired of useless words. If these great people 30,000 feet below him were willing to lose it all, perhaps they deserved to. They would follow false prophets, forgetting that the tractor was only an assembly of nuts and bolts and iron, but the brain of the dullest farmer was a miracle; that the mind of the driver of the car and the tender of the furnace was infinitely more wonderful than the best of their engines or the finest of their factories. To the American the machine, the gleaming complex of transistors and tubes, had become a deity.

Damned fools, mostly, he thought as he had thought many times in the last few months. Mostly a race of damned fools. . . .

PART 2

"Cook the frozen dynamite . . ."

> "I think the B-47 fleet in the hands of professionals could deliver weapons in the year 2000."
> —GENERAL THOMAS S. POWER
> Former Commander in
> Chief, SAC

Chapter One

GROUP CAPTAIN MALCOLM SCOTT accepted the chewing gum that the stewardess offered him. He sat in swaying, cushioned comfort in the DC-8 as it soared smoothly toward Washington over the darkening Appalachians. He had been cocooned in hs imagination, an open American magazine ignored on his lap, when she disturbed him.

His daydreams at the age of forty-one were largely placid, although in his youth he had been prone to charge screaming across the moors with Wallace or to ride with the Light Brigade. Later in life one began to dream more of boating trips on Norfolk Broads or casting in the Dee than of lonely dogfights in a castled sky.

But this evening, perhaps because he was approaching a foreign capital with compromising material in his baggage and a dangerous plan in his head, his fantasies had taken a lethal color. In Staff College he had learned to put himself in the place of the enemy. Just now, when his musings had been interrupted, he had been flying, not east toward Washington across the Appalachians but west toward Washington over the Atlantic. He had been a Russian agent, cold, implacable, dedicated. He had boarded the DC-8 at London under his right name, he imagined, with a proper American visa, because what was about to happen required subterfuge on a scale that made an alias superfluous. Beneath his arm rested a Webley revolver or whatever was its Russian equivalent—a snub-nosed automatic perhaps, cold as death. On his wrist the inexpensive sweep-second chronometer, running on Moscow time and rated for months by the best horologist in Russia.

He glanced at it. Almost halfway across the Atlantic to America, they were: nearing the point of no return. Still out of range of U._S. radar, in the vast mid-Atlantic blind spot between New England and old, with the ceaseless sweep of Munster and Border Control radar left far behind. Forward in the cockpit, innocent of their fate, the captain, first officer, and flight engineer sat, doubtless at the coffee the hostess had taken forward. The first officer was probably working out his midpoint position report.

Everything was moving with historic inevitability, he day-dreamed, or else he would have been paged before he boarded at London. The Russian Bison bomber that would take their airliner's place was hurtling down from the north to a rendez-vous only five minutes away. Fanning out from USSR air-dromes from Murmansk to Cape Zhelenia screamed other Russian craft of the first westbound wave, each a wolf en route to a rendezvous with an innocent lamb. One bomber would meet the BOAC flight to New York, one an Alitalia 707 from Rome to Washington. Too late the Paris-La Guardia Air France passengers would sight another off the wing tip as the French captain sat with a gun to his head; United, TWA, and Pan Am flights to Baltimore, New Orleans, Miami—all would stare at their substitutes in shocked surprise; the SAS flight from Copenhagen over the pole to Los Angeles would already have been joined, passed on its vital statistics, and be on its reluctant way to Moscow. Above the Pacific now the other bombers would long ago have finished aerial refueling, be homing on their victims, far out of range of the U. S. Navy's picket ships and humpbacked radar planes. In each of the airliners heading for California: Quantas, Pan Am, Japan Air Lines, was an agent like himself. The time for him was ... His eyes dropped to his watch. Now!

Quickly he drew strength from whatever source a Russian used: the steppes in moonlight, perhaps, or the golden coming age of utter sameness. Then he imagined himself on his feet, smiling at the stewardess, opening the cockpit door. The men were indeed drinking coffee; he glanced at the captain's name on the door, although it had already been provided him at the Russian Embassy in London.

"Hall," he barked in perfect English, drawing and leveling his gun in a single motion. "Look here!"

Startled, the crew turned. He moved closer to the captain, until his gun barrel was literally touching the neck.

"Jesus Christ!" murmured the first officer.

"If any one of you makes a move," he said coldly, "I must kill this man. Do you understand?"

"What the hell do you want?" demanded the first officer.

"Your airplane."

"We have a flight-plan, mister," the captain ventured. "If we don't check in at the right time off Jersey, you'll see so many F-106s around you'll think there's a war on."

"There is a war on, Captain," he announced. He held out his hand to the first officer, keeping his eye on the pilot. "Let me have the log."

He felt it in his hand. He glanced at it swiftly. Good. The ETAs for penetrating the North Atlantic Air Defense Identification Zone were already worked out; cruising altitude would remain the same throughout the flight. He looked out the starboard window. Against the cobalt northern sky he saw a speck, and it grew until it was a four-engined jet bomber, riding easily a hundred feet away in perfect formation.

"Goddamned Myasischev Bison," he heard the first officer breathe. "I think."

Aldis lamp, Aldis lamp! He had forgotten the Aldis lamp. He demanded it of the flight engineer, kept the gun to the pilot's neck and propped the flight-log on the control pedestal. He took the lamp, pointed it at the helmeted comrade in the bomber, and flashed a greeting. He got a quick reply and began to flick off the checkpoints on the flight-log, using the light because radio silence was part of the plan even so far from America. He finished with the airspeed, course, and time of arrival of the DC-8 at the Air Identification Zone border a hundred miles from the New Jersey coast. There were no queries form the Bison. In Russian he sent: GOOD LUCK.

"Turn right to course zero-four-eight," he told the airline pilot tersely, "and keep your hands off the radio."

"Where do you think you're taking us?" muttered the captain, nevertheless banking to starboard.

"Murmansk."

"When we don't show up in our block of air on time, they'll know something's wrong!"

Ivan Mihailovich Scott jerked his thumb to the bomber continuing on course, a snowflake in the sapphire sky. "He'll take your place. All you must do is fly us safely to Russia."

He smiled the thin smile of a professional agent. His part was almost done. The Bison would take the DC-8's place, as others were taking the places of other DC-8s and Boeing 707s converging on the cities of America; within an hour the first bombers, their transponders converted to standard American airline frequencies, would be showing their proper radar pips and making their reports to New York and San Francisco and Los Angeles in perfect English; within minutes after that they would be circling Washington, Chicago, Boston, while the airliners they had replaced bucked the cold north wind toward Russia. And above the cities and the ICBM silos the bombers would remain, swords over the heads of America while they circled for days, relieved by others, fueled in the air, holding the millions hostage against the loss of the first Russian bomber shot down or the first ballistic missile released. There need not be a life lost on either side as long as the President acceded to what the Chairman demanded.

And what of America; what of the Strategic Air Command? If it happened today, Moscow citizens would look up at a sky spotted with B-58s. But tomorrow, in the 1970's, with the B-58s rusting on Arizona deserts, and the last tired British Vulcans laid to rest, what then?

Polaris subs, they would tell him in the Pentagon; Polaris subs would hold the shotgun to Russia's head. But how many Polaris subs were there and how many Russian bombers?

"Seat belt, sir?"

He snapped his eyes open, back in his seat, the daydream

evaporating. The voice was warm; the face evoked a sad, sweet pang. The eyes were even softer, darker brown; the smile softer, too, and the cheekbones not as high. But she could have been Karen, with some of the baby fat left on. He nodded. "Thank you."

When she walked down the aisle he fastened the belt and put his head back again, and now the fantasies dissolved as if on a cinema screen and Karen was with him, as he had first seen her: a student moving laden with books down a wet Copenhagen alley, wearing the glasses she affected in case the Gestapo had her description. He had waited for her in an agony of fear on the dark corner of Östergade and Pilestraede. The knee he had twisted in the crash was aching; he was washed with recurrent terror, fearing that he had after all misunderstood the instructions and confused the Danish street names. He knew only the name of her group: the *Holger Danske*—there was no way to contact it again if he missed a link in the human chain to Sweden and safety.

She dropped a book directly in front of him. Heart soaring in relief, he crooked his injured knee to retrieve it for her, almost collapsed in pain. She steadied him. The two bent together for the volume and knocked heads. Another book dropped. Suddenly, while he tried to maintain the fiction that they had met accidentally, they were giggling hopelessly together as if they had known each other for years. Out of hand they had gotten, almost, before she looked up at him, the brown eyes dancing, and asked in her Scandanavian lilt: "Flying Officer Scott, I presume?"

He shook the rain from a biology text. "I had better be, don't you think?"

"I'm sorry," she said breathlessly. "Mostly I do better."

"Do you? *My* first crack at this sort of thing."

They had decided that if the Hipos were watching them they had best appear to be young lovers, so together they had moved into a restaurant down the street, where he had spent his last RAF krone for a bottle of Tuborg beer and she had had to slip him the money for the meal under the table.

He was remembering other things now, scenes in a bright, kodachrome procession: the small flat in London in which Dee had been born, and Karen studying child care with all of her Danish thoroughness; the neat home in Nottinghamshire when he had commanded the Group at Farrington; their first Christmas in Russia's bleak cold and the children's department store in Moscow that Karen and Dee had both loved so much.

He was scarcely aware when the wheels of the DC-8 dropped with a jolt and, shortly after, squawked as they met the runway. When the plane stopped, he looked out while the impassive Negro next to him closed his briefcase. As the engines whispered and were stilled, he could see the monolithic terminal building in the distance; he wondered how in the world they had arranged to get the passengers to it.

He stood up and buttoned his tunic. He looked at his watch. He had to make a very important call before he was captured by General Norwood, for after that it might be difficult to break away. He followed his fellow passengers and stepped from the plane directly to the second story of a sort of mobile lounge, done in blue leather and chrome like a U. S. Air Force officers' club. A sallow operator in a blue uniform with a shoulder patch reading: *Federal Aviation Agency* began to drive the ponderous vehicle to the terminal.

"Aren't we mechanized?" commented Malcolm Scott to the Negro.

The black man, who wore a striped school-tie which reminded Malcolm Scott of the regimentals of the Welsh Guard, assessed him for a moment before answering. "Mechanized," he said, "and nationalized. What the hell's the federal government doing running a bus?"

They disembarked from the mobile lounge, entered a vast, almost deserted terminal of gleaming newness, and stood in a row like animals at a trough while a stainless-steel device traveling behind an endless belt shoved suitcases at them.

"Mechanized, nationalized," muttered the Negro. He flicked his eyes at a few black porters near the end of the luggage rack. He motioned at one. "They got seven thousand Negroes unemployed over there in Washington, so they install a thing like this at the Dulles International Airport."

Malcolm Scott, waiting for his suitcase, heard a voice behind him. "Group Captain Scott?" It was a low, guttural growl, somehow familiar. He turned quickly. The man was in civilian clothes, in a white, open-necked sports shirt. He had black eyes, gray sideburns; his head was almost completely bald. He was tanned and solid, over sixty but as straight-backed as a Cranwell cadet. So much for the secret phone call he must make; he was already trapped. Malcolm Scott stiffened instinctively and saluted.

"Good evening, General." He had once sat in a far corner of a lectuare hall of the Imperial Defense College and heard the gruff, flat voice drone interminably of megatonnage dropped, probability of error, saturation of enemy defense. General Halstead Norwood had molded the magnificent bombing instrument that was the U. S. Strategic Air Command. From his Olympian height as Chief of Staff for the Air Force he fought a lonely battle for the manned bomber. He was losing, and he looked tired.

Scott's battered suitcase came sliding down the ramp, and he picked it up. The two walked together toward a flashy red Corvette standing in the almost deserted parking lot.

"I must say, sir," Malcolm Scott said, when he was seated and safety-strapped into the passenger's seat, "that I'm flattered."

"Well," General Norwood shrugged, "I've wanted to meet you since I ran across your article." Malcolm Scott said nothing. They began to flash across the rolling, verdant Virginia countryside at an unwavering eighty miles per hour, their headlights lancing the sultry night. There was a moist breath of tropics in the April air; Scott was glad that within a few days he would be back in the cool of European spring.

They were on a six-lane freeway, and they had passed hardly another car for the last fifteen minutes. "You could have bought a wing of B-70 bombers for what this cost," he was finally moved to remark.

The general looked at him speculatively. "You can say that again."

"I got you a reservation at the Mariott Motor Inn," the general volunteered. "Close to the factory." Suddenly they were sweeping up a serpentine drive, and the Pentagon came into view, lights still on for security, looming on the Potomac River bank amid lawns and parking lots, dominating the river for miles as it poured the last of its human blood into the veins of nighttime Washington traffic.

The Pentagon disappeared as they dipped under an approach to a bridge across the river and darted into a fairyland motor inn which had more the look to Malcolm Scott of a Las Vegas casino than a motel. He gaped as General Norwood drove through an archway commanded by two liveried Negroes in scarlet and brass, checked him in at a drive-in desk without ever leaving the car, and then followed a speeding bellhop on a bicycle past endless wings to a parking place. The bellhop sprang from his bicycle to take the suitcase from the trunk of the car. Malcolm Scott was uncomfortable—the Embassy would have got him a downtown room, cut-rate. God knows how much this luxurious morass would cost him.

General Norwood said: "Don't sweat the rent, Scott. You're my guest here. If the Air Force Association doesn't pick up the tab, I will."

Malcolm Scott, mindful of the American concept of the Scotchman, made a depreciatory gesture. "I can stand it, sir."

"No, we will." The general's eyes flashed. "Okay?"

There were really more important things to worry about, and Malcolm Scott nodded. "Yes, sir." They followed the bellboy down a line of variously colored doors; in the distance Malcolm Scott could hear the ring of youthful voices, splashing and the drumming of a diving board. He began to wonder which of the multihued doors the bellhop would select; he felt like the prince in Scheherazade's story of the hundred portals.

The bellhop found the room and accepted a tip. Under a telephone on the bedside table a red light flashed imperiously; the general explained it meant that he had a message already. Malcolm Scott lifted the receiver, and in a moment was talking to the personal assistant to the Secretary of Defense. When he hung up he had an appointment to meet Charles Van Ness at 11 A.M. the following morning. Things were moving very fast.

General Norwood raised his eyebrows. "Van Ness?"

Startled, Malcolm Scott said: "Yes sir."

"I figured. He assumed I'd pick you up. He decided I'd bring you here."

The incredible fact that a member of the U. S. Joint Chiefs

of Staff and a U. S. Cabinet officer were playing "button, button" with a group captain in the RAF made Malcolm Scott smile despite himself. But there was no smile on General Norwood's face. "Scott, I wonder if you really know how important your article is?"

"I'm beginning to feel I wrote a best-seller, sir." He opened his suitcase; from it he produced a bottle of whisky, and then, remembering that most U. S. motels had ice machines, he stepped outside. Sure enough, he found one. He returned and mixed a drink for the general, noting on the sink an automatic Silex coffee-maker. Gadgets, gadgets, gadgets . . . The virus of automation was infecting the U. S. civil population as deeply as its military. He raised his glass. "Cheers."

The general asked bluntly: "Did you clear with anybody in the Air Ministry before you said your piece?"

Malcolm Scott's heart began to thump. Strictly, he had not, and said so. But the brusque question alarmed him. The general looked disappointed. "The Bomber Command?" he assayed.

This was much closer to the truth, and Malcolm Scott took a deep breath. "I'm sorry, sir. I can't discuss it further."

The general looked partly relieved. "At least, I can assume that this wasn't an individual explosion on your own part. Can I?"

Malcolm Scott was not a fencer with words. He hated the position into which he was backed. "I think you might assume that many of the RAF are concerned about what will happen after our rich uncle sacks the head gamekeeper on the family estate," he said guardedly. "For instance, what will happen if in this decade it turns out *not* to be a game of Russian roulette with ICBMs. If you haven't built a U. S. bomber for eight or ten years, does the RAF Bomber Command have to go it alone?"

"What do you mean by *not* a game of Russian roulette?" the general asked narrowly.

It was the crux of the matter. Whether or not the general looked on him as an ally, at least he must make himself clear. "General," he said carefully, "my article assumes that even in all-out warfare this country would not unleash intercontinental ballistic missiles unless the other side did it first."

"That's right."

"It assumes that neither you nor Russia would destroy yourselves by starting a nuclear conflagration unless you were forced into a corner."

"Neither us *nor* Russia? That's what I read into it. That's why I met you tonight. I couldn't believe it. Your article seriously presumes a war with *conventional* weapons?"

"The possibility of it, anyway. If the Russians want to keep it that way."

"Christ, that's not the argument to use! The SAC bomber force is a *nuclear* force. So's the RAF Bomber Command!"

"Yes," said Malcolm Scott. "But bombers are *capable* of using conventional weapons, too. ICBMs are not. That's the difference. SAC B-52s and the RAF Vulcan mean a *choice*."

"You can use that on the women's clubs," scofffed the general. "Charlie Van Ness and the boys in the Pentagon expect the next war to be nuclear. And they expect to have to use the bomb."

"Does the President?"

The general stared into his drink. He was deeply disturbed, and disappointed, and it showed. "Christ, I don't know. But we can't get manned bombers back in the inventory by promising a conventional war! What about the Army? Restrict them to conventional weapons in Europe and the Russians will go through them like a hot knife through butter. The Army's committed to nuclear weapons! Absolutely."

"Tactical nuclear weapons," Malcolm Scott admitted. "On a scale. There's a hell of a difference in lobbing a nuclear rocket at three hundred troops in the next hollow and inviting the destruction of New York or London by tossing an Atlas at Moscow. Which is what you'll have to do if they have bombers and you don't!"

"All right then," the general said reasonably. "We both advocate manned bombers. I advocate them because they *do* carry nuclear weapons, and will wipe out an enemy more surely than ballistic missiles. You advocate them for reasons which are less clear to, say, the average senator. Suppose you simply back my contention, so as not to confuse the civilian? First, that the manned bomber carries a nuclear load vastly superior to the ICBM. Second, that it delivers it a hell of a lot more accurately. And third, that ballistic missiles, since they can't be tested individually in war games, can't be trusted to work?"

It was a proposition Malcolm Scott had anticipated, and feared. "I couldn't, sir," he said quietly. "For one thing, the ballistic missile *is* a highly lethal weapon, regardless of whether we like it or not. Why do you doubt it?"

"Why shouldn't I doubt it? They're just glorified aircraft, aren't they? How the hell do you know if an airplane is going to perform if you haven't flown it under wartime conditions?"

Malcolm Scott looked at him curiously. "Do you think your ICBM force is unreliable?"

The general shrugged. "I think ICBMs will deteriorate in their silos, no matter how many tests we run. I think the crews will get sloppy, no matter how often they go to Vandenberg to fire one off. An airplane you fly every day. A missile just sits."

There were in the U. S. and the British services a whole spectrum of opinions on the ICBM. He must set the general straight on his own stand. "General," asked Malcolm Scott, "you *are* familiar with the statistical accuracy of, say, the Titan?"

"I'm familiar with what it is *supposed* to be if everything goes right. I *don't* think we can toss one in a garbage can from six thousand miles, no."

"Nobody says you can," Malcolm Scott said. "But if the garbage can were two miles in diameter you'd have a good chance of getting it in."

"Maybe," the general admitted, "if we had enough of them. They don't pack the megatonnage of an airplane, but enough of them might get off. My point is—"

"You must understand, sir, that I *do* think the ICBM is going to work," Malcolm Scott pointed out. "What we have to prevent is the *necessity* of its working. Two miles' error is two miles, after all. It's horribly far. OK for Leningrad; no good for an aircraft factory three point six miles north of Leningrad. You'd ground a bombardier who couldn't come within a thousand yards; two miles circular-error-probability is very, very inaccurate. Inhumanely inaccurate."

The general looked at him oddly. "I see," he said. "Inhumanely inaccurate." He smiled faintly. "War is hell, Scott," he said, "but there's no need to tell a Britisher that." He shrugged. "You may be just the guy Charlie Van Ness is looking for."

"Why?"

"As an example of how woolly-headed we airplane drivers are."

Malcolm Scott flushed. "I'm sorry, sir. That's the way I feel."

The general nodded grimly, got up. He paused at the door. "To quote from your article," he said with some amusement. " 'The history of warfare, from Olduvai Gorge'—wherever that is—'to Hiroshima, proves that no weapon is a substitute for the brain of the man who is there.' So you at least believe that the manned bomber can still get through."

"Of course."

"Tomorrow," the general said, "you'll be talking to your intellectual equals in the Pentagon, not to a used-up throttle-jockey. Be sure they don't change your opinion on *that*."

"They won't," Malcolm Scott said stiffly.

"Good, Scott. Good for you."

The general lifted his glass to Scott, drained it, and left.

Already recognized as a potent threat from high
altitudes, SAC's jet bombers are equally capable of
penetrating enemy defenses from low altitudes.

—PRESS RELEASE
Strategic Air
Command

We are confident that our interceptors can destroy
any bombers that face us.

—PRESS RELEASE
North American
Air Defense
Command

Chapter Two

GROUP CAPTAIN MALCOLM SCOTT finished his breakfast in
the shop off the lobby and left a careful tip for the waitress.
He found a phone booth near the cashier's desk and called his
number. While he waited he watched a procession of well-
dressed young men leave the Inn's glass doors and form a
queue outside, waiting for taxis to the Pentagon a few yards
up the river. He guessed from their crew-cut conformity and
their briefcases, as well as from some familiarity with the
British counterpart, that they were defense industry salesmen-
engineers, species *Americana,* forming for the daily safari
after Pentagon big game. He was about to hang up when a
clipped voice came on the line.

"Yes?"

"Flynn? Scott here."

"Oh yes. Group Captain Scott." The voice was frigid. "I
expected you to ring last night."

"I got involved."

"Matter of fact, I stayed here in my office. Waiting."

Flynn, whoever he was, was an ass; he could sense what

an ass he was across the river and probably half the width of Washington. "Sorry," Malcolm Scott said.

"Quite," said Flynn. "Now, then. I suppose you'd like to fix up some sort of meeting today?"

"No. I'm running a day late. Tomorrow." Malcolm Scott, veteran of Moscow, hesitated momentarily out of habit. "I'll have two more films for you then."

"Films?" the other asked innocently.

Oh, God, Malcolm Scott thought, the man was worse than he had expected. "Never mind," he said. "Where shall we meet?"

"There's a little place close to the National Press Club—Jack's."

He gave Scott the address of a restaurant and they scheduled lunch tomorrow. Then Malcolm Scott phoned Senator Brian Holiday's office and arranged reluctantly to meet the senator. On the way out the door he noticed a newspaper rack. He stopped short. RUSS DOWN U. S. JET. He slipped a ten-cent piece into the slot and extracted a paper. Before he had read three lines he could visualize what had happened. It had not started at a West German airfield, as the reader might infer, but yesterday afternoon in his own office in Omaha. Zachary Chandler must have become curious about some phase of USSR fighter strength. There was only one way to check it; not a very good way, but all that was available. Ten, possibly fifteen minutes later, an F-106 in an alert hangar at Weisbaden had scrambled, flashed into the air in a feint toward the border. Perhaps the pilot had crossed inadvertently; perhaps, impatient or overzealous, he had crossed on purpose; perhaps the Communist planes had actually penetrated to the West to get at him.

At any rate, the 106 had fallen on unfriendly soil. There was no word on the pilot. Malcolm felt sorry for Zach. He was too sensitive a young man for his job. It had happened twice to his predecessor—it would happen again.

Scott looked along the Potomac toward the Pentagon. He could fairly feel the flap that the new incident was causing there; the anger at U. S. instructions from the president, which decreed that when a Soviet plane crossed into Alaska or lanced into West Germany in the unending game of "chicken," it must be escorted politely home.

Thank God for the instructions, though, he thought, signaling a cab. May he not change them in the next few weeks.

He stepped from his cab in the dark tunnel entrance of the Pentagon, walked up a ramp. He had been here once before, in 1950, en route to Korea; Hub Younger, a lieutenant colonel commanding a desk somewhere in the vast labyrinth, had invited him for lunch. Today the building seemed to have grown even more complex. He moved across the garishly lighted basement concourse past all the facilities which would seem necessary to satisfy a full-sized city. It reminded him of Grand Central Station in New York: laundries, banks, a travel agency, gift shops, souvenir stands, book stores. He wondered what the Londoner would say or British newspapers print if Burlington Arcade were moved to the cellar of Whitehall.

He stood for a moment studying a huge chart of the building, trying to pinpoint his own position, keeping aside from the stream of men in mufti and uniform; no military man seemed of less than field grade. He sensed someone beside him, and glanced down at a curly-haired one-star Air Force general with bright blue eyes and a birdlike, inquisitive face.

"Group Captain Scott?" the general asked. He had a bass voice, low for a slight man. Scott liked him instantly.

"That's right, sir."

The general stuck out his hand. "Alf Karman. Washington Air Defense Sector at Fort Lee." The bright blue eyes were regarding him with speculative sympathy, as if the general were a doctor who had been briefed by a colleague on a patient with an incurable disease. "I guess you and I are here for the same reason," General Karman said. "Your article."

"Really?"

The general smiled. "NORAD sends me in to help Van make his pitch whenever they don't want to waste one of the wheels from Colorado Springs. Not that he needs help."

In other words, Malcolm Scott thought, the Secretary of Defense was arming himself with a one-star general to brainwash a British group captain. He must be more worried about Congress than he seemed. He followed the fighter-general briskly through a maze of corridors and ramps to the lion's den.

Chapter Three

MALCOLM SCOTT soon realized, in the paneled office, that the
tone of the meeting had changed. He had had his say, now it
was the Secretary's turn. The man sitting across the ornate
walnut desk under the portrait of Forrestal had as quick and
cutting a mind as he had ever encountered. Charles Van Ness
was a deceptively bland little chap with wispy hair. He em-
phasized his points with quick, chopping motions as if he
were cutting through a hostile crowd with karate blows. After
a false start Scott discovered swiftly that he himself was here
as a student and the civilian Secretary of Defense as an instructor.

The subject for today was U. S. Air Defenses. Malcolm
Scott, apparently, could be presumed to know all there was
about the free world's defensive power, but was seemingly
deficient in background on its defensive strength. Or else why
would he cling to the notion that Russian bombers could get
through? By extension, how could he still believe that U. S.
and British aircraft could penetrate the Soviet guard?

The Secretary availed himself of the latest in visual-aid
techniques. Alongside the rather old-fashioned desk stood a

display board with beautifully drafted and very colorful plexiglass leaves. The Secretary of Defense expounded while a bright, crew-cut young civilian turned the sheets of the display. Malcolm Scott wondered how many times Charles Van Ness had lectured thus. The finished look of the charts and graphs, the permanence of the block figures and skillful renderings of the artist, with the cold, dollars-and-cents language of the Secretary and occasionally his young assistant, made the position of the Defense Department impregnable and the death of the manned bomber utterly inevitable.

The Secretary had not been bombastic at first. He had seemed friendly, but he was oblique, and very subtle. When Scott and General Karman had entered he had arisen, walked around the desk, and pumped Scott's hand, as if Scott were doing him a favor in permitting him to explain his policy; as if, in fact, he were eager to learn. Where Scott had expected antagonism and reserve it was, at first, as if he had found a sincere and enthusiastic student of warfare, open-minded and eager.

The Secretary of Defense was even deferential, before he set sail himself on a billowing sea of facts and U. S. defense figures. "I read your article yesterday in last month's *NATO Journal*, Scott. I agree with some of your contentions."

"You do, sir?"

"Yes. Others . . . Well. Maybe we differ in fundamental philosophy."

"Perhaps."

"Scott," Van Ness smiled, "do you believe that man evolved the weapon or that the need for weapons evolved the man?"

"Man," Malcolm Scott said succinctly, "evolved his weapons, his tools, and his machines."

The Secretary shrugged. "The new anthropology teaches that the weapon in a sense preceded man. That the club or the rock, in one way, is the ancestor of intellect. A weak, nonspecialized animal with a small brain finds he can equalize the odds against a tiger by grabbing a stick or a stone. Or even the thighbone of a previous victim. If he doesn't coordinate hand and brain and eye well enough to use it, he dies and his strain dies too. Coordination, racial survival itself, called for a larger brain, and so on. All to better use the weapon."

"First, man's concept," Malcolm Scott insisted. "First, the imagination to grab the club or make the tool. *Then* the club becomes a weapon and perhaps it takes a larger and larger brain to compete. But *first* the idea, *then* the weapon."

"I think not," said the Secretary. "And I think we've come the full circle. The weapon dominates again."

Malcolm Scott shrugged indifferently. "So, at any rate, there's *one* of my contentions you don't agree with. Right?"

"There are others, too." The Secretary smiled. "They all seem founded on the premise that the manned bomber can get through modern defenses. We don't think so. And we can't afford to gamble on the hope that it can."

Malcolm Scott shifted now in his leather chair next to General Karman. The Secretary explained the effects of continuing the RS-71 program on the fiscal future of the U. S. Defense Department. He pointed out that if the United States had permitted further development of the ill-fated Douglas Skybolt, it might have saved the future of the RAF Bomber Command but the defense budget might now be strapped.

"So much for the strategic bomber."

And, thought Malcolm Scott, if your country goes up in a sheet of Soviet flames triggered by your enthusiastic ballistic missiles and if England goes up with it, and Russia too, who will care a fig about budgets? The Secretary changed gears. "Now, captian, let me modify what I've said. We're going to have brush-fire wars as in Korea and Vietnam; for them the manned aircraft is obviously *not* obsolete. Tactically, the manned fighter plane is certainly not yet obsolete in the *defenses* of the U. S. and Canada, nor in your own. He smiled at Alf Karman. "Right, Alf?"

"Yes sir."

"Tactically," continued Van Ness. "But *strategically?* The ICBM, Captain!"

Malcolm Scott kept his silence.

The Secretary chopped a hand on his desk in rhythm with his points: "For once this country is going to recognize an obsolete weapon before it buys it further. The ballistic missile is the weapon of the future, inhuman as it may seem to you. This country intends, the Congress willing, to stake its future on it. While you're here, you'll doubtless be asked to testify before the Senate Armed Services Committee. Senator Holiday will sponsor you, and between you and General Harwood you may well have an effect on the members. But captain, as you doubtless know, there are three branches in this government. We aren't concerned with the judicial. The arguments in your article, while rather startling, frankly haven't impressed us in the Executive. And the Legislative, while it may rant and rave and appropriate money for obsolete weapons, can't by law spend it. So I'm afraid, Captain, you'll find yourself against a stone wall at the end. Our defense policy, as you know, is already firmed. The computers show we're right."

Malcolm Scott studied the Secretary closely. The man was supposed to have been, before his appointment, an industrial engineer—a very successful one, but nevertheless a man of facts and figures. To Malcolm Scott he seemed more like a salesman, a good salesman, for he seemed to have all the strength of absolute conviction behind him.

"Computers," remarked Malcolm Scott. "I have a suggestion."

"What is that?"

"That we build a huge computer jointly with the Russians. We feed in all the factors affecting the outcome of a war: gross national product, number of trained aircraft workers, scientific and technological skills of each country, acres under cultivation. Then whenever the international situation gets bad we pull a switch and abide by the result."

"It would save a lot of lives, at that," smiled Charles Van Ness.

"It would," Malcolm Scott said. "The trouble is, where do you feed in the stupid refusal, say, of a Russian private to vacate a foxhole under artillery fire? Or the inexplicable, unpredictable conduct of a B-58 crew which simply absorbs everything the Russians can toss at it and drops on the target anyway?"

There was a long silence. "Well," said Charles Van Ness, "it's fairly academic. We, at any rate, utilize computers, limited as their emotional judgment is. The Russians do too. All we can hope is that our computers are better than theirs."

"Mr. Secretary," Scott pointed out, "you've sold your people a defense policy on a promise of 'escalated response' and meeting one blow with another but how are you going to do anything *but* pull out all the stops, as they say, if you have nothing in your arsenal but ICBMs? ICBM warfare is automatically total warfare."

"So is strategic *bomber* warfare," the Secretary replied heatedly, "with nuclear weapons."

Malcolm Scott sighed. He was patently as unlikely to root the fallacies from this man's concepts as the Minuteman missiles from his silos. Van Ness was a committed politician; he could not back off. Words could not change his mind.

Scott nevertheless spoke them, without much hope. "But with bombers, you have a choice, don't you see? It's all very well to have intercontinental missiles, you have to have them, since the enemy does. But you don't throw away the other weapons. Suppose ICBM warfare never happens? Biological warfare never has."

"I see. Biological warfare," the Secretary repeated softly, turning from his charts and graphs. The sparring was over, his eyes grew suddenly hard behind the glittering lenses. "At least, you don't feel that it happened in Korea?"

There was utter silence in the room, broken by a creak of leather as General Karman shifted uncomfortably. Malcolm Scott, his voice cold, said, "Of course not!"

"Good," the Secretary murmured. "I noted a certain anti-American tone, and I wondered." He tapped his fingers. "Suppose, Scott, that you were convinced that the manned bomber could *not* get through. Would you then support the logic of our phasing them out?"

Malcolm Scott thought at length. "Of course."

"Leaving us," the Secretary said dryly, "with nothing but poison gas, germs, and the ICBM?"

"I suppose so. I should want to colonize Mars, perhaps, with a few of my friends, but I suppose so."

"The manned bomber is *not* going to penetrate," the Secretary said. "That makes the rest of your argument superfluous."

"The manned bomber *always* gets through," Malcolm Scott said quietly. "Your own General Younger was in our squadron in World War II. He knows that."

"He'll be in Washington tomorrow," Van Ness said. "And his *present* views are pretty well known."

Malcolm Scott raised his eyebrows. He wondered why Hub was coming to the capital. He hoped he would not meet him. "Ask him some time about a raid on Aarus in Denmark. He was along. No one could get through, but we did. Ask him about a strike on Copenhagen when we skip-bombed the Gestapo Headquarters in the middle of the city of a million people, releasing the prisoners on the top floor, killed 97 SS leaders, and wouldn't have hurt a single Dane if we hadn't crashed one plane."

The crew-cut young man spoke: "That was World War II, Captain. On exercises now, we consider a sector commander of the North American Air Defense command who allows an attacking bomber, *one* bomber, to get through his interceptors to be looking for another job. Right, Alf?"

The general nodded. "Right."

"And *that*, I suggest," Malcolm Scott said wryly, "is not even war, but an exercise."

Alf Karman sat forward suddenly. "You ought to see an Air Defense Direction Center. Will you visit my shop at Fort Lee?"

Malcolm Scott repressed a desire to laugh. It was impossible, incredible, but there it was: the invitation. He wished somehow he could share the joke. He could not.

"When?" he asked carefully.

"Any time it's convenient."

"Tomorrow morning?" Malcolm Scott suggested softly.

"You'll get the real Cook's tour," Karman promised.

"I'm sure." The meeting was obviously over. Scott shook hands with Van Ness.

The eyes behind the bright glasses were studying him speculatively. "No hard feelings," said the Secretary, as if they had just finished a football game.

"None at all." Malcolm Scott shrugged. "It's your . . . What's the phrase? Red cart?"

"Red wagon?"

"It's your red wagon now."

After the Britisher left, Charles Van Ness handed a dispatch to General Alf Karman, watching the general's birdface for a sign of inner turmoil.

Since his appointment as a Cabinet member he had always found it interesting to deal with the military mind. His father had been a battleship admiral, a doggedly bullheaded man; Van Ness himself had once been headed toward the Naval Academy; it had been one of the few dreams that he and his father shared. And then his stupid eyes had weakened and except for two years as an ensign in a Boston supply depot in World War II, he had never worn a uniform.

He wondered sometimes if in the regular service he would have become as innocently predictable as the military men who surrounded him, deferring to his power as their civilian chief. It was seldom that he found originality in them; when he did they seemed always to be on the opposite side of the argument. General Hal Norwood, in his inarticulate way, was an independent thinker, but hardly worthy of his competition. The Scotchman today was another. Aloof, detached as the group captain was, Charles Van Ness had felt a kindred intellect. He wondered why he had stayed in the services so long.

Alf Karman threw the dispatch on the desk, Van Ness noted, in a typically general-like motion.

"He had a wife and kid with him at Weisbaden," Karman grated. "Goddamn it, when can we splash one of theirs?"

The Secretary shrugged. He smoothed the dispatch, which quoted East German newspapers as stating that the young F-106 pilot had died in the crash, set it carefully aside. His assistant read it over his shoulder and merely grunted; it was hardly his problem. Over and over again, through the years, the deadly game of "chicken" had been played along the East-West Border of the Iron curtain, over the sleepy valleys of the Moselle, over the frozen Aleutian Chain, over the China Sea. Both sides toyed at it—a leisurely flight along the border, a lightning lunge toward the enemy's deadline by a Russian MIG or U. S. patrol plane, while breathless radiomen waited in the silent command posts to unearth the latest enemy frequencies and codes; while intent air intelligence officers with stop-watches hung over the shoulders of radar technicians to time response-speeds.

But there was an important difference in the manner in which the game was played, East versus West. Over the years, more than 100 U. S. airmen had been shot down over Communist territory but a U. S. fighter had still to fire the first round at a Russian plane.

"They get more aggressive, and we get more scared to move," Alf Karman exploded. "You've got to ask him again! We owe it to the kids flying them. We can't ask them not to fight back!"

The Secretary studied him carefully. If there were hawks and doves in the U. S. Air Force, Alf Karman was the hawkiest among them. The Secretary half agreed with him; it was the President who would not authorize a change in policy.

"He'll just ask me what good it would do."

Alf Karman stared at him as if he were an idiot. "What *good* it would do? Jesus, Van," he blurted, "they scramble us at *will*. We're having to change our frequencies practically every month. They know how many birds we'll send up from every NORAD base in the country, and where they'll intercept, and for all I know they can recognize the voice of every intercept director we've got in the Centers. And they *get* all this without risk. We don't know what the hell *they've* got unless some poor misguided second lieutenant in an F-106 gets lost and then we're so busy trying to get him back across the border before they shoot him down we never get a chance to see what they scramble after him. They need cooling!"

Charles Van Ness wondered if the time had come to tell Alf Karman about "Operation One-Two." But Alf's boss in Colorado Springs had of course received the memo, Alf in his Washington sector was a minor cog in the overall air defense picture, and besides, the whole nightmare might be a CIA miscalculation. He decided not to tell him, but he had another idea.

Miscalculation or not, the memo had shaken the President. The time might be very ripe to "cool" the next Soviet intruder at that. It might well give the Soviets pause, if they thought they could penetrate U. S. defenses, to lose a plane. There were other reasons, too, political reasons. Senator Brian Holiday was an ex-military pilot; there had been nothing wrong with *his* eyes. He had flown, as any of his admirers would tell you, against the Japanese and North Koreans. Lately he had somehow convinced a large segment of the public that U. S. and Canadian air defenses were a paper wall to be poked at will by Communist planes.

It *would* be lovely, Charles Van Ness thought wistfully, to announce at precisely the right political instant that U. S. fighters had downed a Communist. Lovely domestically, and of some international value; a sure deterrent to further Soviet mistakes in navigation, and obviously a military aid in terms of counterintelligence and NORAD morale. But he doubted that the President would agree. He sighed. "The Boss won't have it, Alf."

"I'll try to remember that," Alf Karman said bitterly. "When the next F-106 pilot asks me why we strapped an airplane on his back at 3 A.M. to go chase a MIG back to Cuba and then wouldn't let him shoot."

Charles Van Ness nodded. His civilian assistant was rolling the charts away, and there was a smudge on the topmost sheet. Remembering that he had to make the same presentation to a group of Pentagon newsmen that afternoon, Charles Van Ness pointed it out.

"That Scotchman seemed like a bright guy," he commented to the brush-cut young man, an MIT graduate and computer expert.

"I wonder why he thinks we can keep the next war in second gear?" speculated the young man.

"He's supposed to be an expert, Jimmy. Did he have any effect on your thinking?"

Jimmy's thinking plugged as neatly into the computers at Rand in Los Angeles or the MIT Univac as if he were connected by an invisible cable. He shook his head. "The manned bombers have had it and he's trying to get used to it. Maybe it takes time," he suggested generously. "Anyway, he didn't get near as steamed-up as most of them."

It was true. The Britisher had given the impression of indifference. Charles Van Ness should have been comforted, and yet . . . There was something reserved about the man, something dangerous, as if he had an ace up his sleeve.

He put the matter from mind and took the two men to lunch in his private dining room.

Malcolm Scott, Group Captain, RAF, sat in the Senate Lunch Room opposite Senator Brian Holiday. The senator was a handsome white-haired man with a jutting jaw; it was difficult for Malcolm Scott to divorce his newspaper image, that of a firebrand hit-'em-now anti-Communist, from the affable and charming person across the table from him.

"Do you," the senator asked incredulously, "seriously believe that the next war will be fought without nuclear weapons?"

"Perhaps without *strategic* nuclear weapons," Malcolm Scott said. "I hope so."

"But why do you *think* so?"

Malcolm Scott and an air marshal three thousand miles away in Whitehall were very possibly the only two military men of significant rank this side of the Kremlin who had even considered the possibility. Scott sat back.

"Senator, the U. S. has nerve gas which, it occasionally claims, would turn every Communist in the world into a quivering mound of flesh. Right?"

The senator nodded thoughtfully. "So I've heard."

"Would you use it? Did you use it in World War II?"

"No," the senator said.

"Why not?"

"Because gas was found ineffective in World War I, wasn't it?" the senator suggested.

"That isn't the real reason The real reason is that we all feared retaliation. Will you accept that?"

The senator nodded. "Yes."

"Now you have biological means of warfare," Malcolm Scott said. "You can infect entire populations and ruin their resistance and even wipe them out. Do you think you'll use these means in the next war?"

"Of course not."

"Why?"

The senator shrugged. "It's too dirty."

Malcolm Scott shook his head. "No. War is always dirty. You won't use biological warfare, Senator, because you know that if you use it the Russians will use it or the Chinese will use it and the end is the end of civilization. That's why you won't use it."

An ancient Negro with thin white spring-coils of hair and a muddy skin refilled their coffee cups. A group of senators on their way back to the Chamber paused, and for a moment Senator Brian Holiday and Scott were on their feet as the senator made introductions. When they sat down again, Malcolm Scott continued: "You won't start biological warfare, and you won't start nuclear."

"We dropped on Hiroshima and Nagasaki," the senator pointed out. "Why would we hesitate to drop on Moscow?"

"In 1945, if the Japanese had had the atom bomb, and the means to deliver it, do you think Truman—"

"Truman *and* Churchill," the senator broke in hotly.

"Truman and Churchill would have ordered it dropped?"

The senator flushed. "We were playing for keeps."

"My question was whether we would have dropped it if the Japanese had had one too."

The senator studied his fingers. "No."

Malcolm Scott sat back. "Well, the Russians have them now. The Chinese do too."

The senator seemed uncomfortable. "I don't like your arguments, but I'm going to have you called. Convince them that the manned bomber can still get through, and we'll worry about the nuances later. OK?"

Malcolm Scott hid a smile. "I'll try, Senator," he promised. "I'll see what I can do."

> "I want flexibility. . . . You cannot change your mind
> and bring the missile back."
> —GENERAL CURTIS LeMAY

Chapter Four

CAPTAIN MORRIS EPSTEIN lifted the lid of the breakfast cart in
his Nebraska tomb, hoping that his partner would not notice.
There was another helping of scrambled eggs inside.

"Help yourself, Morrie," said Dan Frost from the panel.
"I'm stuffed."

Epstein looked up quickly, searching for laughter in his
eye. He slammed down the lid. "No," he said bravely.
"Thanks. Just looking."

It was past 8 A.M. at any rate. The relief crew would be
through its briefing in Lincoln, perhaps climbing into the helicopter for the flight across the prairie. He wondered what they
had learned. Something was going on. Their night had been a
succession of practice alerts and communication checks, the
air alive with orders from the SAC underground Command
Posts and from the "Looking Glass," the auxiliary battle staff
endlessly circling Omaha in an EC-135. They had not had so
little sleep since Cuba.

Epstein sighed. He could not sleep today, either; he had a
class at eleven, and a quiz in Statistics at two. Sometimes he
wondered if he would not have been better off with the

County Probation Office in Los Angeles, studying nights.

He lay down to try to nap before the relief crew arrived, but the warbler began again and he weaved red-eyed to his chair. It was Looking Glass again, checking to see that all crews were alert. Someone certainly had a bug up his ass today.

At nine the relief crew announced itself, and Dan Frost swung the huge door open. The two fresh captains strolled in, stood next to each other on one side of the capsule. It was a time-honored ritual, and the happiest moment on Epstein's 24-hour tour. He and Frost faced them, unbuckled their revolvers, and swung the chambers open. Then they slipped the keys over their necks. Epstein's relief saluted.

"I relieve you, sir."

Morrie returned the salute and handed over gun and key. Leaving, he paused. "What's cooking?" he asked.

The new captain shrugged. "Something, but they ain't talking. Morrie?"

"Yes?"

"I think you're losing weight."

Morrie was about to thank him when he caught the wink between him and Dan Frost. "Thanks," he said bitterly. "Danny's helping me, you know."

But by the time he climbed aboard the helicopter beckoning in the morning sunlight he had recovered his spirits. The past night slipped obediently into line with all the other nights in the hole.

He had four days off, to study, play with his daughters, and work on his thesis. It was not a bad life.

In the first incident since the January and February flights, two aircraft were detected Mar. 15 approaching...the Alaskan mainland. The first passed into U. S. territory at 9:07 P.M. and the second at 9:13 P.M.

—AVIATION WEEK
re USSR Intruders

Chapter Five

MALCOLM SCOTT stood looking out the air attaché's window in the Chancery of the British Embassy, watching the evening traffic swirl around Observatory Circle and spill onto Massachusetts Avenue.

"Group Captain Scott?"

He turned. The florid, apple-cheeked young RAF flight lieutenant who was Assistant Air Attaché was holding out his orders, properly signed and endorsed. From the moment he had entered the office the young man had seemed discomfited by his presence and obscurely angry as well. Malcolm Scott guessed, from his own military-political billets, that he was torn between obligation to his diplomatic bosses and loyalty to a fellow officer.

"Lieutenant," Scott smiled, "let me ask you. Did my article cause a flap here?"

The young man hesitated. "As a matter of fact, yes."

"Would you have written it?" he asked suddenly.

"Sir?"

"Imagine," Malcolm Scott asked, "you were on the Joint Strategic Target Planning Staff. Imagine that suddenly you saw what you thought was a tremendous mistake being made. A mistake so serious, for instance, that the entire effort of that staff, of the U. S. Air Force and the RAF, of the NATO military alliance, was about to be poured down the drain. What action would you take, Lieutenant?"

The young Britisher thought for a moment. Malcolm Scott studied him. A good public school, and then RAF Cranwell, he guessed. The utter rigidity of the well-trained military mind, captured almost at birth. A cliché, for he himself was a Cranwell man; not really true, and yet, the military did attract the type. The flight lieutenant flushed. "Why, I'd take it up with Staff."

"And suppose you found the other members of the Staff in opposition?"

"Well, I guess I'd take another look at my *own* thinking. Right?"

Malcolm Scott nodded, toying with an ornate Wedgwood ashtray on the mantel. "And then? Suppose you reevaluated your own thinking and you found, so far as you could see, that you were *still* right?"

"I'd have to assume, I'm afraid, that the majority of the *staff* was right. After all, we're all on the same side."

Malcolm Scott nodded slowly. "The same side . . . yes. What about their pulling out on Skybolt?"

The assistant air attaché shrugged. "I'm inclined to go along with them. After all, it was an expensive develoment programme for them. And if the manned bomber can't get through, maybe it can't get halfway through, either. Perhaps Skybolt was a waste of money."

It had certainly been a waste of British money, Malcolm Scott thought. It was an air-launched ballistic missile developed by the U. S., but Whitehall had spend hundreds of thousands on a weapons system to integrate with it. At the beginning of its testing, the U. S. Department of Defense had scuttled it with a terse and inaccurate statement that it was failing in development.

" 'There can be no greater error than to expect or calculate upon real favors from nation to nation,' " mused Malcolm Scott. The attaché looked at him questioningly. "George Washington," Scott said. "Farewell Address."

The attaché nodded. He flipped swiftly through a card file to see if there were any messages from London for Scott, found none, stood up to say goodbye. Absently he reached for a pile of engraved invitations. He stood tapping one.

"By the way," he said. "The ambassador's asked us to invite any Commonwealth officers passing through tomorrow night. Show the colors, as it were."

"Thank you, no," Malcolm Scott said.

The attaché looked relieved. "A shame. We expect the President and his wife."

He could not have told why, but on a sudden impulse he reached for the card. He went back to the Mariott Inn and spent the afternoon calling small airports near Washington, searching for a relaxed and trusting operator.

In the green plush Treaty Room off the oval study in the White House, Charles Van Ness sat to the right of the President of the United States at the long table as the other members of the National Security Council gathered their papers and notes and began to leave. The decision on the Soviet-Chinese threat was simply to wait. "God give us the wisdom to recognize that which we can do nothing about," the President had said finally. Van Ness was in the habit of lingering in the White House for a few last words in his chief's study. But today, before he could follow the gaunt, gray-haired man to the sanctum, a secretary from the outer office brought him a phone. It was the duty officer in the War Room underneath the Pentagon.

The North American Air Defense Command was on a yellow alert; three unidentified targets had been "painted" by Alaskan radar. They were approaching the Arctic Circle; within moments would be well into Alaskan airspace if they did not turn aside. While Van Ness talked, word came that they had been intercepted by an F-106, which had identified them as USSR "Bounder" bombers. The fighter-pilot, with his wingman staying well clear, was crowding the Russian flight leader now; soon, one would expect, the Soviet flight would turn north.

The Secretary of Defense told the colonel at the other end of the line to keep him informed. He followed the President into the study, saw the vague irritation that he expected cross the lean features when he explained the latest sortie.

"A game," the President growled, sitting behind his desk. "Draw a line in the dust in the schoolyard, and cross it at your peril. I'm braver than you. Or in the case of the smaller nations, my daddy's braver than your daddy. A hundred years from now people will look back at us and laugh!"

"I doubt it," Charles Van Ness said. "Man is a fighting machine. A hundred years from now he'll still be a fighting machine. The only reason he'll laugh at you and me will be because we allowed them to dish it out so long without doing anything about it."

"And so," the President sighed, "we start another round with them. Who decreed," he wanted to know suddenly, "that the F-106 they shot down yesterday should make a probe?"

"Fighter-Intelligence on the JSTPS in Omaha. It was necessary," Charles Van Ness said vehemently, "or it wouldn't have gone. We ought to be sending up more than we do."

The President did not reply. Charle Van Ness knew that he was thinking of the dead F-106 pilot; he was angry, too, at the attack. There was a grim cast to the lined face. Van Ness thought he saw his chance.

He sat down in the leather chair he liked, close to the desk. He placed his fingertips on his knees, studying them for a moment. They were long and tapering, giving the lie to the clichés about fingers; they were Machiavellian, subtle, and yet he was a practical, hard man of facts and figures. The fingertips should have belonged to an architect or a surgeon. They were wasted on an engineer, superfluous in length even when they flashed across the keys of his desk-calculator. They were the fingertips of an intellectual, and he had always been obscurely ashamed of their grace.

"Mr. President, I think we ought to shoot one down."

The President scowled at him. "We've been through this! What do we have to prove to them? They're always intercepted, aren't they?"

The Secretary of Defense shrugged. "In bad weather, with low-flying aircraft, we can't always be sure."

"What's our batting average?"

"Above 500, I'd say."

"Why do we have to make an example of *one*, then?"

The Secretary began to chop his tapering hand, counting off the points of his argument. He concluded with the matter of public reaction. Ever since Francis Gary Powers had been downed, the public had been aware that probing between East and West was in progress; but it knew only that U. S. pilots had been captured or died. The manned bomber people claimed that the bomber could get through modern defenses. The administration was doing nothing to prove that it could not.

"We will not sacrifice an airplane full of human beings to provide a lesson for the American public," the President said sourly.

"All right, Mr. President. But when do we, and *where* do we, draw the line?"

The President sighed. He was tired. His shoulders sagged. The Secretary noted that he was growing older by the day. "When there's a clear and present danger," the President murmured, "to American lives. Not any sooner."

Charles Van Ness nodded and gave up the argument.

They could wait, after all. The Russians would stretch their luck further and further, and ultimately there would be clear danger to American lives, and then the President would have to act. At least he himself was already on record.

The NORAD concept of air defense is dependent on the . . . digital computer.

—PRESS RELEASE
Los Angeles
Air Defense
Sector

Chapter Six

GROUP CAPTAIN MALCOLM SCOTT made his third landing and taxied the Piper Cub across the grass strip near Arlington, Virginia. The gnarled oldtimer sat bemused beside him. "You fly all right, I reckon," he announced dryly. "Just don't wrestle with it like a heavier plane, is all."

"Righto," Malcolm Scott said. He eased to a stop in front of the weather-beaten Quonset which apparently served the parchment-skinned owner as a combined office and hangar. The man gave off an odor of pipe tobacco and leather that reminded him somehow of early, open-cockpit training days.

"Of course," the old man grinned, looking at Malcolm Scott through twinkling, deep-set eyes like a cheerful monkey, "you wouldn't likely know about heavier planes, from your logbook."

"No," Scott said coolly. "I wouldn't."

"Only forty hours," reflected the instructor. He opened the door but made no move to get out. "Forty hours. . . ."

Thirty-four of them forged, to help you make a decision, thought Malcolm Scott.

The old man shrugged. "Well, I ain't asking questions."

He took a pipe from his pocket, struck a match with his thumbnail. "Man wants to get off by himself for a little morning hop, it's good. Good for me, good for him." He regarded Scott over the flame. "Friend of mine in Houston, though . . . *puff, puff* . . . he rented a plane to a student . . . *puff, puff,* . . . this here student seemed to have forgotten to log a couple of thousand hours in his book, like you. Fellow could fly, though. He flew all the way to Mexico and tried to sell the plane."

"Really?"

The old man nodded. "Well," he said, "I don't reckon an Englishman is stupid enough to try to fly that far in a Piper."

"I don't reckon," Malcolm Scott smiled.

The old man stepped from the aircraft. "Get back by noon," he warned. "I got a lesson at one."

Malcolm Scott nodded and taxied to the end of the runway in a cloud of pipe smoke.

General Alf Karman sat sweating in the balcony of his Command Post alone. He reflected on the ugliness of his domain, far from the sleek fighters he loved. The Direction Center for the Washington Sector of the North American Air Defense Command occupied a mammoth concrete cube at Fort Lee, Virginia, 100 miles south of Washington, D.C. It was as grim and architecturally functional as a brick. WADS, as it was called, had an entrance, a very closely guarded entrance, but that was the only break in its walls. The building was four stories high but it had no windows. If some sort of permanent truce had ever been reached with Communism it could have been turned into an escape-proof prison without the slightest external change by the removal of 65,000 electronic tubes and two 11-million-dollar computers, individually air-conditioned and presumably more comfortable than its commander.

To General Alf Karman, responsible for the defense of the capital and eastern seaboard between the New York and Montgomery, Alabama, sectors, the Command Post at times seemed already a prison.

It was without charm and no more unique than an ice cube. The classic simplicity of his own blockhouse was common to all sixteen of the centers which dotted the U. S. Alf Karman knew that if he were set down blindfolded in a corridor of the Phoenix Center or the Los Angeles one he would have found it difficult until he saw the map in the Command Post itself to distinguish it from his own or that of Seattle, Great Falls, or Oklahoma City.

He had sat a prisoner in the same seat here in the nerve center until after 6 P.M. yesterday when three USSR Bounders had wandered across the Bering Straits and tripped the Distant Early Warning Line. The Washington sector could hardly have been farther from the scene of action, of which there was none anyway, but NORAD had nevertheless gone through sucessive stages of alert, and would do it again today, and tomorrow, and presumably forever, without loosing a missile.

The Command Post was a large amphitheatre. General Karman had wandered into it before lunch today to wait for his British visitor, as one would enter a deserted theatre for a lower balcony seat: the only difference was that the balcony at which he sat was glassed in. Along its front row each comfortable leather armchair for a member of his battle-staff had before it a console studded with lights, switches, and a miniature TV screen. It took months to learn to play the consoles; their full capabilities in instantly displaying information were limitless. Flanking Alf Karman were seats for his deputy, for a communications officer, for an aircraft control and warning officer, for his staff operations officer. Even an Army and Navy officer, plus an FAA civilian to identify commercial flights, were available on his personal staff along the balcony seats.

Below, in what he thought of as the orchestra pit, were other officers at consoles. Alf Karman reflected that in today's Air Force there were a dozen officers manning consoles for every one in a fighter cockpit. Above them, dominating the stage, was a 17-foot-square transparent screen with a vast polar projection of Alaska, Greenland, Canada, and the United States.

It was a very ornate stage: Broadway lights flashed above, left to right, giving the time zones from the Pacific to the Atlantic. As radar 3,000 miles away "painted" hostile aircraft the information was simultaneously dispatched to sectors like his from Maine to Los Angeless and to the North American Air Defense Command Combat Operations Center deep under Cheyenne Mountain near Colorado Springs. The information appeared on hundreds of electronic scopes, and from one of them in the orchestra pit below it was photographed, the film developed, the status flashed on the screen every thirty seconds. A target could be thirty seconds old when he saw it, but the tiny individual scope six inches from his hand did not have even that disadvantage: it was accurate to the microsecond.

Yesterday Alf Karman had been captured here by the Russian foray (or navigational training flight, they would claim today if they bothered to acknowledge the U. S. protest) almost as soon as he had returned from the Pentagon. He had no sooner entered the building than the lights had begun to flash, the status boards to change, and finally, as the unknown aircraft continued south, "Big Noise, Big Noise! Readiness condition one! Air defense: Applejack! Red for applejack! Big Noise, Big Noise . . ."*Ad infinitum,* until finally the air defense warning had changed to a safe "Snow-man" and the Soviet planes were led politely home.

This morning was quiet. The Command Post was deserted. He sat in his chair, flipped his console on to watch an interception directed by a young interceptor-director officer from the "Blue Room" some distance away in the building. A "faker" flashed at 30,000 feet over the Washington sector. It was a "Friendly-Enemy" light bomber sent aloft to simulate a hostile for the training of an interceptor, now pursuing it.

He was sweaty. Three 400-ton air conditioners—enough to cool the Empire State building—were apparently failing at their job. Irritated, he called his Building Maintenance officer. Then he moved restlessly in his armchair, glancing at the time above the screen. Scott was due twenty minutes ago. He had left word at the entrance to be called when the Britisher arrived, for the Secretary of Defense himself could hardly have entered without his blessing.

Alf Karman was a restless man, a fighter-pilot who hated the inactivity that rank and the incresing automation of the North American Air Defense Command was binding around him more tightly every day.

Idly, he pushed a button and spoke to the air-policeman at

the gate outside. No, sir, no RAF officer had yet shown.

His deputy wandered in. "Detroit's out again, I see," observed the colonel.

Alf Karman had not noticed. He glanced at the status board by the screen. The Detroit sector, probably through computer failure, had indeed gone out; it meant only that his own geographical responsibility extended now somewhat farther west until it met that of Chicago. There was no action for him to take.

"I wonder what's wrong?" the colonel asked. He seemed slightly aggrieved. Alf Karman took a grim pleasure in the Detroit computer's affliction. He wondered what would happen if the whole Semi-Automatic Ground Environmental System went on strike. They would have to let the pilots fly the planes again, instead of sit like lumps in their cockpits.

It would not really matter. After all, the computers were mere memory machines for storing pre-computed situations. The complexity of the system sometimes fooled you, made you think that without it you were dead, but the racks of glowing tubes in the lower blockhouse were inanimate and unthinking objects. When the chips were down they were simply aids to the men like himself who must direct and fly the planes, just as adding machines were aids to accountants. He strolled from the Command Post.

Now he was freezing. Maintenance had overdone it. Ordinarily, Alf Karman felt well enough disposed toward his equipment, as he did the experts on his well-chosen, comfortable staff. But this morning he was vaguely disquieted.

He moved through the Computer Rooms, irritated somehow by the familiar odor of heated relays and air-conditioned sterility. The two mighty computers should have reassured him, but they did not. He was master of 10,000 dedicated personnel, of $\frac{1}{15}$th of the most lethal defensive force that the world had ever known, and yet somehow, yesterday, the quiet Scotchman, in his absolute conviction that bombers could get through any defenses, had bothered him. The hell with it.

Impelled, perhaps, by a desire to get closer to the men in the cockpit, he moved through a green-tinted chamber in which the identification people leaned over their display scopes. Here officers endlessly tied-in innumerable tiny radar targets with flight plans so that no enemy bomber could long remain an unknown.

Only high-flying planes showed here, nothing but jets; only the aircraft most likely to be hostile. There were no traces of lightplanes or the numberless low-flying locals, flying below 10,000 feet and under 200 knots. Alf Karman wished that there were some way to check them too. But this was the way it had to be. Fifteen thousand aircraft flew over his sector daily, two hundred coming in from overseas. To show them all would set the screens crazy with tiny comets, turn the identification personnel to screaming idiots.

He passed through a double swinging door and entered his favorite niche in his small empire, the "Blue Room."

It was a cavernous place. The cortex of the Direction Center lay in his battle-staff's amphitheatre upstairs, where the decisions were made, but the medulla oblongata, where the instinctive fighting reflexes originated, was here. All of the tiny facts of a high-flying jet—speed, altitude, direction of flight—were channeled to this room where the intercept directors and their teams worked bathed in the pale blue light from their scopes. As Alf Karman entered through the swinging doors, the senior director, a light colonel, stood up. "Good afternoon, General."

"Afternoon, Charlie."

The senior director followed him down the long line of consoles, each glowing blue, most of them unmanned now.

But one team was working an interceptor to a practice target. A sharp-nosed second lieutenant sat on a stool and peered into the sheen of his scope, his features ghastly blue. The young man wore no wings. The chances that he had climbed more than once or twice into an interceptor cockpit were slim, but he was flying an aircraft a hundred miles away as if he were another Rickenbacker. Or God, Alf Karman reflected grimly. The far-off pilot was a passenger in his own cockpit.

The intercept director—"I.D."—was the most important link in the electronic-human chain from farflung radar antennae through Direction Center to the unarguable scope on the pilot's panel. The young lieutenant's attention to his own screen was unwavering. He flicked Alf Karman not a glance. He was as intent on his task as a pinball addict when the lights began to flash. A flexible steel cable led from his console to a chrome electronic pistol which he held in his hand, finger on the trigger.

Alf Karman peered over his shoulder. Only two aircraft showed on the scope, their "digital information display" tracks—"DIDS"—inching like reluctant BB-sized comets across the screen, one behind the other, hunter and prey. As Alf Karman watched, the intercept director leveled his pistol at his gun and the pursuing comet adjusted its orbit. It was a hundred-million-dollar shooting gallery in a penny arcade, Alf Karman mused; this sallow young man had all the fun and the pilot all the risk.

The chrome pistol substituted for voice commands. If everything worked correctly, the intercept director controlled his aircraft without a single word, simply by pointing the flashgun at the scope and pulling the trigger. When he did, somewhere in the infinite complex of the computers on the floor below an electronic synapse flashed across the circuits and the brute memory searched until it found the best command for the aircraft. It was hard to remind oneself that the system did not think, that until an engineer had programmed into its vast memory every single possibility of enemy and pursuers' courses and speeds and altitudes the computer was moronic. Moronic and stubborn, too: if the programmer had made a mistake, the computer would send the plane the wrong answer each time the interceptor director asked its help.

The young interceptor director was wearing earphones, and the general could not hear the pilot. But there was apparently some lack of rapport between the man on the ground and the man in the air. There had been since time began, thought the general cynically.

"He wants me to go voice," complained the lieutenant to the enlisted technician who sat to his left. "I don't know why."

The general knew why. He had sat too many times like the pilot of the interceptor—feeling like a sack of wheat in the cockpit as the man in the Blue Room shot his plane orders wordlessly. There were parts of "SAGE"—the Semi-Automatic Ground Environmental System—that were utterly necessary—it would be impossible to use old-fashioned methods

of directing supersonic aircraft toward supersonic prey—bu
most pilots were reluctant completely to trust their runs to the
autopilot in the plane or the non-flying intercept director on
the ground.

Most young interceptor directors, the general had observed, did not agree. And this was one of them.

"Okay," the lieutenant said acidly. "Alf Lima 27, continue
port turn to 295 . . . Alfa Lima 27, your target is a flight o
one, measuring angels four-zero. Ground speed 500. . . . You
target should be 12 o'clock, range about six. You got an eye
ball yet?"

It was apparent that the young man had lost all the spor
when he had had to lay down his gun. He watched the screen
for a moment, turned in disgust. "He'd have missed."

As if, Alf Karman noted, he would have been assured a hi
had the pilot stayed on automatic control. Maybe so, the gen
eral thought. Or maybe not. But his sympathy was with the
flier. He glanced at his watch. It was past eleven; the English
man apparently was not coming. He wondered where he was.

Group Captain Malcolm Scott, in the Piper at 8,000 feet
shot his last photograph of the drab gray Direction Center. He
leveled his wings and closed the window against the slip
stream. The plaintive note of the Washington omnibeacon
sang in his earphones and the aircraft jounced gently as he hi
a downdraft. With the last click of his shutter over Genera
Karman's blockhouse his job in America was done. Assuming
that the photos he had taken, and those the others had
snapped, were all right, he could be on his way to England
tomorrow.

If it weren't for the damned Senate hearing! He encased hi
camera and dipped his prop toward the little grass field. Per
haps he could avoid the hearing as he had avoided the tou
today. He hoped that General Karman had not canceled an
engagements to guide him through the complex. He felt guilt
at breaking his promise.

But after all, he had not. He had been there. On time, too.

"The Defense Department is making strenuous efforts to manage the leaks of information to the Press."

—Robert S. McNamara

Chapter Seven

Malcolm Scott had been asked to wear civilian clothes on meeting Flynn; he stepped from the cab outside the restaurant in the same slacks, sport jacket, and somewhat rumpled necktie he had worn flying the Piper. He felt seedy and unkempt; he was enough of a military man to resent the necessity for appearing thus downtown in public. Surreptitiously, after he paid the driver, he rubbed the top of one shoe on the opposite trouser leg, repeated the process with the other shoe, and brushed himself down. Then he walked into the dimly lit, black-leather-and-chrome gloom of the restaurant, heading immediately past the bar to the rear.

He had somehow imagined Flynn as a pale and haggard man, Americanized, a clerk at the British Tourist Bureau or a member of some minor Commonwealth trade mission. A man, at least, unlikely to give himself away as English until he talked. But the person in the rear booth was a portly, florid chap, complete with RAF handlebar moustache. His Britishness fairly shouted across the packed restaurant.

Malcolm Scott, film large in his pocket, moved through

the tables, avoiding the scurrying waiters as best he could. The florid gentleman watched him all the way.

"Mr. Flynn?" Scott asked.

The man nodded. "Group Captain Scott. Sit down."

Malcolm Scott seated himself, studying the agent carefully. He ordered a whisky with ice. They were guarded, fencing. "Been a hot day," Flynn said. "Unusual for the time of year."

Malcolm Scott nodded. "Have you been long in Washington?"

It was foolish, really, but the man seemed determined to play it to the hilt. He nodded mysteriously. He had before him a gin and tonic, which he lifted. "Well, Group Captain Scott, cheers."

Malcolm Scott raised his glass. Sooner or later, they would have to quit playing cloak-and-dagger and come to the point. "Did you," he prodded, "bring the stuff?"

"Stuff?" Flynn asked innocently.

Oh, for Christ's sake, thought Malcolm Scott. Then he remembered the password. "Dunsinane," he said softly. "The Woods of Dunsinane."

Flynn smiled blandly, reached into a dispatch case beside him, and drew forth a series of glossy photographs. With a flourish, he spread them like a fan on the table. Malcolm Scott's heart pumped. Involuntarily he glanced around at their neighbors, but when they seemed to be paying no attention he took the photos and shuffled through them.

They were all but one aerial pictures of varying degrees of clarity. One of them, a shot of Boston from what he judged to be 6,000 feet, showed almost too much of the wing of the Eastern Airlines jet from which it had been taken; no, it was all right. He looked again at another print, taken from a ground station: it was a ballistic missile site in a heavily wooded area, shot from a nearby peak; he judged it offhand to be a site of the 318th Aerospace Division near Bangor, Maine. "Do you have the diaries?"

Flynn tossed two dissimilar notebooks on the table. Malcolm Scott read the names on the frontispieces, leafed through them swiftly.

Under "April 8" he found an entry:

Photograph taken from Apple Hill, eight miles southeast of Bangor. Location ascertained through René Chennault, licensed guide at a rate of $3 per hour, on "deer hunting trip." Total outlay $12 for guide, $4.52 for ammunition. No deer. No shooting. Film exposed secretly while guide was relieving himself behind tree.

Someone was playing games. Well, the picture was all right. He suddenly realized that all of them were all right and, assuming his own films were satisfactory, what had seemed such an incredibly difficult task was very near fruition. The realization made his hands tremble. He shuffled the photos into order.

"Is that all?" he asked Flynn.

"The lot," Flynn said. "Now, I have duplicates, you understand."

Malcolm Scott's eyes widened. "You have *what?*"

"I was told to keep duplicates in my file. Of the pictures. And photostats of the diaries. They're in the office—"

"What office?" Malcolm Scott blurted. "What the hell *are* you anyway, Flynn? It's hard to sit here and discuss this without knowing—"

Flynn raised his hand impatiently. "I don't see that it's particularly necessary that you *do* know, but if you must, I'm the Washington correspondent of the London *Express.*"

That, perhaps, but if so it was only a front. He was an intelligence agent too, Scott knew. Despite this, he was impressed as always by a man who earned a living with his pen. "I see. . . ."

"Now," Flynn said, "the next thing you're going to do is try to discover how much I know about this."

"How much *do* you know?" Malcolm Scott asked.

"I know that if I hang onto prints of these pictures, and all goes well, I'll be rewarded. Professionally. With a 'beat,' as we say. That's just about the extent of my knowledge, I'm afraid. Would you care to tell me more?"

"I can't." He sipped his drink. "You've done things like this before."

"Not precisely," Flynn said. "No, this is an odd one. But

I'm known as a reporter who can keep his mouth shut. And I did develop these films for you myself, in secret, and I acted as a drop, at what perhaps could be some peril. Whatever you're up to, don't you think I'm entitled at least to the prints I've kept, for whatever they're worth?"

"If you've been promised them."

It was none of Scott's business. So far the man had done everything required of him; doubtless he was dependable; he would not have been picked unless he was dependable. "Good show," he said. "Now, would you develop one more roll for me tonight?"

It was impossible; the regular photo staff would be working in the darkroom until past midnight, Flynn knew for a fact.

"Flynn, believe me, as you've been told, it'll be worth your while. As the journalist closest to it, it'll be worth your while."

Flynn changed the subject. "I'm told," he said suddenly, "you're to testify before the Senate Armed Services Committee tomorrow. In a closed hearing?"

Malcolm Scott could not fathom how he had heard of it. Geoffrey Flynn smiled. "I cover the Pentagon as well as the Embassy garden parties, you know. General Younger's testifying today for the ICBM. You're a manned bomber advocate. I suggest you don't even bother."

"Why not?"

"The Pentagon are great ones for controlling the news," the newsman said. "Watch you don't find you're quoted as an *anti*-bomber man, since the hearing's closed. You won't have the protection of the American press, which, my American colleagues tell me, is so vastly superior to ours."

"Is it that bad?" Malcolm Scott wanted to know.

"Don't go, is my advice."

"I have to, don't I?" .

"What can they do if you're on your way to England?"

Malcolm Scott looked at him sadly. "How can I go to England," he asked innocently, "unless you develop my films?"

The puffy eyes danced in sudden mirth. "A typical Scot!"

Flynn chortled. "I'll run them through if I have to wait up half the night. By midnight, then, in my office."

He gave him a card. Malcolm Scott was so grateful that despite the low estate to which his pocketbook had fallen he ordered lunch for the both of them.

Chapter Eight

GENERAL HUB YOUNGER waited his turn in a spectator's seat in the high-vaulted marble hearing room while General Hal Norwood sat at bay in stubby, glacial calm in the witness chair, his five stars a little dull, his chest a carpet of faded decorations. Younger had never been called to Senate testimony before, and now, as the members of the Armed Services Committee digested his senior's last answer, he tried to assess the odd discomfort he had felt at the apparent openness of what was a closed hearing.

He had come to the new Senate Office Building with Senator Joe Peroni, riding the underground from the Capitol where he had met the senator in the office of the Majority Leader.

He had met Peroni before, when the senator and two of his cohorts now on the dais before him had inspected ICBM sites near SAC Headquarters. He had felt rapport with the squat, black-eyed Italian-American; his questions in the silos had been studied and he seemed to have a mathmatical bent.

He was the senator's boy at this hearing, the senator's and the Pentagon's. Charlie Van Ness, veteran of a dozen such inquisitions, had said: "Just follow Peroni's lead, Hub, and

you can't go wrong. He's had me up there three times already.
You can see, I'm all right. Bruised, but all right. . . ."

The knowledge of that was all that was keeping him from
utter panic at the feeling that he was going to be forced to give
away military secrets of the U. S., Britain, and Canada, in a
truly traitorous style.

He had expected the hearing room to be guarded by Capitol
police, or at least by men identifiable as being from the forces
of the Senate Master-at-Arms. But he had entered with the
senator through no guards at all, faced the dais rapidly filling
with committee members, glanced at the spectator seats, half-
empty but nevertheless half-full, and quickly asked Senator
Peroni: "This *is* a closed hearing, sir?"

The senator nodded. "Don't worry, Hub. See those gals?"

Behind the dais at which Brian Holiday presided stood
three unobtrusive young women. One of them was studying
his face intently. He smiled automatically. All at once she
moved to the girl in the center and made some inquiry. The
second girl, who apparently recognized him, nodded reassur-
ingly and all three went back to their study of the faces in the
spectators below. This was the sole security, apparently, and
he must accept it.

General Norwood was not winning friends for the manned
bomber. He had been gruff even with his own sponsor, Senator Holiday, and with Senator Peroni almost acid.

"General Norwood," Brian Holiday said now, "you've tes-
tified that the ballistic missile will not necessarily be difficult
to defend against in the future. What do you base this on?"

Hal Norwood's squat frame shifted impatiently. "I didn't
say I thought it would be not '*difficult*' to deal with. I said it
would be not '*impossible*' to deal with. There's a difference."

"All right, General. There *is* a difference. Why do you
think it will be not 'impossible' to deal with?"

General Hal Norwood arose suddenly, moved across the
room to a map of the world. "Hell, gentlemen, the ICBM isn't
the ultimate weapon!" He put his finger on the North Central
United States, traced an arc over the Pole toward Russia.
"From this silo in Wyoming, say, to the center of Moscow!
There's only *one* possible trajectory that an ICBM can take.
Gentlemen, there are no others! You know this already. It's

got no brains. It *has* to travel along an imaginary tube in space from the time it's launched to the time thirty or forty minutes later when we hope it hits the target. Thirty or forty *minutes*, gentlemen, not seconds! Thirty or forty minutes is something you can get your hands on. And it will never go any faster and General Younger here has to admit it, because it's obeying the laws of motion! It's out there in space, and it's blind, and once you toss it out there it's not going to make a damn what you do, because you've left its boosters behind."

For the first time he became animated: "Now the Russians know as soon as that nose cone pokes over the rim of the earth *exactly* where it was launched and where it's headed. It *has* to curve along an imaginary tunnel if it's going to hit at all. Along that invisible tube, gentlemen, it's got to be here, and here, and here, at precisely the right second."

He jabbed a stubby finger three times at spots on the map. "If it isn't, they got nothing to worry about anyway! If it *is*, all they got to do is to launch an anti-ICBM along the same tunnel with a proximity fuse and a nuclear warhead, and when they pass near each other"—he snapped his fingers—"that's the end of your ICBM. Now, gentlemen, the bomber is something else again."

"Just a minute, General," Senator Peroni cut in. "The theory is fine, but do you think the USSR is ahead of us in anti-ICBM missiles?"

The general shrugged. "Nobody knows."

"And yet," the senator reminded him. *"We're* nowhere close."

The general flushed and returned to his seat. "We have some high-acceleration missiles coming up that ought to do it. Like 'Sprint.' We've had hits even with the Nike Hercules. Every offense has in it the seed of its own defense. We'll develop something. They will too."

"Look," Senator Peroni objected. "If they can develop an anti-ICBM missile to knock down a warhead traveling at 15,000 miles per hour, why should they have any trouble intercepting a bomber? Even a Mach three bomber, traveling at say 3,000?"

The general's hand slammed on the desk in front of the witness stand. "Because, Senator, the manned bomber doesn't have to fly through that tunnel! It has a choice of altitude, and it has a choice of direction! It has a choice of speed! It has a choice of tactics! It can sneak under radar at low altitude! Or come in behind weather! Or confuse radar by dumping quail! And it'll be equally capable of doing this in ten years or twenty, regardless of what defenses are brought up against it!"

"General Karman was in here last Friday," Senator Peroni observed. "He said that in exercises like 'Skyshield' and the 'Friendly Enemy' sorties, practically nobody in the attacking forces ever penetrated successfully. He wondered how you motivated your SAC crews to believe that they'd penetrate in the first place, let alone get back alive."

"He did, did he?" Hal Norwood growled. "I'd like to see him handle a saturation raid someday. Like Ploesti or some of the Hamburg raids or—it's a nasty word, but war is war—Dresden. The *Luftwaffe* was going to shoot down everything that flew, but the RAF broke a hell of a lot of china there!"

"That was World War II," Senator Peroni protested.

"It doesn't matter," the general said doggedly. "World War II or World War III. We had two percent attrition when the intelligence guys told us we'd lose our whole damn strike force. If you double two percent attrition for the next war, or triple it, isn't it still worth the crews in terms of strike damage?"

"What about the future, General? The Pentagon, and the Rand people, and the scientific advisers to the Secretary of Defense say that in ten years the manned bomber will be a sitting duck. They're dealing with facts, General. Not conjecture or . . . well, nostalgia."

General Hub Younger could see the red tide crawling up Hal Norwood's neck. The squat, compact old man looked as if he was coiled to rush the dais. With a great effort Norwood controlled himself.

"In ten years," he said softly enough, "the ballistic missile will be your sitting duck. The Mach three, Mach four bomber will be more flexible, not less. Some day a Mach three bomber will prove it. But you know something, Senator?"

"What's that?"

"It takes six years to build one. Unless you vote the funds

now, and unless the Pentagon spends them, that bomber will be Russian."

There was a long silence, but Hub Younger sensed that not a vote had been changed. The pro-administration senatorial faces were granite. "Some of us feel," Senator Peroni said, "along with the Secretary of Defense, that if we try to add a bomber program to the space and present defense budget, the Russians won't need to build bombers. We'd have to sell them ours. General Norwood, thank you."

As Norwood walked up the aisle toward Hub Younger he hesitated for a moment, and Hub looked deep into the flinty eyes. The Old Man paused, almost spoke, then shook his head and continued. Hub Younger knew that it was his own turn to bang the remaining coffin nails into the SAC Bomber Force.

Then he was sitting in the witness chair himself, sworn and ready for the last-ditch onslaught by Senator Brian Holiday, his own inquisitor. . . .

"General Younger," Senator Holiday said, reminding Hub Younger of a rattlesnake backed into a corner. "Could you give the committee your estimate of the megatonnage you would assume that the United States would be ready to drop on the USSR and China today?"

General Hub Younger swallowed. He sensed as he had from the beginning that people were leaving and entering the room almost at will. It was obvious that the entire security precautions resided in the three sets of eyes behind the senators, hopefully sharp. Presumably the girls were Senate secretaries who knew everyone in the room by sight; if someone entered that they were not sure of, it was to be hoped they would stop the hearing until they *were* sure.

Senator Brian Holiday, from the end of the committee table, looked down at him through his thick horned-rimmed glasses. "Well, sir?"

"These are, of course, top secret figures..." Hub began tentatively.

"This is a closed hearing, General," answered the senator.

It doesn't look like one, thought Younger. He thought of the overzealous major who suspected Malcolm Scott. Now he was being just as old-womanish himself. He took a deep breath.

"We now have a total of 205 Titan and Atlas ICBMs," he began, "plus a total of 600 Minutemen. Each Titan and Atlas will carry a warhead of approximately ten megatons, and each Minuteman about one megaton. So you see we have today somewhat over 2,600 megatons total ICBM capacity."

The committee scribbled a few notes, which General Hub Younger hoped would be destroyed.

"What's our total deliverable megatonnage by your SAC bomber forces?" Brian Holiday demanded. "Today?"

"Well, sir, we have a total of a little over a thousand B-47, B-52, and B-58 bombers. And their present deliverable megatonnage runs around 25,000 megatons."

"So today," Brian Holiday said, "we could deliver around twenty-six *thousand* megatons by bomber, but only twenty-six *hundred* by ICBM?"

Hub Younger nodded. "But those figures are misleading, Senator. For one thing, we feel that—"

"General Younger," Senator Holiday broke in, "before you go on, let me pursue this a little further. Take the middle of the 1970's. How many Atlas and Titan ICBMs will we have then?"

Hub Younger colored. "None, sir. They're to be phased out." Which you damn well know, he thought silently.

"Phased out?" the senator said thoughtfully. "I see. And what ballistic missiles will be taking their place?"

"We'll have at least 1,000 Minutemen by the middle of the 70's, plus a projected 656 Polaris Missiles."

"I see. Giving a total deliverable megatonnage of what?"

"Around 1,600 megatons," Hub Younger said. "About one megaton per missile."

The senator's handsome, tanned face broke into a series of incredulous lines, as if he were having trouble digesting the horrible truth. "Do I understand, General, that you plan *no* increase in deliverable megatonnage—that is, ICBM megatonnage—over the next ten years?"

"That's correct, sir."

"All right. We'll come back to that. Now, as for the manned bomber forces. Are you one of those, General, who have advised the Department of Defense to ask no funds for further development of manned bombers in this fiscal year?"

"Yes sir," Hub Younger said bluntly.

"Why, General?"

"Because I feel that the manned strategic aircraft is becoming obsolete. I feel that we should devote the same funds to further development of intercontinental—"

The senator held up his hand. "General Younger, this force of bombers which is SAC—the fine SAC Bomber Command you have inherited—assuming no new inputs, how long will the aircraft last?"

"With proper maintenance, good upkeep...without too much attrition, up to 1975."

"Becoming more obsolete each year?"

"Certainly."

"Becoming, in effect, useless by the early 70's?"

"Useless now, some think," Hub Younger said.

"I see. General, how many megatons can a B-52 carry?"

"It depends, sir. But at least twenty-four."

"And your biggest ICBM? The Titan? How many megatons?"

Hub Younger sighed. "Less than ten megatons."

"And the Polaris missiles?"

"Less than one megaton."

"And Minutemen?"

"Around the same. One megaton."

Senator Holiday sat for a moment, as if shocked speechless. An actor, Hub Younger thought bitterly, posturing on a stage. Perhaps they were all actors, the men behind the table, in an unreal world in which the effect of what one said was more important than what one really felt. He was a man being pummeled by shadows.

The senator bent over the pad on which he had been scribbling. "If I'm right, General, we now have ninety percent of our megatonnage riding in manned aircraft, and ten percent sitting in silos. By 1975 the ninety percent deliverable by bomber will no longer be deliverable because the aircraft will have rusted or turned obsolete. We will have only some ten percent sitting in untested, untried missiles, even smaller than the missiles we have now."

"Senator," Hub Younger said, "that's not quite true. It's impossible, as you know yourself, being a pilot, to maintain aircraft one hundred percent alert. As a matter of fact, today only one out of two of our total bombers is on alert. All missiles are one hundred percent alert all the time, roughly."

"That doesn't change the fact," Senator Holiday pointed out, "that you are advising that we eliminate all but ten percent of the deliverable megatonnage we have today!"

In a way, it was true. Hub Younger believed that there were sound strategic reasons for it. Some were complex, some dealt with the industrial capacity of the United States and the gross national product and the very ability of the taxpayer to bear the burden of useless military expenditure. In the past, the military had grasped at every cent it could get; he liked to think he was the forerunner of a new breed, calculating the overall economic picture instead of battling with other commanders for their place at the congressional trough. But it was impossible for him to explain without lapsing into nuclear socio-economic jargon, into strategic concepts that had taken him years to absorb and could hardly be simplified for the politicians behind the table. It was as if a family in conference were asking a surgeon to explain suture by suture a modern operation on a relative as opposed to an older technique of which they also knew nothing.

Hub Younger sighed. It *had* to be simplified, and quickly. "It's academic, Senator," he said, falling back on the one thing he knew would impress the layman. "We have to face it, Mr. Chairman, Senator Holiday, Senators. The manned bomber simply cannot any longer get through. And it will be less likely to get through in 1975. Our phasing-out of it will coincide with its increasing obsolescence. This is the neat, clean way to do it. Further research programs arise simply from a desire to justify the use of weapons which we have trained men to fly but which are really obsolete. The manned bomber cannot get through!"

His last words took effect. Where most of the members had been doodling, some even reading, now he saw that he had their attention. Senator Joe Peroni was looking at him approvingly. Now he stepped into the breach.

"I think we understand that," he said soothingly. "It's certainly been the consensus of opinion. Everywhere in the military, in the technological branches, in the scientific world and in the office of the Secretary of Defense. My opinion is that we've gone far enough and should dispense with further hearings."

"No!" Brian Holiday rasped stubbornly. "We've got an RAF officer coming in tomorrow who, incidentally, is one of the top target planning people on this gentleman's staff. I think this committee should hear what he has to say. For the record, if nothing else!"

The Chairman nodded sourly. "So be it. We'll hear him as scheduled. Now, do I have a motion to adjourn?"

General Hub Younger moved up the aisle to wait for Senator Peroni. They had obviously carried the day. Tomorrow Malcolm Scott, especially in his present detached mood, would not change things in the least.

He would find him tonight, after feeling the CIA's current pulse on "Operation One-Two," and warn him not to feel badly if things did not go his way.

> "It is totally unrealistic to imagine that a Head of State would authorize the irretrievable launching of a retaliatory nuclear strike [simply] on advanced information that hostile weapons were on their way."
> —MARSHAL OF THE ROYAL AIR FORCE
> SIR DERMOT BOYLE, G.C.E.,
> K.C.V.O., K.B.E., A.F.C.

Chapter Nine

MALCOLM SCOTT bent to a steaming shower at the Mariott Motor Inn, letting his tensions run down the drain with the soft Virginia water. He had spent the afternoon like a tourist in Washington, had ridden the elevator to the top of the Washington Monument, moved through churchlike quiet in the wood-chambered Library of Congress, finally finished the tour amidst World War I Spads and Nieuports in the Aviation Hall of the Smithsonian Institution.

He had returned, sent Lennie in Omaha a postcard, sent another to Zach and Pixie. Then it was time to prepare for the cocktail party at the Embassy; he had still not the slightest idea what had prompted him to take the invitation. Curiosity, probably, or a desire to see the President in the flesh. He had met Khrushchev in Moscow at a similar affair and the Queen at the Presentation of Colours to a new squadron at Tarrington; he supposed that deep down he was a snob, or perhaps that he simply wished to add another head-of-state to his collection for old-age reminiscence.

He turned off the water and dried himself, banging his elbow in the tiny cubicle. Why was it, with a continent to build on, American architects felt an obligation to squeeze everything into an area that would have fitted into the bomb bay of a Vulcan?

He had bribed the bellhop to press his uniform; now he inspected it critically. He put on his trousers and poured himself a drink. As he sipped it he scanned the photos he had collected from Flynn. He would pick his own up tonight on the way back from the Embassy reception; he hoped they were as clear as the others had shot.

There was an authoritative rap on the door. His heart jumped. Swiftly he jammed photos and diaries into a corner of the suitcase, closed and locked it. It was Hub Younger. Scott was surprised and a little disturbed. He poured him a drink. "How did you know I was here?" he asked the general.

"General Norwood's office told me."

"His office? Are you two not speaking to each other?"

"I'm afraid not very much, after today. I'm not exactly his protégé. He'd have been a lot happier if . . ."

"If you'd got the sack instead of SAC." Scott smiled. "British humor."

Younger nodded mirthlessly. "Well, I didn't get the sack, and I think he will. That's one reason I thought I'd look you up tonight."

"The other being that you're staying here anyway," guessed Scott.

Younger nodded. "Scotty, don't feel badly, but I think we sewed it up today."

Malcolm Scott shrugged. "That's the way the crumpet crumbles," he said. He felt detached, above the triviality of argument.

Younger looked at him strangely. "You don't seem perturbed."

"Hell, I've known it for weeks," Scott said.

Hub Younger continued to regard him strangely. "What do you think of Major Chandler?" he asked suddenly.

Malcolm Scott felt a spurt of alarm. The last night he had seen his assistant, Zach had beaten the bushes very close to the truth. Suppose he had not been put off, after all, by the flimsy flying-school explanation? Suppose he had transmitted his suspicions to Security?

"Why do you ask, Hub?" he probed.

"Well, for one thing, I sign his efficiency reports."

That was one thing, Malcolm Scott thought, but was there anything else? "I think he's one of the hardest-working young officers I've ever met. I just hope this F-106 that got splashed, if he instigated the flight, doesn't shake him too much."

"He instigated the flight," Younger said casually. "But it was justified. No, I just wondered how stable a man he was. How easy is he to shake?"

Scott sensed something beneath the general's words. His mind raced frantically. He hated to malign Zach, but he could not afford to be stopped now. He said thoughtfully: "I think he's probably a very stable fighter-pilot. He's inclined to be a little nervous about paper work."

"Paper work?"

"You know. He tends to overclassify information, for instance. 'Secret' stamp where 'confidential' would do. That sort of thing. Otherwise, he's one of the best."

Hub Younger seemed relieved. "I suppose so. Maybe I'm too cautious too. I couldn't see any security in that hearing today, and it was like describing my sex life." He finished his drink and stood up. "Why don't you meet me for breakfast tomorrow? Pick me up in 217?"

"Righto."

At the door Hub Younger paused, hesitated, as if he were on the verge of asking a question. For a moment the two men stood in awkward silence. "Yes, Hub?" Scott urged.

Younger was looking at him strangely. Suddenly he shook his head. "Nothing, Scotty."

The door closed behind him. Slowly, preoccupied and worried, he knotted his tie. Something was wrong, very, very, wrong. He called BOAC and tried to change his reservation from the day after tomorrow to tonight. Barring a cancellation it would be impossible; tourist season was just beginning. But he could call back later in the evening to make sure. Jumpy and irritable, he hung up. He may as well after all go to the cocktail party. From downtown Washington he could try again to contact Flynn; if the film was ready, perhaps he could wait at the airport for a cancellation. He winced. For a moment he had forgotten the breakfast with Hub. If he was suspicious at all he would grow more so if he checked out early. What a flap he would cause when he missed the hearing! Hub would hear about that, too. And yet, what could anyone do? Once he was out of the country he was home free, as they said.

He resolved to call the airlines later in the evening.

The taxi turned off Massachusetts Avenue through ancient iron gates to the ambassador's residence. Next to the building was the six-story Chancery in which Scott had checked in with the air attaché. It was drizzling, hot and a little sultry. Malcolm Scott felt that his heavy RAF uniform was losing its press. The cab turned into the portico of a dirty red brick mansion, stopped in the shelter of an overhang. Scott, whose cab fares were eating further and further into his cash, began to curse inwardly the instinct that had brought him.

He had after all seen the President many times on TV; besides, his nerves were jangled. He honestly felt that he was facing an evening of boredom not to be eased even by liquor dispensed at the Crown's expense.

He entered the massive doors to a deeply carpeted hall with a soaring ceiling. He gave his uniform cap and invitation to a dark-uniformed Welshman, who indicated a door some fifty feet down the hall. From it issued brittle laughter from women too highly strung and a cacophony of cocktail-party sounds which depressed him even more.

He had made a mistake in coming; he was an absolute stranger here, and would suffer for it. He was not yet a prisoner and could escape by simply picking up his hat and leaving. Besides, he should try to call Flynn again, pick up his damnable pictures, his luggage, and wait for a plane to get the hell to London.

Instead he walked into the room.

The red-haired girl was drinking too much, but her clear young eyes gave promise that here was an intelligence well able to rise above a more-than-moderate lake of Embassy whisky. She was a Shropshire lass, as she put it, but her accent was that of London; she had lived there almost all her life until she had come to America as a clerk on the Embassy staff. "And you, Group Captain Scott?" she asked.

He was feeling better, for she was really a lovely girl, somehow less fragile and more friendly than the wives of the diplomats and the few single women, perhaps civil servants like herself, who were standing around the crowded room. They had taken a stroll through the garden when the rain had stopped: "Really, Group Captain Scott, you should see it later. We have a garden party on the Queen's birthday—"

"I met her once," he said shamelessly. He was on his third drink. "I imagine I'm a sycophant, or a name dropper, or something, but do you honestly know why I came?"

She smiled. "Why?"

"Because I wanted to see the President." They glanced at a small knot of men around the President and the British ambassador, Sir Swarth-Evans.

"And now you've seen him," she said, "how would you like to meet him?"

Ordinarily he carried his liquor well, but there was no explanation for what he said: "Certainly."

"Surely I can introduce a group captain in the RAF to the ambassador."

Malcolm Scott began to have second thoughts. "From your plebeian position," he suggested, "perhaps a group captain looks a bit bigger than he is. You're likely to be transferred to Singapore."

"I'd like Singapore," the girl said. "Shall we try?"

Before he could remonstrate, she was moving through the groups of people, across the room. He followed her, more reluctant at every step, but he found himself regarding the British ambassador, a tall, mahogany-skinned gentleman who recovered quickly from his clerk's effrontery. Two unsmiling gentlemen moved closer to the group—Secret Service, Malcolm Scott thought with a thrill.

"Yes, Miss Chelsey?" the ambassador murmured, leaning down a little. Scott felt the girl grow tense. There was a moment of stiff embarrassment. The poor child had completely lost her nerve. He took a deep breath.

"Your Excellency," he said, watching himself from another planet, "Group Captain Scott, sir. I asked Miss Chelsey if she might introduce us." He had a sudden stroke of fortune—he remembered another Swarth-Evans. "I had the pleasure of having one of your relatives in my squadron at Tarrington, in Nottinghamshire?"

He had been right. The ambassador relaxed. "Yes. My brother's eldest son."

"One of our best chaps," he said. He would not have known him had he been there tonight.

"Really?" The ambassador evaluated Scott for a moment. The girl began to breath again. Another man joined the circle. With a start, Malcolm Scott saw that it was Charles Van Ness. The Secretary of Defense nodded, smiling, but behind his glittering lenses his eyes were curious.

The ambassador made up his mind. He addressed the smiling gaunt man standing a little detached from the group. "Mr. President, I wonder if I might introduce our Miss Chelsey, who works in the Embassy here, and Group Captain . . . Scott?"

The President smiled, a charming smile that lit his lined face and made him look ten years younger, and put out his hand. Malcolm Scott saluted instinctively, bowed slightly and took it. Like a *Wehrmacht* lieutenant, he thought in one part of his mind, and that's what a lifetime in the service does for you. But again, as if from a distance, he heard himself saying the right things.

"Mr. President, I've always been an admirer of yours."

The President smiled, saying nothing, regarding Malcolm Scott with fatherly eyes. And Scott, tongue loosened by alcohol or a sudden explosion of adrenaline, or impelled by some inner drive which had brought him here in the first place, went on: "I'm in Washington, though, more or less to oppose one of your Administration's decisions."

The ambassador cleared his throat. Charles Van Ness' eyes narrowed grimly. "Mr. President," he began, taking the President's arm, "there are some people *I'd* like you to meet over here. . . ." The President stood fast. He was still smiling at Scott, but his eyes were puzzled. "What decision was that, Captain?"

"The decision not to ask for manned bomber funds."

The President smiled grimly. "Well, you see, Captain, in our position we're invariably damned if we do and damned if we don't. Now Van, here, who has the best advice *we* have available—"

Charles Van Ness broke in. *"And,"* he said significantly, "who's made no objection to your giving your thoughts to the appropriate Senate committee, Captain . . ."

"That's right, sir. And we in the RAF appreciate this. But there's still a question in some of our minds. In my mind, for one. And the President is the only one who can answer it."

There was a cold silence in the group. And in some of the adjoining knots of people, too, as if they sensed a ripple in the calm which must invariably surround a chief of state. They were quiet, listening. Malcolm Scott went on: "It's a question, sir, of what you, or really, one of your successors might do ten yers from now in a certain emergency."

"I hardly know what will come up tomorrow," the President said mildly, "let alone ten years from now."

"At any rate," Malcolm Scott said, "we know that there'll be no proper U. S. bomber command around at the time. Assume that the eastern bloc, as they will, will still have modern, lately developed manned aircraft. Assume that they choose to send them to attack the continental United States with *non*-nuclear weapons. When this country can retaliate only with weapons of nuclear mass destruction, weapons which can't, once committed, be called back . . ."

"You're proposing quite a nightmare, Captain," said the President somewhat distantly.

"Perhaps. But I just wonder, if these bombers were directed toward your shores, at what point a President of the United States would decide to doom the world."

"At a point," the President said, "at which this country faced annihilation."

"But," Malcolm Scott pushed, feeling like someone who has already stepped off a precipice and may as well do a swan dive on the way down, "suppose the enemy refuses to propose *total* annihilation? He has a choice, and you have none. With you, it's all or nothing. At what point, Mr. President, do you think your successor might press the button?"

"I believe, Scott," the ambassador said frigidly, "this is hardly the place to discuss it."

"I agree," growled the Secretary of Defense.

"Am I to believe," Malcolm Scott asked the President recklessly, "that if, say, Boston were threatened by conventional bombs you would launch ICBMs and trigger the loss of all the rest? New York, Washington, Philadelphia, Denver, Los Angeles? Destroy Moscow and know that Paris and London would go?"

"You'd better believe it," the Secretary of Defense said harshly. "And so had the Soviets."

Malcolm Scott, dead serious, paid no attention. He was looking into the President's eyes. "Am I to believe that, sir?"

"Yes," the President said sadly. "You are to believe it."

The Secretary of Defense shot a last-minute, highly malevolent glance at Malcolm Scott. He steered the President away. The ambassador shook his head in profound despair, and followed the two of them. Scott looked after them. "I'm sorry," he murmured to the girl. "God knows what I've done to your future here."

She seemed not to hear him. "Do you really think they would?" she murmured.

Malcolm Scott took the night elevator to the 9th floor of the National Press Building. He passed frosted doors labeled with the name of every imaginable newspaper on five continents. The place had a schoolroom smell of pencils and erasers and sweat and old wood.

He stopped outside the London *Express* office, tapped at the door. It was unlocked, so he entered. The office was hardly more than three cubicles set end to end, three jumbled rows of press clippings and files, rows of *Encyclopaedia Britannicas,* reference books, bound copies of *The New York Times*. Flynn led him to the back room, where the sour-sweet smell of film developer and sharp tang of hypo brought tears to Scott's eyes.

Rolling from a chromed drying drum crackled two copies of each of the photos he had shot. Quickly he looked at them, the missile site near Lincoln and the Washington Air Defense Sector blockhouse at Fort Lee. They were satisfactory, although the Air Defense blockhouse could have used more exposure. He watched while Flynn extracted his duplicates.

Flynn straightened. "I don't suppose, now we're through, you'd care to tell me more about this?"

"No," Malcolm Scott said. "I do, however, appreciate it."

"Thank you," Flynn said rather bitterly. "And when are the missing links to be supplied?"

"In due time," Malcolm Scott said.

"Thanks a lot," the reporter said. "Suppose I take you down and buy you a drink at the Press Club downstairs."

"Wouldn't help," Malcolm Scott said hurriedly. "But may I use your phone?"

Flynn nodded, and Scott phoned BOAC. His heart leaped. There had been a cancellation, and if he could be at the airport at 7 P.M., with passport and proper papers . . .

He slammed down the phone joyously. "Instead of the drink, could you drive me to Virginia and then to Dulles Airport?"

The reporter looked at him incredulously. Finally he shrugged. "Suppose I may as well. You've mucked up my evening enough already."

At 8 P.M. Malcolm Scott settled into a coach seat of BOAC Flight 506 en route to London. In his suitcase were the pictures and the diaries, and in his heart was a song.

"Young Lochinvar is come out of the west, through all the wide border his steed is the best . . ."

He was not young anymore, and he hardly fitted the image of Lochinvar now, if ever he had, but the first phase of the plan was over, successful beyond his wildest dreams. He settled back in his seat and slept like a child all the way across the Atlantic.

General Hub Younger sat in his room at the Mariott Motor Inn waiting for Malcolm Scott. He was already shaved and in uniform. It was 8 A.M. Since Malcolm Scott was to appear for the Senate Committee in the morning session, it was time they started for breakfast. He picked up the phone.

"Group Captain Scott? I believe he's in Room 118."

There was a pause at the end of the line. "I'm sorry, sir. He checked out late last night."

"He *what?*"

"He's checked out, General. Through the night clerk. For a BOAC flight."

"I see," General Younger said. Very slowly he replaced the phone.

He called BOAC, his heart beating fast. Yes, Group Captain Scott had changed his reservations, and presumably now was well across the Atlantic.

Hub Younger began to pace the motel room. He had still not really the slightest grounds for suspicion. Somehow, to stir Air Force Intelligence into action here in Washington now and then to find out that he was wrong in the end was even more horrifying than if he had taken the same action in his own command at SAC Headquarters. And yet, the same ugly threat of compromise hung over Scott that had made Chandler's suspicion take root in his mind in the first place.

On a sudden inspiration he called the Pentagon War Room. "This is General Younger."

"Yes *sir.*"

"I want you to patch me into Offut Air Force Base, and from there to Major Zachary Chandler of the JSTPS."

From force of habit he glanced at his watch as the clicks and buzzes on the line indicated scurried response. In nine seconds he was talking to Chandler. Not the best time, but not bad, either.

"Major Chandler?"

The major's voice was heavy with sleep. It was only 7 A.M. in Omaha. "Yes sir?"

"You made last year's UK inspection tour with Malcolm Scott. If I asked you to go on it with him this year, would you know where to tie into him?"

"He's probably still in Washington, sir."

"No, Major, he isn't still in Washington. He left for London this morning. Could you find him if I sent you over?"

"Yes sir. I think so. He's probably going to Whitehall, for one thing, to check in with Air Vice-Marshal Kimball. And High Wycombe, I guess, to the Bomber Command, and probably RAF Tarrington. Yes, I think I could find him, assuming—"

"Assuming what?"

The assumption, of course, was that he was simply not

getting off the plane to London and on to one to Moscow, but neither man could bring himself to speak of it. "If he's in London, if he's in England, sir, I can find him."

"Get yourself a set of orders. The deputy commander will sign them."

"General?"

"Yes?"

"My actual mission . . ."

"Your actual mission is to do exactly what you did last year, goddamn it! Do I have to draw you a map?"

"No sir," the major said very softly. "I understand, sir."

General Hub Younger slammed down the phone. Damn it, some things were better left unsaid.

He supposed that he should inform Senator Holiday that his prize witness had just flown the coop; at the very least, he had to tell Charles Van Ness. But neither of them would be at work yet. He took off his blouse, lay flat on the floor, and began to do his sit-ups. There was no reason, no matter what, to let one's muscles lose their tone.

PART 3

"But oh, beware my Country,
when my Country grows polite!"

"To me it is quite clear that if the East and the West have the known ability to retaliate, neither will risk a nuclear war, because it must bring disaster."

—MARSHAL OF THE ROYAL AIR FORCE
SIR DERMOT BOYLE

Chapter One

THE stubby British airport bus rumbled stolidly through late-afternoon Heathrow traffic toward London. A recent rain had scrubbed the air; Malcolm Scott could see it on the road and hear it in the moan of the tires as they passed through a puddle and whiff it in the musty, plush-seat smell of the bus. The morning was vivid and green-tinged. To Malcolm Scott the storefront colors and the advertisements seemed twice as bright as those in America. It was an unfair comparison, he knew, compounded of latent homesickness and a quite unrealized weariness with things American. But the green little plots of ground in front of the row-houses, the bright red bricks, the Dunlop Tyre billboards, all seemed to glow with a depth of color he had forgotten.

When he had left London two years before he was reeling from Karen's death; his UK inspection tour last year with Chandler had been tinged with sadness because he knew that he would be revisiting places for the first time that Karen and he had known together; now, with the pain receding, he felt more content than he had in years.

This happy breed of men, this little world,
This precious stone set in the silver sea....

He turned to his seat companion, a little old lady, unmistakably British, he had noticed getting off the plane. "Good to get back," he said.

She smiled. "Yes. Tomorrow there'll be rain, or smoke, and it won't be nearly as lovely. But I don't think I'll rush off again."

Tomorrow. Tomorrow there was so much to do, and the day after, and the day after that, that his joy plummeted with the press of it all. He began to try to fabricate for Hub Younger a reason why he had left a day early, and there was Senator Holiday too....

By the time they reached Hyde Park the headlights snaking around Marble Arch were on; as he bundled his suitcase into a good, staid London taxi it began to rain. When they drew up outside the RAF Club, the trees across the street in Green Park were sodden. The cabbie touched his cap. "Thank you, Governor."

It *was* good to be back, rain or no.

Malcolm Scott gazed from Air Vice-Marshal Sir Ronald Kimball's office at late-morning mist steaming from the Thames. Behind him the marshal was studying the photos and diaries. Scott was still cold from the shock of seeing his deterioration; a clammy knot of fear had settled in his chest. He wondered if he were about to lose another link with happier days. He speculated on what the medical answer was: anemia, or jaundice, or diabetes? He heard the air marshal shuffling the photographs. Almost reluctant to look at his old friend again, he turned. Air Vice-Marshal Sir Ronald Kimball, D.F.C., A.F.C., had been thin and ascetic a year ago, but still handsome in a wiry way. Now he seemed a skeleton, his face pale and etched with lines of pain, his eyes pouchy, tired and lusterless. The hands holding the photos were translucent and veined with blue. And shaking, as well.

The marshal looked up with a trace of his old smile. "Well, Scott, I should say you've done your usual excellent job."

"Thank you, sir."

The air marshal looked down at the photos, balanced the diaries in his hand. "Suppose you'd had a Russian accent? Or suppose Kimberly had, or the chap in Maine?"

Kimberly was a Royal Navy officer on loan to the Boston Navy yard; the chap who had shot the missile site in Maine was an RAF Regiment major studying plant security in New England. The RAF Regiment was, in the view of the average air officer, trigger-happy infantry more suited to its duty of guarding Her Majesty's Aerodromes than a job of espionage. Scott had recruited the rock-ape anyway. The major's diary told the story; he had used none of the special privileges of an ally, and his pictures were as clear as any of the others.

"We located our targets from scratch, posing as civilians," Malcolm Scott said deliberately. "I think we'd have been able to get those pictures if we'd been uniformed generals in the Chinese army. The diaries prove it."

The marshal nodded. "Can this journalist I got you in Washington . . ."

Malcolm Scott shrugged. "He has copies of the photos. He has photostats of the diaries. All we have to do, I should think, is supply the missing link."

"Very well," the marshal said. "None of you got caught, which is better than I had a right to expect. Now it's up to us. This brings us to what I've been doing."

Air Marshal Kimball grimaced suddenly. Scott stepped forward. The air marshal shook his head, tried to smile, but Scott saw the tips of his fingers on the desk grow red, then white, as he clenched the desk top. The attack, whatever it was, seemed to last forever. Finally, the marshal relaxed.

"Stomach," he said briefly. "Ulcer."

Ulcer, hell, Scott thought.

"At any rate," Kimball said. "The political end of it hasn't been quite so easy as I'd hoped, but I won't go into that. It's enough to say, Scott, we're right on the knife-edge of not doing it at all."

Scott's world plummeted. "Has it been that bad?"

The air marshal nodded. "The politicians are entirely on the fence about it. They want the results, without the risk. I'm going ahead anyway, as far as I can. I can always cancel it before they start."

"Before *they* start?" Malcolm Scott said softly. "What do you mean? I'm leading it. I hope you understand that."

"Wing Commander Harry Boyle is leading it," the air marshal said sharply. "You're doing exactly what you're told to do!"

"Sir," Scott said, "this whole bloody thing was my idea! If you remember, I conceived it! The whole bloody thing was my idea!"

"It's refreshing," the air marshal said mildly, "to find someone who doesn't want to pretend that he never heard of it. However, after you give the crews a final briefing, your active participation is over. Even if the operation goes."

"Why?" Scott demanded hotly.

"I've had second thoughts."

Scott leaned over his desk. "Sir, I've *got* to lead it. You can't let these men go without me! I can't sit it out any more than Marshal Embry could have waited out the Copenhagen strike! *He* went, and there was a price on his head in Germany. There's no price on mine in America."

Not as of yesterday, anyway, he added silently, wondering what had happened when he failed to report to the committee hearing. He had already called Washington for Senator Holiday, who had refused to speak, and for General Norwood. "Hub, Air Vice-Marshal Kimball ordered me back. He thought I'd involve the RAF with the Senate. You should be glad." General Norwood's reaction had been frigid: "Who the hell do you think you're working for?" It didn't matter. Within ten days, they would all know.

"Why do you compare Dunsinane with the Copenhagen raid?" the air marshal asked innocently. "Do you consider it equally dangerous?"

Scott sat down in a leather chair opposite the marshal's desk. "Sir," he said honestly, "let's not fool ourselves. Of course it's dangerous."

The air vice-marshal pushed his chair away from the desk and sat back, peering over his fingertips. "I've spent the last two months, Scott, explaining to one frightened civilian after another that there was really no danger at all."

"I hope to get away without a scratch," Malcolm Scott

said. "But we can't deny that there's danger, and that's why I want to go."

With an effort Air Marshal Kimball got up, walked to the window. The London drizzle was beginning again. A quarter of a mile up the Thames Big Ben sounded. He sighed. "I'm getting very, very old, and you're getting older too. You'd think we'd be over the foibles of youth, wouldn't you?"

"I consider myself so," Scott said rather stiffly.

The air marshal turned, wincing slightly as he did so. The spasm of pain, whatever it was, passed more quickly this time. "You're in good health. You have twenty, thirty years to live. On a pension, probably, the last ten or twenty of it. Why do you want to risk it all? Normal flying's risky enough."

"This is *my* project," Scott said. "I want to go."

The air marshal sighed. "Let me tell you something. I've left the leadership of this raid in the background, in discussing it with the politicians. They're assuming that it's a normal squadron operation, led by some young wing commander or other. At most, a wing commander."

"They're assuming wrong, sir."

"They are not!" The marshal's eyes flashed. "Now, if it all blows up in our faces, and it's led by some hot-headed junior officer, what do they do? They cane him, so to speak, to satisfy our rich Uncle, and in a year it's all forgotten and he goes on with his career. If it's led by you, it's officially sanctioned!"

"My God, sir, I'm just a group captain! You're talking as if I were carrying your baton!"

"You're a forty-one-year-old group captain who should know better. And you're *slated* for a baton," the marshal said. "If you led it there'd be no way of pointing to it as an operation conceived by a bunch of lunatics around the Swan's Head up in Tarrington. No, Scott, they'd know it for exactly what it is. Why do you think we left the Embassy out of it? Why do you think your contact in Washington was a journalist, instead of the RAF attaché?" The air marhsal smiled suddenly, and it was as if twenty years had dropped away and he was Malcolm Scott's squadron leader again in the bleak, damp officers' club at Brussels. "I wish I could go on it myself. But you see, I can't. Nor can you."

"I don't see why," Malcolm Scott muttered, a dull ache in his throat. "I can't see why at all."

The air marshal shrugged. "At any rate, let's go on."

Without getting up he rolled his swivel chair to a cabinet secured with a heavy iron bar and padlock. He unlocked it and with some effort began to slide the bar upwards. Scott moved swiftly to help him. Kimball rolled back behind his desk on the chair. Taking the contents from a thick manila envelope, he described the status of "Operation Dunsinane." He had been busy. The men were chosen, the plans were laid. Scott took the envelope. At the door he paused.

"Sir, I'll ask again. May *I* recruit a crew? May I go? As we planned in the first place?"

Air Vice-Marshal Kimball rubbed his eyes. His hand hid his sallow, death's-head face, and Scott felt a wrench of agony in his own body as he saw that whatever physical pain had brought his old friend to this state was racking him again. "Can I get you something, sir?" he asked quickly.

Kimball shook his head. "Nothing. And you *can't* lead this. You're too senior."

Malcolm Scott moved back to the desk. "That's not really it, is it, sir?" The air marshal did not answer.

"What it really is," Scott blurted, "is that you don't want me broken if it fails. You don't want me court-martialed. You want me behind that desk some day, but you see, *I* don't give a damn! I want to go!"

The air marshal shook his head. "That's all, Scott."

As Malcolm Scott passed, burning with anger, through the outer office he hesitated by the marshal's secretary. She was a chunky, black-haired woman. To Scott she had always seemed the embodiment of the great unloved. All that nature could do to stifle her life had been done: she had rough, reddened skin, a body like a barrel, lifeless black hair done into a bun, a square face. Her black eyes, which were not unattractive, were guarded by lenses that looked a good half-inch thick. She showered on Sir Ronald Kimball, Scott had noticed, the affection of a slave for a gentle master. Her name was Miss Blackman—she could have had no first name—and Sir Rodney called her Blackie, so Malcolm Scott did too, but he had observed that few others ran the risk of drawing too close to the gush of her lonely friendship. She was licking an envelope, and for a moment their eyes met and they were frozen in a brief tableau. Outside, a lighter on the Thames groaned once. A telephone down the corridor rang. Malcolm Scott nodded toward the inner office.

"What's wrong with him, Blackie?" he wanted to know. "It's serious, isn't it?"

Her eyes clouded with sudden tears. She nodded, sealed the envelope, but did not answer. He left the room thoughtfully.

After a preliminary review, tissues from 170 patients were found sufficiently well preserved to warrant histologic study. . . . Lamentably, an exact comparison by distance from the bomb is not possible on the basis of the material.

— Joint U. S. Commission for the
Investigation of the Atomic
Bomb in Japan

Chapter Two

MALCOLM SCOTT sat on the top platform of a lurching London bus heading toward his daughter's flat off Sloan Square. Across from him a bespectacled matron was studying his RAF uniform with carefully undisguised contempt. She had "Ban-the-Bomb" all over her, and Malcolm Scott felt an insane impulse to pull the straw hat she was wearing down over her ears. He had never seen London so prosperous, the traffic so jammed, the autos so gleaming. The city seemed more variegated than he remembered, with shaggy-haired West Indians and sandaled beatniks jostling Strand fashion plates, their bowlers set squarely and umbrellas crooked over forearms as if they had all been turned out of some monstrous sartorial machine on Saville Row.

The house in which Dee had her flat was moldy brownstone, three-stories high, married tightly to a Victorian neighbor. A stone stairway behind an iron fence led below. He descended to a bright red door, grasped the brass tongue in the mouth of a polished lion, and tapped.

He had a strange feeling that she was directly behind the

door, gathering her courage. He tapped again. It opened immediately.

She was a tall, slender girl. When they had been stationed at Tarrington she had taken to wearing low shoes so that she would not tower above her dates. She had not been popular, but in his eyes she was lovely, with Karen's wide forehead and strangely non-Scandinavian brown eyes. She was wearing slacks that accentuated her molded legs. Her hips were more round; she had grown more womanly than he remembered her and nobody but a fool now could deny her beauty. There was an indefinable warmth about her too, a softness, a penetrability, that had somehow not been a part of her a year ago when he had visited her at the University, but there was still an awkward coltishness about her that he treasured. Now she wore her hair in a long pageboy cut. She was without makeup, glowing with excitement and yet strangely troubled in her eyes.

He held her close for a moment, followed her into the apartment. The place was immaculately clean, like an artist's studio swept for a show, or a barracks for inspection. The flat was a room and a kitchen with a small fridge, a gas stove, and a series of cupboards unsuccessfully hidden by a counter at one end. A couch with a black cover must have doubled as a bed. On it lay in careful abandon orange and dark green pillows shaped like the scones of his childhood. Two familiar Turkish saddle-seats that he had bought in Istanbul crouched opposite a new leatherette-covered easy chair in flaming red, with a reading lamp placed just so.

It was very much as he would have expected, save for the paintings. They were everywhere: oils, watercolors, clown portraits, in every nook and corner. And there was another oddity, one which quenched his joy at seeing Dee. A man lived in this room, Malcolm Scott sensed, as certainly as if he had spotted a pipe rack or a humidor full of cigars.

When she was young they had been very close; during the years in Moscow, with no English children in the Embassy and few Russian diplomatic children allowed to play with her, he had been her closest confidant.

"It's lovely," he said of the apartment. "And you are too."

She ignored the last. "I think it's lovely," she agreed. "A

bit of a bore commuting. The agency, you know, is on Old Bond Street. But Evan works there too, and we have this perfectly wonderful little Vespa—" She colored suddenly, as if she had said too much.

"Who's Evan?" The father in Malcolm Scott felt an odd tug of malice. "And I wonder if you ought to be tackling London traffic on that sort of toy."

He felt like an idiot. She had been on her own for two years, and he was suddenly a father telling her in the first breath not to play with the neighbor boy and to stay off the street with her new tricycle. He moved to a watercolor of dark barges moving up the foggy Thames. "Is Evan an artist?"

"A very good one. I think."

"Full time?"

"Hardly anybody is full time, Daddy. He's an advertising artist, really. But he sells quite a lot, too. In fact, he's at Green Park today. Every Saturday and Sunday."

He had seen the young artists at Green Park, opposite the RAF Club. He had thought of them almost as sidewalk painters. He sat tiredly in the leather chair, feeling an intruder in her world. He was almost afraid to find out more about Evan, whoever he was. He absolutely knew that if he moved to the closet door and opened it he would find it full of men's clothing. He fought down quick, Presbyterian rage at the defiler of his daughter. "I'm sure he's a nice chap."

"He is," she answered, and he could hear the teapot spout rattling against the rim of a cup. "Is it still two of sugar?" she asked unsteadily.

"Yes."

She brought a tray and a few sandwiches to the table by the chair, set it down, and seated herself at his feet, sitting sideways on one of the tricky saddles.

"And how is America now?" she asked.

"America," he told her softly, "is very, very lonely."

"Have you . . . have you met anybody over there?" she asked with an effort. "What was her name? Lennie? Do you still see her?"

"At work. But what about Evan?"

She swallowed. Suddenly he knew. He knew so certainly that he must have subconsciously known when first he came into the room, alerted perhaps by her new softness or perhaps by some new fullness of breast or clumsiness. He put down his tea so that he would not spill it, sat back, and waited for the news.

"I'm preggers, Daddy. I hate that word. I'm pregnant, is all. There's no use making up euphemisms for it, is there? I mean, you're either it or you aren't. There's no such thing as a little bit, is there?" She was rambling; and he could tell the strain from the intensity of her brown eyes, which she refused to take away from his face no matter how much she must have wished to, clinging to the delicate thread that remained between them. Much as he loved her, dour Scottish Presbyterianism glowered at him from the pulpit. His impulse was to recall Karen from the grave, point to her sanctity and compare their love to whatever tawdry affair this was.

But the thought of Karen, who would have given the girl nothing but sympathy, saved him. "It's all right, darling." His voice was husky, and she began to cry. He stroked her coarse brown hair. "Now," he said, "I guess the next thing is, where is the scoundrel?"

She looked up at him, smiling through tears. "I have his car number, anyway." She grinned. Illegitimate child or not, blotch on the family escutcheon be damned, he had more rapport with her this moment than he had had since she was ten, and the glow of it suffused him like a double dram of whisky. He must not snap the thread. "As to where he is," she said, "he's standing in the drizzle outside Green Park, trying to hold his temper while fat American women decide whether his last seascape matches their eyes."

"Do you love him?"

"I love him."

"Why not marry him? Or is that old-fashioned?"

"I want to marry him. He thinks he can't."

His heart dropped. "Is he married?"

She shook her head. Scott grinned in relief. "He's Jewish? Hindu? Colored? A Communist? Tell your old Dad. Some of my best friends are—"

"Daddy?"

"Yes?"

"He doesn't want the *child*. He won't let me have it. I

mean, he wants to get married, but if we do, I have to . . ."

Malcolm Scott tensed. "You're not serious?"

"Yes."

He got up and began to pace. "When the hell does he get back?"

She swallowed. "No! Daddy, I've been honest. You have to promise you won't do anything. I mean it!"

He looked into her face. She did mean it. It was none of his business; if he interfered, he would break the thread forever. "Listen, Dee. Aside from the morals of destroying a helpless individual, it's illegal, and it's dangerous to you! Send this son of a bitch packing, have the child, and I'll jolly well see you don't want!"

"I want to have the child," she insisted. "But I want him too."

Her voice was dead, as if she had expected his reaction all the while. But he could not keep the anger from his own. "Dee, Dee, he's not for you! Can't you see?"

"When you meet him—"

"Unless he walks in this door while I'm here, I have no intention of meeting him at all. Unless you want me to knock his bloody teeth down his throat!"

She snuffed out a cigarette with a gesture of finality. "Then I don't want you to meet him. I *never* want you to meet him."

"Listen," he said, fighting to gain the ground he had lost. "Listen, darling. My anger—my *entire* anger—is directed at a man who'll seduce a nineteen-year-old girl—"

"Twenty," she corrected. "Almost twenty-one."

"A twenty-year-old girl, and confront her with a choice like this! My anger isn't directed at you."

"It takes two to make a seduction," observed his daughter.

"That's true," Malcolm Scott said. "But *you're* not the one proposing the choice! He is!"

"I knew it, though, you see? He told me. He's utterly honest, about everything, and that's one reason I love him so much. He's a little like you."

"Thanks," Malcolm Scott said dryly.

"He's honest, and he's kind . . ."

Malcolm Scott moved to the eye-level window, looked out. The place was a dungeon. It had begun to rain. Three feet from his eyes, across the stone steps leading down to the door, water dripped in Chinese-torture fashion from a tin spout onto a loose tile. If one depressed one's head far enough one could see a six-by-three-foot patch of leaden northern sky. He whirled suddenly, throat tight. "He's got you living in a bloody palace, hasn't he?"

"If you met him, without histrionics, you'd like him. After all, you and Mommy slept together before you were married, didn't you?"

He hesitated. Occupied Copenhagen in wartime was hardly a parallel to peacetime London. Or was it? "Yes."

"Wait for him?" She moved next to him at the window. "Now it's raining, he'll be home directly. He'll be rushing about, throwing all the canvases under the tarp. The trick is to outlast the others, you see, in case some tourist wanders along; he has this thick curly hair, which looks simply heart-rending in the rain, and he's made some of his best sales in absolute downpours. We're getting a Volkswagen bus very soon, and then he can show from the back of it."

"And still get his hair wet, I presume?" he asked bitterly.

"And still get it wet. Daddy, I do want you to meet him. When you've cooled down."

"I am not," Malcolm Scott said stiffly, "likely to cool down. It's easy to talk about being a broad-minded father, but Dee, how the hell he could give you a choice like that?"

"It's because . . ." She looked into his eyes. "Oh, I can't explain it. Evan could, but I can't. I'm sorry, Daddy."

"Why can't you? Why can't you, Dee?"

The veil they had drawn aside so briefly had dropped between them again. Scott felt as if he were enveloped in a flimsy curtain of chintz, a gauze he could not quite peer through. "I'm leaving London tomorrow or the next day," he told her. "I'm going to RAF Tarrington."

"You're at the RAF Club here, aren't you? Opposite Green Park?"

He nodded.

"He shows directly across the street," she pled.

Malcolm Scott struggled to tear through the shroud. But the dull resentment rose to his throat; he simply could not find it in himself to say what she wanted.

"I don't care to meet him," he said.

"Ever?" She was very close to tears.

"I'll be back in London within the week," he said. His voice seemed to echo strangely in the room. For a moment the two stood in silence as the rain dripped on the tile outside. He had a strange, dull feeling of dread in the pit of his stomach. He shook it off, cupped her face between his hands, and kissed her gently on the tip of her nose, as he had not since she was a child of six. "I'll be back," he promised softly, "to see *you*."

As he hailed a cab on the glistening street, he looked down into the dungeon. Her white face peered up at him. She was crying, but she managed a smile and a wave. He waved back, and stepped into the taxi.

1ST SOVIET PILOT: "The target is burning. The tail assembly is falling off the target!"

2ND SOVIET PILOT: "Look at him. He will not get away. He is already falling!"

3RD SOVIET PILOT: "Yes, he is falling. I will finish him off, boys. I will finish him off on the run. . . ."

—U. S. STATE DEPARTMENT TRANSLATION OF
MONITORED RUSS INTERCEPTORS SHOOTING
DOWN 17 U. S. AIRMEN IN AN UNARMED
C-130 TRANSPORT NEAR THE TURKISH
BORDER, SEPT. 2, 1958

Chapter Three

MAJOR ZACHARY CHANDLER, U. S. Air Force, stood at the arched window of the reading room in the RAF Club and looked gloomily across Piccadilly Street to the lush emptiness of Green Park, glittering in falling rain. He was becoming anxious. He had come directly from the airport to the RAF Club because a year ago, on the inspection tour with Malcolm Scott, they had been billeted there while in London. To his relief, yes, Group Captain Scott was staying there. So at least he had not disembarked from the BOAC aircraft onto an Aeroflot to Moscow.

Perhaps it was the heavy English midday meal he had had in the lonely mess below, or perhaps the gray rain outside, or perhaps the polite and utterly uncommunicative club members he had seen, but now the anxiety was beginning to return. For all the world like the American cartoons of London clubmen, three of the members sat in deep leather chairs in the reading room. One of them, sure enough, was reading the London *Times*, a second was devouring a military journal, and a third was skimming *Punch*. Three airborne Colonel Blimps-in-training. Glaring down from the paneled walls were portraits of the RAF great. An ancient servitor in a white work-jacket was moving a stepladder from one to the other, shining the brass nameplates beneath them. Now he dropped, in this silent vacuum, a can of cleaning fluid. It clattered down the steps and fell on the polished floor, splattering crazily. Not one of the three young men looked up.

Zach moved through a corridor emblazoned with squadron crests, down stairs under the clear Anglo-Saxon eyes of Billy Bishop complete with leather puttees, high-collared tunic and Sam Browne belt. He strolled into a sterile television room. Leather chairs were lined up precisely in rows. He flicked on the set, sat down to see whether the BBC had improved in the last year. It had not. He would almost have preferred the idiotic quiz shows which would have been on in Nebraska with emasculated intellectuals discussing Malaysia.

He flicked off the set, wandered through drafty, empty halls to the reception desk, ascertained that Scott had not returned to his room. His apprehension began to weigh on him again: suppose he had simply come to London as a smoke-screen, or to see his daughter for the last time, and was climbing aboard a Tupelov 110 at London Airport at this instant?

He burned with resentment at General Hub Younger for not having had the courage to imply what his real mission in England was. If Malcolm Scott defected, he would hold himself as much to blame as if he had been detailed to stop him; yet he could not stop him at all, really, unless he gave full-blast vent of his suspicions to British authorities, who would probably only laugh at him.

And, Zach Chandler reflected, another ounce of guilt might be the straw that would break his back. With sudden determination he went to the room they had assigned him. He found stationery in the battered desk, looked up an address in his wallet, and began to write a letter to the widow of the F-106 pilot who had died because he, Zach Chandler, had had a passing interest in a Polish airfield.

The letter was almost impossible, but he struggled through it:

And so, Mrs. Samuels, Frank's flight was not wasted. It could help to save the lives of his buddies if the time ever comes.

With sincere sympathy,
Zach Chandler, Major, U. S. Air Force

He was undoubtedly sticking his neck out in sending the letter. But if a fighter-pilot named Frank Samuels, whom he'd never seen, could risk his life at the whisk of a pen in Omaha, the man who had held the pen could risk censure to console his widow. He was sealing the letter thoughtfully when there was a tap at the door. "Come in."

It was Malcolm Scott. The Britisher's face was red, and his eyes hard. "They told me you were here," he said, "and I couldn't believe it."

Zach Chandler sighed and began the great half-lie.

Malcolm Scott sat, his feet on the ice-cold radiator, regarding his American assistant through half-lowered eyes. His head ached from the meeting with his daughter or the shock of finding Chandler. "I still don't understand," he said, hiding his irritation as best he could.

Zach Chandler licked his lips. "All I know is, Scotty, the general called me from Washington and told me to join up on you here. It's entirely on account of the F-106 incident."

"It is?" Malcolm Scott doubted it. "Well, it's too bad the chap was lost, but it's questionable whether it's necessary to send the local expert all the way to Europe to brief the Bomber Command on what we learned. Seems we do have normal means of communication. Teletype, codes . . . I might even have been recruited to sound the alarm. If the American taxpayer were milked less frequently for useless travel expenses he might bear the cost of a few Mach three bombers. Anyway, welcome to our tight little island."

"Thanks. I thought for a minute you were going to send me home."

"Why?"

"You don't seem to be jumping with joy."

Above all, he must seem pleased. "I am, Zach." His mind

whirled. Somehow he must find a way to detach the American from himself. He had crews to brief; with Chandler about it would simply be too sticky. He would need help; help from on high.

"I'm going to Whitehall, Zach. I'll drop you at Adastral House to get your orders endorsed. Then I'll introduce you to Kimball and take you to a little restaurant in Soho and we'll have some of the best fettucini this side of Alfredo's. Right?"

As they signaled a cab outside the RAF Club Malcolm Scott saw the last of the artists across the street tying a tarpaulin-covered packet of his wares onto a motor scooter. He was a tall young man, and he carried himself with a certain ease that made a good impression.

"Come on, Scotty," Zach Chandler said. "You want to drown us?"

Malcolm Scott took a last look at the long, lean young man as he stepped onto the motor scooter, looked back for traffic, and chugged into its stream. "Adastral House," he said. "Theobald's Road West."

The taxi pulled away from the curb. Zach Chandler began to forward him messages from Skipper and Pixie and the lost, lost Lenore. But Malcolm Scott hardly heard him.

Malcolm Scott watched Air Vice-Marshal Kimball as he telephoned the commanding officer of the RAF fighter school. A long day's work had not helped the lines of fatigue on Kimball's face. Scott wished that his old friend would tell him what the trouble was; it must be serious.

"All right," the air marshal said, hanging up the phone. It was the fourth of his four calls. "It's all set. Your friend Chandler has a full schedule." He glanced at the paper on his desk. "Tomorrow, he's to visit the Lightning Squadron at Billingsley. The next day, he's to address the Operational Plans people at Bomber Command, High Wycombe; on Wednesday, he'll be talking to a group at the Imperial Defense College; by the time he's ready to join you at Tarrington, agent or not, there'll be nothing for him to agent."

Scott nodded. "Sir," he asked suddenly. "We've known each other too long. What is it?"

The air marshal stiffened. "Perhaps we haven't known each other *that* long, Scott!" Suddenly he relaxed. "Or, perhaps we have." He managed a smile from the death-head. "I've avoided our own medics and dealt with the civilians," he said. "One of the advantages of socialized medicine."

"I thought that," Malcolm Scott murmured. "Well, what is it, sir?"

"Cancer," the air marshal said.

"I'm sorry, sir . . ."

Kimball shrugged. "I don't imagine you'll see Elizabeth, or Peter—do you remember him? He's quite the university don, now. But I'll ask you at any rate not to mention it. Elizabeth's on the continent traveling, content it's really nothing, thank God, and he's at Oxford, but I'll have to call them in soon enough, I suppose. I'm supposed to be in the hospital now. One doctor gave me six months, but the other was much more optimistic—six weeks. Yes, Scott, I'm afraid I've bought a packet."

Malcolm Scott had a deep desire to comfort him somehow, but there was no use mouthing platitudes. "I'm sorry."

The air marshal smiled. "I am too. You look forward to the declining years, you know; that's really what we soldiers search for, isn't it? The rose garden in Surrey, with the flying-helmet and scarf hung in the study, and the postman with one's check each month?" He shrugged. "But we did have some days, didn't we?"

Scott found his throat was too tight to answer. He nodded.

The air marshal continued: "The Low Countries, of course, and the Rhine. Hell mostly, but a few triumphs. The Copenhagen thing . . . Well, some of us got near the top, eventually. Me, I suppose you'd say, and then of course Hub Younger in America, and I suppose you're destined for the best."

Malcolm Scott said thickly: "Thank you, sir. I don't really care, do you know, anymore."

"I don't suppose you do." The air marshal shrugged. "It doesn't matter. Now, to get back to your amateur spy from America. Where is he now?"

"Having his orders endorsed."

"Good." He glanced at the paper on his desk. "It seems we've rather tied him up. What's your own schedule?"

"I'm going to RAF Cranwell tomorrow," Malcolm Scott said, heart thumping. "There's an electronics officer there who should check our figures on Dunsinane, for the jamming and the other ECM. And then I'll go on to Tarrington." He paused. "Sir, please reconsider? I *have* to go on this!"

"No!"

Blackie tapped on the door and announced Major Zachary Chandler, U. S. Air Force. Zach arrived and apologized.

"Typical U. S. red tape at our liaison office, sir," said Zach. "Sorry I'm late."

"Not at all," said Kimball smoothly, without blinking an eye. "Your boss here and myself were discussing some property I've optioned near Oxford, to keep us in our old age."

Zach Chandler started visibly. "Property, sir?" There was such eager hope in his voice that Malcolm Scott knew that his alibi had never gone down; perhaps this would do it.

"Yes, Major. One of the airfields you chaps built us during the war, abandoned now."

"He mentioned," Zach Chandler said, "starting a flying school."

The air marshal did not overplay it. He simply nodded and flipped a schedule to Zach and went on with Act Two. "I'm going to peel you off from Scott, Major. I need you."

"I told the marshal how disappointed I was, Zach," Malcolm Scott said. "But he wants you to speak to these chaps before you join me. So I'm afraid that's it."

Zach Chandler seemed about to speak. The two Britishers waited, smiling placidly. Chandler gave up. "Yes sir. Whatever you say."

As the major left, Malcolm Scott lingered behind. His old squadron leader was fighting the pain again. It seemed to last for hours, although the clock on the wall had clicked hardly one stop forward when the marshal groaned and relaxed. Scott took his hand.

"Goodbye, sir. Directly this do is over, I'll be back to see you."

The marshal nodded. Incredibly he patted the back of Scott's hand. "I hope so, Scott. Now goodbye."

At the door Scott gave him one last look. The air marshal was sitting back in his swivel chair, breathing hard, his eyes closed. Zach Chandler had already moved through the outer office, and was waiting in the corridor. Scott paused at the secretary's desk.

"I think you'd better look after him," he said. "If he's taking anything, he should have it."

She shook her head. "He's not. Oh, sir, whatever it is he's hanging on for, I do hope it won't be long. He should be quiet in bed."

"It won't be long," Malcolm Scott told her. "It won't be long at all."

Then he followed Chandler out of the office.

"May it not be that the very power and destructive-
ness of these [nuclear] weapons is the greatest
guarantee against their use?"
—MARSHAL OF THE ROYAL AIR FORCE
SIR DERMOT BOYLE

Chapter Four

MALCOLM SCOTT awakened in the RAF Club with Sunday
morning blues. He had had them, since Karen died, all over
the world: in the BOQ at Omaha, in officers' messes and hotel
rooms from Tokyo to Hong Kong to Madrid. They sat now
like a gray, indigestible lump on his stomach.

He dressed slowly, trying to kill them, and had a bite of
breakfast with Zach Chandler, who retired to the writing room
to send a letter to Pixie. Scott wandered to the library, poked
about in the racks of newspapers until he found the *Gazette
Service Supplement*. For some time he amused himself by
reading of the comings and goings of the flying fraternity.
"Group Captain Roger Guest, O.B.E., K.G., posted to 108
Squadron, Gibraltar"; "Air Marshal Sir Harry R. Townsend,
K.B.E., A.F.C, retired this date."

He sighed, got up, moved to the window. Yesterday's
storm had passed; it was a bright April morning outside, but
he would have found more cheer in rain or fog. There was no
reason, really, why he should not go to see Kraft at Cranwell
today instead of tomorrow. He could dine at the staff table in
the great vaulted hall, surrounded by the young faces and

cheered perhaps by the echo of his youth as a cadet.

Across the street by Green Park, the artists were laying out their wares. He wondered if anyone could display there, or whether one was licensed by the City, or whether the laws of private enterprise and competition simply weaned out the amateurs. He could never recall having seen a poor picture in the lot.

Far down the line he saw the tall young man again, taking his canvases from the covered bundle on the rear seat of the Vespa. He moved with unconscious directness, completely at variance with the posings and the uncertainty of the other artists Scott could see. There was none of the posturing of the virtuoso placing a canvas, with the dubious head cocked and minute adjustment. Evan moved like a man who knew exactly what he was doing before he moved at all.

Suddenly Scott found himself passing down the front steps, cutting diagonally through the traffic to the quiet shade of the sidewalk around Green Park. His heart was thumping and his face was hot as he slowed, walked along the line of early-bird artists jockeying for studio space on the stone wall under the iron picket fence. He found himself near the end of the lot, where the young man was placing his last canvas. Scott stopped, staring.

It was a portrait of Dee, done in the light from the casement window in their cellar flat. A wisp of hair fell over her forehead. He remembered the errant curl she had had there when a child: *"There was a little girl and she had a little curl right in the middle of her forehead. And when she was good, she was very very good, but when she was bad she was horrid."*

The young man had caught such love and softness in the line of her cheek and the fullness of her lips that Scott forgot his agony. He turned to the tall youngster and said: "How much is this?"

The boy had been studying him intently. "It's not for sale, sir," he said softly.

Malcolm Scott looked at him curiously. "Then what's it doing here on display?"

"I . . . I don't really know." The young man grinned. He had even white teeth, though one of them was broken; his smile, his dark blue eyes, and his thick curly hair gave him an Irish look. "I bring it quite often, but when I have an inquiry I say it's sold. I like it there, that's all. Now, any of the others . . ."

Scott relaxed a little. "But you see, I'm not interested in any of the others."

"It's really not for sale, sir."

"At any price?" Malcolm Scott asked curiously.

"At any price, sir." The young man was regarding him narrowly. Suddenly he said: "You're her father, aren't you?"

Traffic roared by on Piccadilly, and then there was a momentary lull. From a branch overhanging the iron fence above them a bird chattered angrily. Malcolm Scott nodded. "Yes."

"I thought you might be here, but she said you wouldn't."

"And, well, here I am," said Scott.

"She'll be down in a few minutes. Do you think we might have a talk first?"

"I'd like it," Malcolm Scott said, surprising himself. The young man moved to a diminutive station wagon from which a bearded man was wrestling canvases. He delegated him in Spanish as agent for his own and led Scott into the park to a bench by a gravel walk. The two men sat down."

"She's told me," Evan began, "that it's the choice I've given her has you tensed up."

"You're damned right, it has!" Scott swung to face him. "What kind of bloody ass are you? You can't force a girl like her into a thing like that."

"I have. She's agreed. Last night."

"Then," Scott said tightly, "you've ruined it for the two of you. She'll not forgive you."

The young man's blue eyes never wavered. "Where were you in 1941?"

Scott stared. "Finishing RAF Cranwell. And then I imagine at some airdrome or other."

"I lived in London. Bloomsbury."

Bloomsbury had been hard hit, but this young man could scarcely have been four years old. "You're not going to give me the 'scarred by war' rot, are you? At your age?"

He ignored him. "I was three. My dad was in Africa. I've heard my mother was going to evacuate us to the country but she seems to have put it off. And one afternoon . . . She was killed. Killed? Her bloody *head* was blown off!" He peeled back his arm, showed a deep burn. "I only got this." He shrugged. "Head was blown off." He patted the bench on one side of him, then the other. "It was here . . . She was here. I was in the middle, you see?" He tried a grin. "Where do you turn?"

Scott's disbelief must have shown, but it did not seem to disturb the young man in the least. "People think I imagined it. You know, three years old and all. Imagined it? Hell, I can close my eyes . . . she was wearing a green sweater . . . pullover . . . her arm was twisted, so . . . her hair had got dirty . . . she had a patch of mortar on her skirt . . . like a chalk mark. . . . I've painted in every medium there is, but I can't yet draw in chalk. . . . But I could paint that picture, Group Captain Scott. I could jolly well paint that picture, in three-D!"

"I believe you," Malcolm Scott said finally. "But it has damn-all to do with your risking my daughter's life!"

"It won't be risked, if it costs us every farthing!"

"But why do it? Why *not* a child? Hell, you survived. Are you sorry you were born?"

"Not at all. Not at all. But you see, actually the odds on my surviving were quite good. The odds on my mother's surviving were good despite the facts. My father *did* survive, in Africa. After all, how many children were hurt? How many mothers were killed? How many fathers?" The young man shrugged. "One out of one hundred and fifty of the home population. Not bad. Acceptable. But! How many Japanese casualties at Hiroshima? With a sick little atom bomb? One out of two! What sort of odds are those? And the next one? Nine dead out of ten? Nineteen out of twenty? When the odds get *less* than even, I do not intend to bring a child into the world to test its luck."

Scott's head began to ache. "You're one of the 'Ban-the-Bomb' lads, aren't you?"

"I've had all that. It's stupid."

"You're predicating a war. You treat it as if it were inevitable." The young man merely smiled at him, his eyes unwavering. Scott felt all of the platitudes slipping away unsaid.

"Perhaps you're right. Why aren't you doing something about it?"

"Time. I'm an artist. I've barely enough time to paint what I have in me to paint. I have no more *time* for useless endeavor, don't you see? I'm not Lord Russell, and what has he done, actually? No, war is coming. And there is nothing that Dee and I can do, except cut the casualty list by one."

"That's the stupidest statement I've ever heard! The child lives *now!*"

"Not consciously," the young man said. "It's the knowing that hurts."

Malcolm Scott leaned back. He was very tired. "Do you have to predicate *nuclear* war?"

"What do you mean?"

"War may be inevitable. Nuclear war is not."

"You've just come from America. Are you telling me their bloody big rockets are just for show? What the hell!"

Malcolm Scott leaned forward. "I'm telling you that man means to survive! Maybe he won't finish warfare with the stroke of a pen. It doesn't follow that he means to blow up the world!"

"I see," said the artist. "A nice, clean, non-nuclear war." A little boy on the gravel path toddled away from his Nanny, fell over Scott's feet. Evan picked him up and set him right. The child glared at him and tottered onward.

"It won't be nice," Scott went on, "and it won't be clean. But it need not be nuclear! What's to gain, either side? Man's a thinking animal, even in war. Has he suddenly gone round the bend? Hell, no. He's the same calculating animal he always was, and he doesn't intend to get wiped out."

The young man seemed nonplussed. "I can't see it. It isn't set up that way."

"I'm a professional."

"You're a professional, but I read the papers. It just isn't set up that way!" He wavered. "Is it?"

Malcolm Scott pressed his advantage. "Maybe not. But maybe we just can't see it. It isn't a nice equation in logic or arithmetic. We'll have war when we think to gain by it, and we'll be shortsighted enough for centuries to think we *can* gain by it, but doesn't mean we've gone mad! Wait and see."

Evan was looking past him down the path. Scott turned. His daughter was walking swiftly toward them, through a shaft of speckled sunlight filtering through the trees. Her face turned radiant.

"I'll wait and see," the young man said absently.

Malcolm Scott grasped his knee. "But the child," he said swiftly. "Is it to be allowed to wait and see? Evan?"

The blue eyes met his. "Could we speak of it again?"

Malcolm Scott nodded. "When I get back to London. All right?"

The young man grinned. "All right, sir."

"You'll wait?"

"We won't make a move."

"I crossed the street to buy a portrait I liked," Malcolm Scott told Dee. "This chap wouldn't sell it to me."

"But since I've the real thing...I'm going to give it to him."

Dee's face shone. Malcolm Scott smiled at her man. "I'll take you up on it when I come back. Since you have the real thing."

> "The challenge of the missile does not mean that
> the flying machine is outdated."
> —PRIME MINISTER HAROLD MACMILLAN
> To RAF Cranwell cadets, 1959

Chapter Five

GROUP CAPTAIN MALCOLM SCOTT sat in the back seat of the
car which had been sent from the Royal Air Force College to
pick him up at the railroad station. It had just rained, and a
pale yellow sun was glittering on the elms which lined the
road to Cranwell. Malcolm Scott felt a touch of nostalgia for
the verdant plateau of Lincolnshire. Over twenty years before
he had come here as a gangling Edinburgh boy clutching a
Scottish Certificate of Education and a passion to spend his
life flying in the RAF.

The driver swung through the entrance. Across the vast
oval Parade, glistening in the rain-scrubbed air, white col-
umns beneath the central bell tower stood stark against red
brick walls. In perfect symmetry the two college wings
stretched against the flat Lincolnshire horizon.

He had seen the massive turrets of the U. S. Military Academy at West Point, and RAF Cranwell could not compare in
grandeur or even beauty. He had visited Annapolis, too, and
Cranwell could not match its charm; he had seen the stark
simplicity of the U. S. Air Force Academy of Colorado
Springs, and found it inspiring. Cranwell was hardly in the

running with Sandhurst or the Royal Navy's Dartmouth either, but from its plain portico 600 men who were to receive decorations in World War II had passed. This was the alma mater of the few to whom so many owed so much, the heart of the service which for a few weeks had held the bridge and saved the world.

He alighted at the entrance, passed beneath the blue-and-gilt Royal insignia *"Superna Petinus"*—"We seek the things that are above." He moved nostalgically through the entrance hall along Founders Gallery. Across the Atlantic, military men were basing their hopes on buried hulls of titanian and the drive of fuel and liquid oxygen; in Washington the computers whirred and the West Pointers forgot that the man was the heart of the weapon. But Old Boys from Cranwell had chased buzz-bombs over London, felt their Spitfires dissolve around them, and known that others would take up the chase the next day. No one who had trooped the colors here or lifted tankards in the bar or dined in the Great Hall under the regimental standards would ever forget that the human heart would triumph over the tools of the human brain.

At the reception desk he put in a call for Flight Lieutenant Martin Kraft, who was teaching electronics to second-year cadets. Then he strolled to the senior mess to wait.

Martin Kraft had pale blue eyes, bad skin, and a pugnacious dimpled jaw. He had receding brown hair which he arranged over a bald spot at the crown of his head. Scott felt the pale eyes upon him and leaned forward in the red leather chair. They sat beneath the gaze of a gallery of Victoria Cross winners. There were no cadets in the mess, although Malcolm Scott knew that when lunchtime arrived it would be full of young faces and white collar tabs.

"I think," Kraft said reluctantly, "you're serious. Am I right?"

Kraft had flown on his crew for two years at RAF Tarrington. Scott respected his skill as a technician so greatly that until this moment he had never really considered whether or not he liked him.

"Of course I'm serious," he said brusquely. "Now that

we've determined that, will two jamming aircraft per bombing aircraft do it?"

Kraft worked his pocket slide rule, looked up. "I should think so. Theoretically." He paused, made a church of his two hands and rested his chin lightly on the steeple. "What prevents them from launching SAC?"

"We expect them to," Malcolm Scott said again. "SAC *aircraft.*"

"What the hell," Kraft demanded, "prevents them from launching ICBMs?"

"Oh, now really," Malcolm Scott said. "For nine attacking planes?"

"Let's hope you haven't underestimated their trigger-happiness, that's all." Kraft arose, walked across the room and knocked his pipe out. Coming back, he gazed thoughtfully at a portrait on the wall. "As you know, Scott," he said quietly, "I'm a university-entry type. Imperial College of Science and Technology, to be quite honest—not even your Oxford or Cambridge school-tie spirit, you see. Perhaps if I'd been at Cranwell here, some of it might have seeped in. But you see, I wasn't, and it hasn't. Scotty, I think you're mad. Are you going?"

"No, worse luck. But the jamming part's all right?"

Kraft returned his slide rule to his pocket. "The jamming part's all right." The two men shook hands. Malcolm Scott cautioned the electronics officer not to speak of the matter, called for a car, and departed for Tarrington. He was somewhat deflated. He had hoped Kraft would be enthused.

Chapter Six

IN pained surprise, General Hub Younger regarded the Secretary of Defense in the paneled dining room of the Secretary's
Georgetown home. The Secretary had just asked him to make
a speech.

"Armed Forces Day?" he protested. "I've got my own shop
to look after! I've been here four days already!"

Claudia Van Ness and her two daughters arose to clear the
table, for it was Thursday and the maid's night out. Charles
Van Ness offered Hub and Alf Karman cigars, leaned back in
his chair. "Hanson Baldwin and a couple of military analysts
from the West Coast will be there. I'd sure appreciate your
doing it."

"Van, for God's sake! What about this 'Operation One-
Two Punch'?" he said softly. "Aren't we considering it anymore?"

Van Ness shrugged. "What's there for you to do but wait?"

"What's Operation One-Two?" asked Karman.

"I thought you knew," winced Hub Younger. "Well, don't
feel bad, Alf. I'm not allowed to tell my own JSTPS in
Omaha. Too many foreigners."

"We want to protect our sources," Van Ness said succinctly. "It's pretty thin stuff, Alf, but the CIA says the Peiping peace team in Moscow has sewed it up. Kiss and make up."

"No!"

"The Chinese will move against Vietnam. The Cubans will boot Castro, install his brother, and get missiles back into Cuba."

"I don't believe it," Alf Karman said.

"I've doubled the alerts in the holes," said Hub, "and the bomber boys have been doing Minimum Interval Take Offs all week."

"NORAD's been pushing, too," recalled Alf Karman. "Well, it's nice to know."

"What about the speech, Hub?" prodded the Secretary.

Hub Younger sighed resignedly. SAC ran automatically: it was always ready. He balanced the work he must do in Omaha against the certainty that General Hal Norwood was resigning from the Joint Chiefs of Staff; the apex of his military career glittered like a diamond within reach. The speech was a minor matter, hardly likely to influence the selection one way or the other, and yet, he could not bring himself to leave a poor taste in the mouth of the Secretary now, of all times. Years ago, perhaps—but rank, and the desire for it, did this to one.

General Alf Karman was watching him, reading his mind perfectly. All right, damn it, Younger told him silently, what the hell can we do? There's always the political boss, and always a moment of truth when the velvet civilian hand turns to a mailed fist. Until the day we retire, there is always that moment of truth.

"All right, Charlie," he said reluctantly. "I may fly to Omaha, but I'll be back here tomorrow night."

Charles Van Ness smiled, lit his cigar. "Alf," he said to Karman, "I saw the President today."

Alf Karman sat up straighter. "Yes?"

Van Ness seemed happy. "I pointed out to him again your thinking and other NORAD thinking on our tolerating snoopers. I told him that if he looked at the last USSR chicken raids over Alaska and Greenland and Turkey and projected them for another six months, we'd find them over Fairbanks and Thule and damn near to Istanbul. I hit him pretty hard with it."

"He ought to be hit hard with it," Alf Karman agreed. "Don't you think so, Hub?"

Younger had been paying only dim attention to the conversation. He sipped his brandy. It seemed sour. In the past few days the seed of suspicion in Malcolm Scott's case had sprouted to a poisonous plant. He resolved now that unless he heard from Chandler within the next twelve hours he would throw the whole thing at the feet of the Central Intelligence Agency, bypassing Air Force Intelligence simply because he could not face their screams of anguish when they learned he had waited so long. "Pardon me, Alf?"

"Don't you think the President ought to be jostled about our policy with snoopers?"

"Oh, yes," Hub Younger said vaguely. "You can't let them reconnoiter with impunity. It tempts them too much."

Charles Van Ness smiled like a sleepy, bespectacled bear. "The President's beginning to understand that."

Alf Karman sat up even straighter. "He *is?*"

The Secretary of Defense nodded slowly. "Next time, I think, *pow!*"

"Is this official?"

"Not yet. But you'll see."

"Well, thank God for that," Alf Karman said. "It's nice for the throttle-jocks in Germany and Spain to know that the next bogey can get more than his wrists slapped."

"I hope to hell NORAD goes easy," Hub Younger said uncomfortably. "There's such a thing as a genuine error in navigation, you know, SAC aircraft make them too."

"What's that got to do with it?"

"Well," Hub Younger said, "I'd hate to give them any more excuse than they already have for knocking down my bombers."

"What the hell difference will it make?" asked Karman. "They do anyway. This may be the lesson they've been waiting for."

Claudia Van Ness, a cheerful, corseted woman, poked her head from the kitchen. "A phone call, Hub. From London, yet. Take it in the den?"

He sat amid the Secretary's gallery of photos, political trophies of the hunt, and heard Major Chandler's voice ebb and flow with distance. When the major was finished he said: "Whose idea was it to split you up? The marshal's or Scott's?"

"Air Marshal Kimball's, sir."

"And Kimball explained the flight-school thing?"

"Yes, sir. He's his *partner* in it!"

Hub Younger sighed, relaxing for the first time in a week.

"Okay, Major, you got a free ride to London. Finish your job for them and come home."

He hung up. Sorry, Scotty, he thought. I'm glad we didn't panic, but I'm more glad you'll never know how close we came. He sipped his brandy for a moment alone. It seemed suddenly very, very good.

> "Man is the most efficient and flexible control device you can install in an aircraft. Furthermore he can be produced cheaply by unskilled labor."
> —Scott Crossfield
> Test Pilot, X-15

Chapter Seven

ALL of the way from Cranwell, in the back seat of the RAF car, Malcolm Scott had felt the torture of passing through the little towns of Lincoln and Yorkshire. Karen and he had loved to ride Idle, through East Retford and Gamston and Tuxford, along tree-shaded roads and shaggy hedgerows so English that it would make Karen giggle.

Just past Bawtry the driver hesitated. "Right, toward Epworth," Malcolm Scott said mechanically. The last time he had traveled this road with her had been in an RAF ambulance. She had slipped in the bathtub in their quarters. "Serves me right for being so Scandinavian-clean," she had murmured when she came finally back to consciousness, and it had seemed nothing, but an hour later they were roaring under the dark elms toward London. It was a blood clot, and she had fought her way to clarity only once again, near here, reached out a hand and squeezed twice. It was their own private signal of danger and fear and hope, from the week in Copenhagen when the Hipos passed close and they walked on the knife-edge of death.

Now they drove through an unguarded gate. Good. The

less fuss, the more chance that his group would get away clean. They rode down the main street of RAF Tarrington in the lurking dusk. Malcolm Scott glanced down one of the side roads toward the married officers' quarters. Lights were on in the two-story brick house; in an upper window an adolescent girl, who might have been Dee, was silhouetted playing a violin. The glint of sunset caught the windowpane in a blaze of copper. Life went on in the little home as it had before they had come; it would go on after the present tenants were forgotten.

Somehow, the short glimpse had made him feel better. He directed the driver to the officers' mess and thanked him. Before he entered the massive doors to the warmth and comradeship of men he knew, he looked back past the Administration Buildings at the hangar area and the long strips of concrete slashing the grassy fields. A lorry drew up outside a hangar, headlights bright already. It discharged an RAF regiment sentry with tommy gun and a leashed German shepherd. Searchlights suddenly struck back at the creeping darkness. A line of graceful, snow-white Vulcans leaped dramatically from the shadows. Maintenance crews clambered over them. He wondered if these were the Dunsinane planes. He would know soon enough.

He sat on the right hand of Group Captain Reginald Smythe, commanding the base, a sad-eyed officer with a hangdog look of patient despair. Smythe had foregone dinner at home to officiate at Malcolm Scott's homecoming, but he showed little enthusiasm for discussing the problems of the next few days. Down the long tables little WRAF waitresses enlisted from the nearby towns of Lancaster and Haxey and the farms on the river Torne served the pudding and followed it with port.

It would have been easy for Malcolm Scott, even had he not known the majority of Dunsinane volunteers from reading the operations-order, to spot them during dinner from their suppressed excitement. Winn, Bons-Vickers, Kiwi Barcus, Guy Hollister, Wallace, and Peter Welsh—they were his men from years before, and they were mad to go. He burned with anger at not being allowed, himself. He had two glasses of the port, and by the time dinner was finished he felt better.

They moved to the bar and Malcolm Scott cornered Smythe alone. He had been in his entry at Cranwell but Smythe was regarding him as if he were a leper. "Reggie," Scott said, "I'll want a few things."

The base commander looked as if he were about to cut and run. "So far as I know, Scotty," he said emphatically, "this is a mass Lone Ranger flight to Nairobi and back. Its purpose is training: in-flight refueling operations. It's under Air Vice-Marshal Kimball's Special Plans Office of Bomber Command. My entire function is to be that of local filling-station operator. I shall even clean your windshields, if necessary, but I do not wish to be consulted about it further."

"I can see that," Malcolm Scott said dryly. "And aside from that, Reggie, how is duty at Tarrington?"

"Smashing," Smythe said sourly, "until you and Kimball and God knows who else dreamed up this bloody do."

"*Whatever* it is." Malcolm Scott smiled.

"Whatever it is. I suppose you'll want a briefing room?"

"That room next to base ops would do very well," Malcolm Scott agreed, "if it's still available. A rock-ape to guard it twenty-four hours a day, but unobtrusively, as though they're watching the whole corridor, you see? The weather at hourly intervals from tomorrow morning on. A telephone patched direct to Kimball's office, and I'll have a participating crewman standing by on this end from tomorrow morning on."

"Anything else?" asked Smythe acidly.

"No, Reggie."

"If it all blows up," Smythe said, "I expect Whitehall or Adastral House or High Wycombe or someone will have a clear-cut press policy for you here?"

"Expect that Sir Ronald won't let us down," suggested Malcolm Scott. "It'll be much easier on your nerves."

"Time, gentlemen, please," called the pub-keeper at the Swan's Head. Malcolm Scott drained his bitters and regarded Flight Lieutenant Michael O'Moore across the scarred table, polished with the elbows of two generations of Tarrington airmen.

"Cheers," he told his old copilot. "We'd better get cracking."

"The whole bloody lot's going on it!" Mike O'Moore growled over a glass of whisky and soda. His brisk red handlebar moustache quivered like the antennae of an angry lobster. "I'm the best bloody copilot, or pilot if you must know, at Tarrington, but I'm non-U. *And* Irish, and it's all too bloody much to fight."

O'Moore was forty now, or thereabouts, one of the horde of military men who had lived their whole lives in two or three years of war, and for whom all else would forever be bland and tasteless. His day was a long reminiscence of the Hamburg raids or Cherbourg or the bash in London after Antwerp. He was an anachronism; a reincarnation of some seventeenth century mercenary, a man without fear, erratic, alcoholic but a superb pilot because flying had become his life in formative years. His drinking had scotched his promotions; he would die a flight lieutenant.

"So," said O'Moore, "I know something's up. Or I think I do. That clot Boyle's to lead it, and I can't *buy* myself a bloody seat!"

"Nor can I," observed Scott. "Nor can I, Michael, my lad."

"Who the hell carries the can on this show?"

"What do you mean?"

"When they come back, if they do, all covered with glory and with the blue of heaven shining through their wings, who do they point the finger at? You or the great skull Kimball or who?"

Malcolm Scott swallowed his anger at hearing his friend so described. "At least, it wouldn't be you if you *were* going."

"One of the advantages," Mike O'Moore said bitterly, "of juniority."

"It's your own damn fault." Malcolm Scott shrugged. "If you'd ask for staff college, or even sit a promotion exam, you'd soon be a squadron leader."

O'Moore leaned forward. "Get me on it? Dunsinane?"

"Shut up!" Scott whispered. "So help me, this is as top-secret as the emergency War Order. You have no need to know."

"Why was I left out? Is it because Kimball thinks I like the whisky too much?" All of the rapport between them was shattered, suddenly. O'Moore slammed his palm onto the table viciously. "Or is it because I'm an Irishman, and the Irish talk too much?"

"Shut up!" Malcolm Scott spat. There were half-amused, half-bored glances at the two from the civilians at the bar; young pseudo-squires with car agencies in Leeds or Manchester. Scott regarded his old friend closely and stood up. "Are we ready to go?" he asked O'Moore tersely.

"I'll stay for a bit," Michael O'Moore said.

"It's closing time. You can't get a drink."

"Oh, come off it, Scott," O'Moore said scornfully. "You think I'll spill the beans?"

"I think," Malcolm Scott said gruffly, "you're getting to be a bloody drunk!"

He jerked him to his feet and they left.

Mens Agitat Molem—*Mind Controls Matter.*
—Motto, Number 102
Bombing Squadron,
RAF Finningley

Chapter Eight

MALCOLM SCOTT inspected the nine aircraft of Operation Dunsinane and found them not wanting. He looked over the briefing room that Smythe had provided, checked the weather on the teletype in one corner of it, and picked up the phone to call Air Marshal Kimball. He got Blackie. She was crying.

"Sir, he's gone!"

"Gone?"

"He's dead!"

Malcolm Scott stared at the walls, covered with charts and maps, and saw nothing; the teletype in the corner jangled and he did not hear; the door opened and the sentry poked his head in, recognized him, snapped to attention, and Scott did not even see him.

"What did you say, Blackie?"

"He was admitted to Royal Hospital yesterday morning. His wife and son got in last night. He died this morning. He's dead, sir, he's dead . . ."

"I'm sorry, Blackie. It's best for him, but I'm very, very sorry. Tell Elizabeth and the boy."

Slowly, he hung up the phone. His throat was tight, his

chest ached. He had not even found out about the funeral. He must call back. Thirty years, and Kimball had left behind him really nothing. Not even Dunsinane, for now the flap would start for certain and when it was over, there would be no flight.

He felt a great emptiness. He would, he imagined, go to London tomorrow, meet Zach Chandler, together with him complete the inspection tour and return to Omaha. And the B-58s would rust on Arizona fields and the missiles would crouch in their silos and the Americans, secure in their convictions that no man born of woman could slip past their guard, would sleep while the factories of Russia hummed and the bomber lines in Leningrad and Minsk spawned another generation of craft. He was quite at a loss as how best to pick up the pieces. He supposed that the first thing to do was to phone back and tell Blackie to destroy the diaries. They were compromising documents which could embarrass their writers. But there was time for that. He left Operations and went to the mess for a cup of tea.

Major Zachary Chandler stepped from the rear seat of the RAF sedan into London drizzle outside Whitehall. The Union Jack, he noticed, was at half-mast. He told his driver to wait; with some irritation shouldered his way through the glass door to the Information Desk. He showed his identification to an aging pensioner, asked that he be announced in Air Vice-Marshal Kimball's office, and learned that Kimball had died. Shocked, he made his way to the office regardless.

This morning he had arrived at High Wycombe, prepared to brief Bomber Command brass on Soviet fighter tactics, and found himself totally unexpected. He had been pleasant enough amidst the confusion there, but all the way back into London he had seethed. Now he knew how it had happened; Kimball must have been scheduling him on a day-to-day basis. The stumpy woman he had seen before in Kimball's office was sitting despondent before documents stacked on her desk. She had been crying.

"I'm so sorry, Major. I expect you heard?"

Zach Chandler nodded. "And I'm sorry too."

"Well," she said distractedly. "About you, sir, I hardly

know what to suggest. He was going to arrange for you to talk elsewhere, but I have no idea where. I could go through his last day's desk-diary..."

Zach Chandler shook his head. "Unless you think he's got something scheduled, why don't I just join up with Group Captain Scott? Like last year?"

She seemed relieved. "Would you, sir? He's at RAF Tarrington. It would be one less thing for me to worry about until someone comes to take charge."

Zach Chandler produced his orders, and she found a stamp to date them. She would call the auto pool for him and make sure that he had the use of the RAF sedan. Awkwardly, he expressed his condolences again. Suddenly she remembered something. She reached down the side of the desk and lifted a battered dispatch case.

"Sir Ronald sent word from the hospital last night. He asked to be certain that Group Captain Scott had this. Could you take it to him, sir?"

Zach Chandler nodded and left.

Malcolm Scott waited for his tea in the library of the mess. A white-jacketed batman looked in: "Group Captain Scott? You have a message from weather."

Disconsolately Scott went to the phone. A low off the Alaskan coast had deepened. Another trough off Labrador was growing in size. There was predicted considerable thunderstorm activity along the east coast. Scott replaced the receiver and turned away, sick. Now that the show was off, they would have precisely the sort of weather which would have made it succeed. The batman brought his tea. He sipped it, gazing up at the two crossed standards of the two squadrons at Tarrington. Number 18 Squadron: "With courage and faith," and his own old Squadron 101: "Press on."

He began to pace the room. Wing Commander Harry Boyle, disheveled in a flight suit, entered. He had a message in his hand. "Scotty, did you hear?"

Scott nodded. "On the phone."

Boyle was a fine, broad-shouldered young officer with tanned skin and piercing gray eyes. Malcolm Scott had never seen him shaken, but he was now. "I expect this jolly well blows it?" Boyle asked.

"I suppose so."

"I mean . . . there's no one higher than him to back me? To back *us,* I mean?"

Scott studied him. He could not shake off a feeling that Boyle was glad. "No one who won't get the wind up now."

"Bloody shame," said Boyle. "All this work . . ."

Malcolm Scott nodded. "All this work."

"And Sir Ronald wanted it so badly too. When he first came up here with it, he picked me to lead because I was so keen on it."

"Are you still?"

"What?"

Malcolm Scott said, "Harry, suppose I sent you anyway?"

Boyle swallowed. "My God, sir, you're not even properly in the RAF at present. You're on a staff in Omaha. And do you think you have enough rank to protect me, after all? Shouldn't I look a bit of an ass pointing to you, if it went off wrong, and saying: 'He told me to'?"

"Perhaps."

"No, but actually, sir?"

Scott's heart began to pump. He could feel the tingle of action. He got up, deliberately restraining his excitement. "Harry, how would you feel if I went with you?"

Boyle winced. "I'd go, if ordered in writing, but—"

"This is a volunteer do," Malcolm Scott said. "No one will be ordered in writing."

"I'm sorry, sir. It's not the physical danger. But professionally—"

"Would your crew go with me?"

"I'd prefer," Boyle said stiffly, "to keep us in one piece. We're Select Star, you know."

"Oh," Malcolm Scott said dryly. "Select Star. Very well, Boyle. Barring Air Ministry cancellation, I'll recruit a crew if I can and take your place."

Boyle flushed. It was incredible that Kimball had picked him; this man would never have carried it through unless it all went perfectly, and it could hardly do that.

"Sorry, sir," Boyle said uncomfortably.

"Don't be sorry," shrugged Scott. "It's all for the best."

He had no doubts about O'Moore as his copilot. He called Martin Kraft at RAF Cranwell. He got him out of class, but he may as well have saved the trouble. "My God, sir, not me!"

Well, there were other air-electronic officers here at Tarrington. Or in a pinch, he and O'Moore might handle the scope. He set up the briefing for next morning.

"The 'V' Force, even without Skybolt, will continue
to spearhead our deterrent until the late sixties."
—EARL MOUNTBATTEN OF BURMA
Chief of the Defence Staff

Chapter Nine

GROUP CAPTAIN MALCOLM SCOTT looked out the window of
his room, past Base Ops to the flight line. Bathed in the security searchlights, the nine white Vulcans seemed to stretch to
infinity. Around each he could see from time to time its
sentry, bundled for the cold, silhouetted against the lights with
his canine helper.

He tried on the flight suit Harry Boyle had lent him; it was
not a bad fit, actually, and Boyle's white plastic bone-dome
fitted his head as if it had been molded for him.

He lay on his bunk in the flight suit, for he had scheduled
the final briefing early. He would need his sleep; tomorrow
would be a day in which all of his responses—and God
knows how they had atrophied over the past two years—
would have to be instantaneous; a day on which perception
and judgment and intellect must be razor-sharp.

He heard footsteps on the stairway leading from the entrance hall below, pausing as if someone were looking for
numbers, approaching again. There was a tap at the door.
"Yes? Come in."

It opened and he saw the stoop-shouldered silhouette of

Martin Kraft. He flicked on the bedside light, hunching himself toward the head to rest his shoulders on the iron bars. "Marty! Have you changed your mind?"

Kraft was haggard. His face seemed crumpled and uncertain, like a paper bag that someone had balled up and then decided to keep. "No," Kraft said. "I started to think about it, though. Air Marshal Kimball's died. How can you go through with it? They'll not let you off the field."

"You worry about the jamming. I'll handle clearances. Officially, this is a flight to Nairobi and back."

"Who's to take the rap, now the Air Marshal's gone? All of us?"

Scott suppressed a smile. "Not if you're not going."

"If I *should* go."

"Me."

"You've gone daft!"

"I say, Kraft, did you actually motor all the way up from Cranwell to advise me on my career?"

Kraft did not answer. Scott said, "Did you by any chance bring your flight kit?"

Kraft hesitated. "Yes."

"Get a room here. Or sleep in that chair. Briefing's at 0630 hours."

Kraft left and Scott turned off the light, but now he found sleep impossible. He tried to visualize the result of the raid. He saw the aircraft returning to Tarrington, landing, the crews exhausted. But there was no one to meet them but stern rock-apes, tommy guns at the ready.

In the shadows stood a hulking civilian from the Air Ministry, by a huge G. I. can striped with red, white, and blue. As each aircraft commander passed, he was made to drop a roll of film into the can; Malcolm Scott peered in to see the bottom already lined with the diaries and the photographs they had so painfully taken in America. There was a sudden smell of gasoline, a dull *whoosh* as the lot went up in flames, then, as if in a movie, he saw them all standing in gloom before a court-martial. Sitting in a coffin next to them, quite dead but contesting every bitter point, was Air Vice-Marshal Sir Ronald Kimball, D.F.C., A.F.C.

When he awoke it was to the tapping of the batman on the door, but it was as if he had not slept at all.

Malcolm Scott leaned with pointer in hand on the podium at the head of the briefing room off Operations, as he had so often stood when he was stationed at Tarrington. He felt for a moment as if the two American years hardly existed; as if this evening he would return to the little brick quarters at the end of the road.

In the middle of the room was an island of stand-up desks, at which one could fill in one's flight plan before handing it through the eye-level window into the next room. The window was now closed and locked. Around the walls were charts and maps and notices to airmen; in a place of honor was the map of England on which Royal flights were traced in regal purple to insure a wide right-of-way against other traffic.

Forty-four officers of Her Majesty's Air Force faced him, sitting in chairs lined up for the occasion. He had this morning consulted the officers' rosters of the two Tarrington-based squadrons. From the lists, he and Kraft had eliminated all the nav-bombardiers and nav-plotters with families, then chosen a quick young nav-bombardier named George White and a stolid, heavy nav-plotter named Humphrey Latham. They had volunteered straight off. Now they sat next to O'Moore in the first row; the three were the only men in the room who had not read the Operation Plan. He doubted that O'Moore knew where the flight was bound.

He smiled at the men of Operation Dunsinane. "I expect you're wondering why I asked you here today," he began. It drew a laugh. He asked a rosy-cheeked young pilot officer in the rear to check the door, studied the faces before him. Except for the absent Harry Boyle, he decided, Air Vice-Marshal Kimball had done a good job. He knew each of the captains personally: Squadron Leader Victor Ladd, D.S.C., A.S.C., a florid, enthusiastic man with bright snapping eyes, who was one of the best captains in the whole V force. Squadron Leader John Gregory, M.B.E., who would captain Live Oak Three, was a quick, flashy type, a bachelor by repute deadly to abandoned officers' wives and pink-cheeked WRAF lieutenants. Flight Lieutenant David Ricardo, D.S.O., D.S.C., was a graduate of the Test Pilot School; Kiwi Barcus, trained in the Royal Australian Air Force, seemed saturated with the need to prove that all one heard of Aussie courage was true.

"For the benefit of my own crew," Scott said, "I'll run through the Op Plan. In brief, you new chaps, the key is this: two jamming aircraft screening each of the attacking planes, and complete electronic silence from the attacking planes. Right?"

They nodded, and he began the briefing, glancing at the paper before him.

"Mission:" He looked up at the men. "In short, gentlemen, we shall strike at three pairs of targets, each pair consisting of a military installation and a nearby city. Only three of our aircraft will actually attack. I shall hit the Washington Air Defense Direction Center at Fort Lee, Virginia, and then Washington D.C. itself—"

"Washington!" yelped O'Moore. "The bloody Yanks!" O'Moore hated Americans. Oversexed, overpaid, and over here, he had chanted interminably in the war. He was still chanting it.

Scott went on. "Ricardo will hit an ICBM site near Bangor, Maine, and continue on to hit Boston. Kiwi Barcus will strike an ICBM site near Lincoln, Nebraska, and swing northeast to his SAC Headquarters in Omaha. Each attacking aircraft will be assigned two screening planes, which will stand off, jamming continuously." He searched the faces. "Any questions on the mission?"

There was no reply. Someone cleared his throat. Malcolm Scott went on. "All right, gentlemen. *'Enemy forces:* The North American Air Defense Command is a joint U. S.-Canadian organization with headquarters in Colorado Springs. It is divided into sectors in accordance with the amount of air traffic each sector must monitor.'" He moved to the map of North America behind him, pointing out the sectors as he spoke. "Operation Dunsinane penetrates only the Bangor, Boston, New York, Washington, Ottawa, Chicago, and Sioux City Air Defense Sectors."

"Only!" O'Moore groaned delightedly.

Scott turned back to the room. "Interceptor aircraft to anticipate are F-101 Voodoo, RCAF Canucks, U. S. Delta Daggers, F-106 Delta Darts. These kites are virtually controlled automatically, from the ground. The pilot seems to be practically a passenger. They will be equipped with Falcon radar-guided and infrared heat-seeking missiles. Plane and missile make up an extremely long-range weapon; our chances for success depend on escaping detection, not on avoiding them once we're detected."

"Sir?" asked Ricardo. "Are the orders as to identifying ourselves still the same?"

Malcolm Scott nodded. "Absolutely." He turned back to the chart, swept his pointer around the North American land mass. "In addition, antiaircraft missile batteries manned by Air Force and U. S. Army personnel have the Nike, the Hawk, a twenty-mile missile, and the Bomarc, with a four-hundred mile range. Treetop altitude is essential after coastal defenses are penetrated to avoid enemy ground batteries. Nobody will get you with any one of them if you're below the radar horizon. Any questions on that?"

There were none. *"Weather:* It's top-drawer: The attack will await a frontal situation with the usual electrical storms over the North Atlantic and Great Lakes, to confuse enemy radar.' Gentlemen, we have that situation now."

The weather officer briefed them. For a moment Scott felt like Admiral Drake at bowls on the Hoe, standing aside to let the weather work for England as the Spanish Armada swept up the Channel. He looked back at his paper when the weatherman was through.

"'Enemy radar:'" He turned to the chart and swept a line across Greenland and Alaska: "Here to the north, gentlemen, the Ballistic Missile Early Warning sites do not concern us; our refueling area and our route lie south." He pointed to the chart near Greenland. "Radar aircraft of the Greenland-Iceland-United Kingdom Barrier should not be a problem, for the same reason." He touched the pointer off New England. "'Warning Star' Constellation aircraft of the Atlantic Barrier Line *will* concern us and must be jammed." He drew his pointer from the northern tip of Newfoundland across Canada to Alaska, and then along the Aleutian Chain of islands.

"This, the mid-Canada radar line, definitely concerns us and must also be jammed, at least its eastern portion." He drew a line along the U.S.-Canadian border. "Next south is the Pine Tree Line. It has to be jammed for the attack on Omaha and Boston. Last, are the contiguous radars along the Atlantic Seaboard, which must be jammed. I hope not to be concerned with U. S. Navy radar picket ships farther south." He pointed to the Central United States. "Kiwi, if he doesn't trip the Pine Tree Line, should have no trouble once he's past Chicago, provided he stays under the radar horizon."

"'Ow low?" Kiwi asked in his Digger twang. "'Ow low do you suggest, sir?"

"Not above a hundred feet," Malcolm Scott said.

"Twenty-five, I should say," amended Kiwi.

"Aircraft participating:" Malcolm Scott continued. "Nine Vulcan B bombers. Also, three Vickers Valiant refueling aircraft. We will refuel westbound at 1300 hours Zulu precisely, 500 miles south of Greenland, each three-plane section being fueled by one of the three Valiants. Any questions about westbound refueling?"

He looked around the room. There were no questions. *"Schedule:* At 1325 Zulu after west-bound refueling the three sections will split away from each other. In addition, simultaneously in each section, the two screening aircraft will veer off until they are fifty miles apart, maintaining their altitude of thirty-thousand feet. At the same time the one attacking aircraft in each section will begin his descent, so as to be well below the coastal radar horizon by 1400 Zulu hours. Thereafter, he will maintain an altitude of fifty feet to one hundred feet above the terrain or the ocean. At precisely 1400 hours my two screening aircraft, Live Oak Two and Live Oak Three, will commence ECM jamming of the Constellation aircraft of the Atlantic Barrier Line, screening my penetration through this line all the way to the contiguous radar along the Atlantic Seaboard. They will maintain their station off Delaware until I've completed my attack. Similarly, in the second element, Live Oak Five and Six will screen Ricardo, jamming the Atlantic Barrier Line and the Pine Tree Radar System while he attacks his target near Bangor, Maine. Screening aircraft during this attack orbit off Nova Scotia.

"Gentlemen," he said, "this is important—they'll jam *simultaneously* and maintain the fifty-mile distance to make it impossible for the Atlantic Barrier Line and Pine Tree Radar Line to triangulate successfully and pinpoint them. The third section, with Kiwi Barcus leading, will penetrate the northernmost radar aircraft of the Atlantic Barrier Patrol, cross over the Coast of Newfoundland near Hopedale. The screening aircraft will take station between the mid-Canada Line and the Pine Tree Radars, jamming as Kiwi heads south for the Nebraska targets, passing over the Great Lakes at wave-level altitude. The attacks are simultaneous, at 1615 Zulu, which incidentally is 11:15 Eastern Standard Time in Washington and only 10:15 in Chicago, because of the time change."

"It's a big country, isn't it?" observed someone.

"The bigger they are," exclaimed O'Moore, "the harder—"

"All right," interrupted Scott, "upon the completion of their attack, the three attacking aircraft will switch on their *own* jamming to further confuse Pine Tree, and mid-Canada radar. They'll also drop chaff and launch decoys. They'll report when over international waters, blind, as follows: 'Live Oak Four—or Seven as the case may be—international waters.' They'll proceed individually to the second refueling point for the homeward trip, which will have moved to a point one hundred miles east of Nova Scotia. Jamming aircraft will screen the refueling operation from a point twenty-five miles south, while they wait their turn to refuel. The order of refueling is in Appendix A of Operation Dunsinane. I'm sure you are all familiar with it. Any questions?"

There were no questions.

He went on: "Refueling aircraft, coming and going, are unaware of our true mission and believe this to be a routine Ranger training flight." He put away the pointer. "I want you to know, gentlemen, that this is an absolutely up-and-up operation. You all of you have your target photos. These photos were made by people who avoided taking advantage of the fact that we were friendly military officers. A Soviet spy could have had the same. Each of these persons kept a diary for the length of his 'espionage.' Each shows precisely how he arranged to get the pictures. So there's no possiblity of the Americans claiming foul."

He paused, leaned on the podium. "I want this to be a success. Just as Sir Ronald did. Does his death change any of your feelings? Does anyone want to be counted out? You chaps? White? Latham? O'Moore?"

"Not half!" exploded O'Moore. "No sir," said White. Latham shook his head.

"All right, gentlemen. Let's teach the Yanks a lesson in applied military science. Breakfast, and departure time is 0912 hours. Right?"

He began to move toward the door after the men he would lead. The briefing should have covered everything, and yet he had a nagging doubt that all the strings were tied. He tried to think where he had gone amiss, projecting himself twenty-four hours into the future. When the raid was complete, when the point had been proved, would it have *really* been proved? Yes, copies of the photos were in the Press Building in Washington, with the unflappable Mr. Flynn; the bombardier-navigators had each his individual target-photo; there was no proof that could be lacking.

He was leaving the room when the teletype in the corner rang three times. It was a priority message, Malcolm Scott knew. The weather officer paused to read it. He stiffened. Malcolm Scott knew precisely what the teletype said. His first thought was that someone in London had arisen very early to send their hopes crashing to the ground. The weatherman tore the sheet from the machine, handed it to him wordlessly.

It was addressed to Group Captain Smythe, as officer commanding RAF Tarrington. It was also sent to the squadron commanders of the two squadrons, and to Scott himself. No one in the Air Ministry had taken any chances on its going astray. And no one in the Air Ministry was officially admitting that he had even known of Operation Dunsinane. For it was signed simply: AIR MINISTRY.

It read: OPERATION DUNSINANE CANCELED THIS DATE. PROCEED WITH ROUTINE RANGER TRAINING MISSION.

Malcolm Scott tensed. He looked at the weather officer. "There's another teletype on the base still, isn't there?"

"Yes, sir. In Communications."

"Normally, what happens to a message like this?"

"Here in Operations, it's acted on immediately. In Communications Central, it would be sent to the base commander and the two squadron commanders during working hours."

"What time do they go to work?"

"Around nine or thereabouts."

Malcolm Scott folded the message carefully. Heart drumming, he put it in a pocket in his flight suit.

"You haven't read it?" he begged the weather officer.

He was a little man with a large red nose and runny eyes. He had a miserable cold. "I expect not, sir."

"*I* didn't see you read it. It isn't addressed to you. Can I count on it?"

The young man nodded mutely. Malcolm Scott squeezed his arm and followed his crews from the room.

> "I convinced our Group that we would go straight in
> and we did. We never did take any evasive action.
> Antiaircraft was going to shoot every bomber down
> that came over. We had a loss ratio of less than 2
> percent."
>
> —GENERAL CURTIS LeMAY
> re W.W. II bombing of
> occupied Europe

Chapter Ten

THE sedan drew up before the Officers' Mess Building at
RAF Tarrington. Zach Chandler remembered from last year
that breakfast hours were over at 8:30 A.M. He had missed a
meal. He was sure that in the case of a transient American
officer the cooks would whip up a breakfast but he hated to
ask. He shook hands with the man who had been driving him
for the past few days and suggested that he get something to
eat before starting back to London. Then he pulled Sir Ronald's briefcase from the car. A group of RAF flight officers
passed, leaving after breakfast. There were at least a dozen;
all were in flight suits. Zach wondered why Saturday was so
busy. He checked in with the batman at the desk. Yes, Group
Captain Scott was living in the mess; no, he had not seen him
this morning. The batman assigned him a room near Scott's,
selected a key from the rack behind him, picked up the briefcase and led him to the stairway.

As they climbed Zach Chandler looked up at another group
of officers in flight gear. Whatever operation was proceeding,
it was apparently going to pass over desolate territory; each
man had a revolver hanging from a shoulder holster. Round-

ing the first flight of stairs, he heard an Irish brogue: "Philip, my boy, I've been waiting for this day for the last twenty years."

He squeezed to the right to allow the group to pass. The man who had spoken glanced at him distastefully. Doesn't like Americans, decided Zach.

"It looks as if there's something planned for today," he hinted as the batman opened the door to a plain but comfortable room.

"Yes sir. It's one of our Lone Ranger flights to Nairobi. Non-stop. For refueling drill, you know?"

Zach Chandler had heard of them. The batman laid the briefcase on the bed. "Did you want to see Group Captain Scott, sir?"

"Yes."

"He's going on this flight, I believe."

"Going on this flight?" Zach Chandler said. Obviously, Scott was getting his hand in before he returned to the desk in Omaha. Well, if he missed him now he would see him tonight.

He glanced at himself in the mirror. In London he had not had time to shave before word had come that his car was waiting below. He had stuffed his razor, a clean shirt, and a change of underwear into Air Marshal Kimball's briefcase, because he and Scott would be returning through London and there was no use bringing his suitcase to Tarrington. Now he shaved. When he was through he put the razor in a drawer in the battered bureau, dumped his shirts and underwear from the briefcase, and froze.

Tumbling out behind a uniform shirt was the cheap yellow diary he had seen in the map-case of Malcolm Scott's sports car in Lincoln, Nebraska.

He checked it, his mind racing. Why had Scott left a personal diary with Sir Ronald Kimball? Instinctively, he reached into the briefcase. There were two other similar books inside. He leafed through the first. It was in a different handwriting, but the general tenor was the same: "Ascertained an ICBM squadron in area from real-estate salesman, by posing as a worried potential buyer of a home. Assured me that it was in fact fourteen miles north of the tract." He picked up the second diary, a gray pocket-sized notebook. It was printed in a neat English hand: "Managed four photos from Number 34 seat of Eastern Airliner into Boston."

He stood up, trembling. Suddenly it was all becoming clear, very clear. There had been something wrong from the very moment he landed in London; it was ridiculous on the face of it that he should have been separated from Scott in the first place. There was only one answer—the departed air vice-marshal was a party to the defection. Whether the two were acting from motives they thought transcended patriotism, whether the air marshal had ever himself planned to defect, he was certainly helping Scott. Zach was surrounded by enemies. If an air vice-marshal in the RAF had lied to him, who could he tell?

He sat on the bed, forcing his thoughts into order. This was no time for panic. He had to put together the pieces, and swiftly. Until he put them together he must somehow prevent Malcolm Scott from leaving England. Whether he had a full crew of defectors—he must have at least one to overpower the other crew members—or whether he had only a traitorous copilot and would omit manning the other seats was beside the point. Obviously, he intended to pretend trouble somewhere not too far from takeoff, cut loose from the Nairobi group, turn north, and head for the continent.

He wondered what sort of arrangements Scott had made to penetrate Russian defenses. They must expect him. That too was beside the point. He must be stopped. And he would not be stopped by an American Air Force major. If there was one certain outcome of the innocence he himself had so far displayed, it was this: he was hopelessly out-gunned and out-ranked. He needed help. He needed it quickly.

He stuffed the diaries back into the briefcase, lifted the mattress on the bed, changed his mind, moved to a closet, reached up to a shelf. He shook his head, backed away from the closet, looked wildly around the room. He got to his hands and knees by the bed and slipped the briefcase under the rug beneath the headboard. He stepped back.

He had left a hump in the carpet, but it was hardly noticeable. If British batmen vacuumed the room as seldom as American charge-of-quarters cleaned Air Force BOQs, the briefcase would be there well into the next week.

He left the room swiftly and moved to the hall phone.

Malcolm Scott walked with Michael O'Moore toward the huge bat-winged Vulcan gleaming in the morning sun. Across the pad he heard the auxiliary power units on Live Oak Two and Live Oak Six sputter into life, then caught the shriek of the mighty Olympus engines as they wailed across the English countryside with the howl of 64,000 pounds of harnessed thrust.

They had precisely thirty-three minutes to pre-flight the aircraft, climb in, and start their engines. And yet the nagging doubt persisted that everything was done that had to be done. It was formless, and yet it seemed to swirl around the ghost of Air Vice-Marshal Kimball. Sir Ronald's job was over, though; he had organized the flight, all was prepared for its success, he had left out nothing. The only change was if it went awry Malcolm Scott would bear the punishment for it, and this he was prepared to do. And yet . . .

"The diaries!" he blurted.

"What's that, Scotty?" O'Moore demanded.

Malcolm Scott stood stock-still forty feet from the aircraft, turned and started back to operations. "Where the hell are you going?" O'Moore called.

"Pre-flight the kite! I've a call to make!"

And then he was sprinting toward the Operations Building.

Zach Chandler sat sweating at the phone at the end of the corridor outside his room. It was 3 A.M. in Omaha. A jet started in the distance, and then another. He jiggled the hook, "Operator, it's important!"

"I'm trying, sir . . ."

Three thousand miles away a male voice answered: "Offutt Air Force Base."

"I have a collect call for General Hub Younger," said the Omaha operator.

"Collect? Aren't you paid, operator?"

"Collect," said the London trans-ocean girl.

The SAC operator sounded amused. "We can't accept collect calls!"

"Look," began Zach. There was an ugly click. "I'm sorry, sir," said the British operator. "They won't accept."

"Tell him—"

"He's left the line, sir."

Zach gave his home number. Another engine started outside. He would have to talk fast, but Pixie could somehow contact Hub Younger, who might still be in Washington. His own phone was ringing now; Pixie, sleepy, would stumble to it, and then . . .

"Hello? Who is that?"

His heart dropped. Jennie! Her nursery door was near the telephone. She slept lightly; her mother did not.

"Jennie? Honey, get your mother . . ."

"What?"

"This is your daddy! Get your mother, and wake her up . . ."

"Is this 294–2318?" The Omaha operator wanted to know.

"Daddy?" said Jennie.

"Damn it, Jennie, wake up your mother!"

"She's asleep," Jennie said decisively. "Daddy, when are you coming home?"

"Very soon, darling—"

"Is that a child?" the Omaha operator wanted to know.

"Of course it's a child," Zach Chandler exploded. "I'm trying to get her to wake up her mother!"

"I'm sorry, sir, but on a collect call—"

"Jennie! Get your mother!"

"She's asleep," insisted Jennie. He heard her yawn across an ocean and half a continent. "Goodnight, Daddy."

There was a rattle and the unmistakable sound of a phone left off the hook. Zach Chandler felt trapped in a nightmare. "Okay, okay," he said to the operator. He felt for his notebook. Swiftly he leafed through it. Lennie, Lennie, Lennie . . . She would know how to get Hub Younger. "I have another Omaha number," he said. Lennie would know what to do.

Malcolm Scott slammed down the telephone in the Operations Building. He glared at it as if it were responsible. "Damn, damn, damn," he muttered.

Mike O'Moore entered the clearance area, looking wildly

about. He moved over quickly. "Now, Scotty. You'd best get out there! We've only twelve minutes to engine start!"

"That poor, benighted idiot of Sir Ronald's! She turned over the whole key to this operation to my Omaha assistant, who was sent over here to keep an eye on me!"

Mike O'Moore's eyes widened. "What the hell rot are you talking?"

"The diaries," murmured Malcolm Scott. "She tried to send the diaries to me with an American!"

"What diaries?"

"I can't explain! It would take too long!"

"What American?" O'Moore wanted to know.

"Chap who works for me in Omaha," Scott said absently.

"Yes, but what does he look like?"

"Round face, curly hair, kind of a babylike chubbiness about him."

"A major?"

"Yes," Scott said, surprised. "How'd you know?"

"He's here."

"What?"

"He was checking into the mess when we left. I saw him on the stairs."

Malcolm Scott thought swiftly. Chandler had obviously not looked into the briefcase, or they would have heard about it. On the other hand, to meet him in flight clothes would trigger him to all sorts of conjecture. "Go to the mess," he said. "Tell him I sent you to pick up the briefcase. Tell him you need it now for the Nairobi flight. Tell him I'll see him later this morning. Double-time, Mike!"

"It'll make him suspicious," warned O'Moore, "if you make too big a flap over it."

"Muck off, will you now?"

O'Moore was right, in a way, but he could not bring himself to leave the diaries with an American.

He watched O'Moore trot from the Operations Office and turned back to the airplane. His heart was beating fast and his lips were dry.

Zach Chandler wiped his brow. The jets howled outside. It was so late that he would have to stop Scott physically, somehow, but if he could get word to the general first . . .

"When you get my number," he told the Omaha operator, "tell her it's her boss, and to accept charges."

The phone rang interminably. The operator spoke, and then he heard Lennie's voice: "Zach! Where are you?"

"Still in England," he said swiftly. He was so relieved that he paid no attention to footsteps behind him. "Get General Younger, wherever he is. Tell him Scott's taking a Vulcan—"

The phone was yanked suddenly from his hands. He whirled to stare into a snub-nosed revolver. It was trembling violently, and from its cylinder four leaden slugs glared at him balefully while the hole in the muzzle seemed to grow in size. The flight lieutenant with the moustache was not holding it as one saw on television. The man's face was screwed into a mask of hatred, and he was aiming at a spot precisely in the center of Zach Chandler's forehead. Zach, enraged and frustrated, felt the dank breath of death cooling his anger.

"For Christ's sakes," he breathed. "Put it down!"

The man shook his head slowly, and his moustache seemed to grow in size. "No! Bloody Yank spy! Where's your room?" The man was Irish. Weak in the knees, Zach Chandler arose, led him to the room, not trusting himself to speak.

"Now, then," the Irishman wanted to know. "Where's the briefcase?"

Zach Chandler became all at once certain that the man was going to kill him anyway. As long as the briefcase existed, there was some reason to leave him alive. "I didn't bring it," he heard himself say. "I forgot it in London."

Another engine started in the distance. It seemed to distract the Irishman, who looked as if he had a hangover.

"All right, Major," grated the Irishman. "Come with me."

And then Zach Chandler found himself herded down the steps, the barrel of the revolver jammed in the small of his back, and the Irishman's stale breath, reminiscent of whiskey and cigarettes, heavy in his nostrils.

Malcolm Scott started numbers three and four engines, too intent on the instrument panel to notice the men climbing from the jeep off his left wing tip some fifty feet away. He heard them scramble up the ladder behind him and turned. "What in the name of God?"

Zach Chandler was looking at him with exactly the expression of a Boy Scout who finds that his scoutmaster is the local rapist. The young man looked ready to cry, not in grief, but in sheer, childlike anger.

"Scott," he spat, voice high, "you no good son of a bitch, I hope you rot in Siberia!" He whirled on the three crew members behind the hatch, who had swiveled from their aft-facing position and were gaping at him. "Do you know these two bastards are going to defect? Or are you Commies too? You better do something, or you're going to end up in the Russian can!"

"My God," murmured Martin Kraft. Malcolm Scott had a mad desire to laugh, but the situation was not one for laughter. O'Moore appeared behind the American.

"What the hell did you bring him up here for?" Scott demanded.

"I found him on the phone, spilling the beans. Did you want me to leave him there?"

"Who were you talking to?" Scott asked. Chandler refused to answer. "Hub Younger, Zach?" Chandler was mute. "How much did he say?" Scott asked O'Moore.

"Not much. You were taking a Vulcan, some such rot."

"Did you get the diaries?" Scott asked O'Moore wearily.

"He says he left them in London."

Zach Chandler nodded blandly. "In the Embassy safe."

"I'm sure of that," O'Moore growled. "I'll get him to tell us."

"You couldn't," Scott sighed, "if I let you. What shall we do with him?"

"Take him," decided O'Moore.

Malcolm Scott considered the situation. He wondered whether, if he could convince Chandler of the nature of their mission, he could safely trust the young man to be left behind, on parole as it were. "If I told you," he said slowly to Chandler, "that the reason for all of this was a mock attack on NORAD defenses, could I leave you here on a promise of twenty-four-hour silence?"

"Yes, *sir!*" Zach Chandler smiled, eyes full of hatred.

"You can trust me absolutely, Group Captain Scott."

Malcolm Scott sighed. "Close the hatch," he said dully.

Hands flashing over the panel, he started engines one and two. Then he waved to the seat beside him. "Let him sit there, for takeoff, O'Moore. He won't touch anything. And he and I have a little talking to do."

He picked up the microphone, checked with Live Oak One through Nine. In two minutes they were rumbling toward the downwind end of the runway.

They were airborne at 0919 Zulu hours, seven minutes late.

> "In the event of war, this nation will be hit, and probably seriously. No defenses can be 100 percent successful. But there is a difference between being hurt and being killed."
> —GENERAL HERBERT H. THATCHER
> Commander, Air Defense
> Command

Chapter Eleven

LENNIE NORRIS lay in bed and listened to the first faint stirrings of life in suburban Omaha. In the far distance, tires squealed around a corner; much closer, a dog barked once. A few blocks away she heard the low-throated growl of the anonymous milkman's truck; she wondered why anyone would choose to live his life while others slept. She yanked her second pillow over her head, rolling restlessly and pressing it close to her ear so that the rattle of the milk bottles would not reach it.

She wondered if she had slept at all since answering the ridiculous call from England. She was tired; she had gone to a party at Cal's old fraternity. She was growing to love him more and more. Already the image of Malcolm Scott was fading. It had been ridiculous from the start; he was a fascinating man, a strong man, but really they had nothing in common.

It had been folly on her part; thank God she had at least escaped pregnancy. And now she had Cal. They would be very happy, she knew, happier than ever she would have been with Malcolm Scott; she would never have been at home in England.

Then why had Zach's mention of him on the crazy telephone call excited her? For half an hour after the call had been cut off she had sat sleepily waiting for Zach to call again. Had it been earlier in England, or later? Or was it really from England he had phoned? Obviously he must have been drunk, or he would simply have called Pixie Chandler at home. "Scott's taking a Vulcan..." Back to Omaha, no doubt, but why ask her to tell the general?

Yet he had not sounded drunk. She had a sudden impulse. She hated to wake Pixie, for she knew her only slightly, but there was something in Zach's tone that gave the call importance. She rolled over in bed, too heavy-lidded to turn on the light, and dialed information. When she had the Chandler number she hesitated again.

If Zach had wanted to call his home, he could have. Perhaps the message was a confidential one. The Vulcan was a military plane, after all. Its movements might be classified.

In a sudden spurt of activity Lennie swung her feet over the side of the bed. Her mouth was stale with fraternity beer; she had not liked it. She put on the West Point bathrobe that years ago a cadet had given her and creaked down the stairs to the kitchen to start a pot of coffee.

It was simply too early to try to get General Younger. So far as she knew he was still in Washington. She could call his deputy later, at some reasonable hour.

From the perculator the aroma of coffee drifted toward the kitchen table. It smelled wonderful. She got up, bleary-eyed, and poured herself a cup. When it really woke her up, she would call Washington and start trying to track down the general.

Zach Chandler watched Malcolm Scott ease the throttles off to 90 percent power at 30,000 feet. He was very conscious of O'Moore's presence behind him, but he was damned if he was going to favor the Irishman with a glance simply to see if he still had the gun out. Sitting in the copilot seat, he was quite helpless anyway; O'Moore could easily overpower him from behind. Presumably the three crew members were picked defectors too. Malcolm Scott spoke into his mike.

"Live Oak aircraft from Live Oak Leader. Coming to two-niner-one. Thirty-thousand feet. Acknowledge."

Slowly, ponderously, the great bat-winged craft swung to the rising sun. Looking behind him, Zachary Chandler could see the other banking. He felt a gentle nudge against his shoulders as the airspeed built up in level flight. He looked again at the gyrocompass, puzzled. If their basic course was west, they were certainly not heading for Nairobi, but they were not heading for Soviet Russia either. Malcolm Scott had caught the glance. He reached under his seat, dropped it, and adjusted the back.

"Now, sonny," he said, with an edge of bitterness in his voice, "suppose you and I have a little talk."

Zach Chandler only glared at him. But he listened.

"Most of the SAC's striking power is still carried in bomb bays."

—GENERAL THOMAS S. POWER
Former
Commander-in-Chief,
SAC, September, 1964

Chapter Twelve

GENERAL ALF KARMAN awakened in his quarters at Fort Lee to the ring of the telephone by his bedside table. It was the command duty officer at the Washington Air Defense Sector, and the line was direct. "General, we're going to a yellow alert."

It was a normal occurrence, probably indicative of the 4713th "Friendly Enemy" Squadron from Stewart Air Force Base taking advantage of Armed Forces Day to confuse their interceptor comrades in NORAD. Alf Karman approved the Pearl Harbor technique. He was not worried. Armed Forces Day in his sector passed over operational personnel with scarcely a ripple. You after all let the intercept directors and the pilots alone to do their job; the public information people and the housekeeping personnel were sufficient to display the Air Force's wares to the curious taxpayer.

He glanced at his watch. It was 8:30 A.M. He hoped that the phone had not awakened Hub Younger, sleeping in his guest room. He shaved quickly, kissed his wife, and told her not to wake up. "I'll be back as soon as I can."

He slid behind the seat of his Air Force sedan and started

it. While the engine warmed he picked up his microphone. He reported to the Washington Air Defense Sector: "WADS from General Karman. I'll be in my mobile for the next five minutes."

"Roger, sir. Wait, sir. The command duty officer wants to talk to you." In a moment his duty officer was on the phone. "It's going to escalate, I think, General."

Alf Karman rubbed his eyes. He felt a flicker of annoyance, which he knew he would overcome when he had the reins firmly in hand. "Okay, Jake," he told the colonel. "What's the hassle?"

"Somebody's jamming the northernmost Connie on the Atlantic Barrier Line."

"Ah-hah," Alf Karman smiled, "I wondered when theyd start doing that."

"The question is, General, who's they?"

"What do you mean?"

"I don't think it's the 4713th. The evaluators say the jamming doesn't look like anything we've got."

Alf Karman's heart began to beat harder. A USSR probe? Or, perhaps, Soviet aircraft screening a ferry-flight down the Central Atlantic and into Cuba?

He remembered all at once the change in Presidential attitude that Van Ness had predicted. If it was a Soviet probe, the Russian pilots had better hope that they did not go too far. And if it was a ferry-flight? God knew what might happen then.

"I'll be right there, Jake." He pulled swiftly away from the curb.

At 30,000 feet south of Iceland, Zach Chandler stared across the throttles at Group Captain Malcolm Scott. His head was throbbing and he could hardly believe what he had just heard. But there was no doubt about it; for an hour, while Scott had explained what he called "Operation Dunsinane," Zach had been sneaking glances at the gyrocompass. Every fifteen minutes or so the stocky navigator behind them would write a new course on a slip of paper, turn, hand it to O'Moore. O'Moore, standing behind Chandler, would clip it on the panel so that Scott could use it.

The courses varied somewhat, as the navigator apparently corrected for changing winds, for they were running into the cirrus clouds above that meant serious weather ahead. Even at 30,000 Zach Chandler could sense the turbulence that lurked below and the elemental forces riding a front ahead. But though the headings varied, they varied only to the westward, as the great-circle course toward the North American Continent would arc first toward the North Pole and then sweep to the southeast with the curve of the earth.

He had to believe Scott: it was too late for trickery—they were heading for Canada or America. "Okay, Scotty. I'll accept it. It's a mock raid. But do you honestly sit there and tell me that you haven't cleared this with *anybody* in the Defense Department? At *any* level?"

Malcolm Scott, his hands on the oddly shaped yoke, turned to him. "Of course we haven't! My God, we've been having ordinary training exercises for the last fifteen years! For what? What about Sky Shield? You didn't learn anything from that!"

"The only Sky Shield I ever participated in," Zach Chandler said coldly, "I sat up there in an F-106 with SAC and RAF targets as big as an orange on my scope, wondering how the hell they ever got anybody to be a bomber pilot when we could knock them down like pigeons."

"So you *didn't* learn anything." Malcolm Scott smiled. "You may today."

"If you penetrate the U. S. Air Defense Identification Zone without clearance," Zach Chandler growled, "it's going to look like North American Aviation's moved the F-106 assembly up here!"

"Is it?" Malcolm Scott asked. "We'll see."

"You're crazy!" Zach exploded. "What'll you prove?"

"For one thing," Scott said, "we'll show your President he isn't likely to launch ICBMs until he has to."

"And you're going to kill us all doing it!"

"I'm scanning," called the air-electronics officer from the seat directly behind Scott, craning his neck forward. He turned back to his radar, said: "I say . . . I have one. The Atlantic anchor of the mid-Canada radar line, or maybe an aircraft of the Atlantic Barrier Line."

"See if you can pick up our refueling craft up ahead," Malcolm Scott said.

"Very good, sir," said the air-electronics officer. He bent back over his scope.

"Scotty," O'Moore said from behind Chandler. "Hadn't we better let me up there in his seat."

"Get down, Zach," agreed Malcolm Scott. "It's time we went to work."

General Hub Younger awakened instantly in the Karman guest room. He sat up in bed. Betty Karman was shaking his foot.

"Hub? Hub, boy! Reveille!"

"Thanks," he said. "What time is it?"

"Almost nine. There's a phone call for you."

"Nine!" he had not slept so long in years.

"I'll start your breakfast."

He crawled into trousers and padded to the phone in the hall. It was Offutt Air Force Base. He recognized the operator's voice. "Younger, here."

"I've got a call for you, sir. Odd one. It's a girl. She works for JSTPS, or I wouldn't have bothered. She says the deputy commander won't do. Do you care to take it, sir?"

"What's she want, a raise?" he asked impatiently. "All right. Put her on."

In a moment he heard a young and tremulous female voice. "General Younger, this is Lennie Norris. I guess you'll think I'm crazy, but . . . well, I work for Group Captain Scott and Major Chandler."

He remembered the girl, an attractive, diffident person he had seen in the European Section over the past two years.

"Oh? Yes, Lennie?"

"Sometime last night, or, this morning, really I had a trans-atlantic phone call. Collect. It was Zach . . . Major Chandler. It sounded like him. I'm sure it was."

"Yes?"

"He said . . . well, as nearly as I can remember, this is what he said: 'Tell General Younger Scott's taking a Vulcan.'"

"Go on."

"That's all! He was cut off."

"That's all?" General Younger thought swiftly. "Has anything come in from him since? To your office? Or mine?"

"I'm at home, sir. It's Saturday."

"Okay, Miss . . . Okay, Lennie. Thanks. It's probably nothing. Now I want the Offutt Air Force Base operator."

The man had never left the line. "Yes sir?"

"Check and see if a transatlantic call came in from Major Chandler last night."

There was a strained delay. "He tried to call, sir. I wasn't here. The man I relieved told me."

"What happened?"

"He tried to call collect. We can't accept collect—"

"Oh, for Christ's sake!" General Younger exploded. "He's on the staff!"

"Yes sir. Well, that's what I told the man I relieved."

"I want that man's name on my desk when I get back! Now, patch me into the British Air Ministry," he demanded. "The duty officer there, please."

In five minutes he had discovered that Malcolm Scott had been airborne for two hours, en route from RAF Tarrington to Nairobi and return, on a regular Lone Ranger exercise. And with eight other aircraft. His spirits soared. No one was defecting with nine airplanes. He had simply wanted some flight time with his old outfit and told Chandler to clear it with Omaha if he could. Hub Younger wondered if the time would come when he could sit with Scott over a drink and tell him of the crazy days of suspicion. He supposed not, at least until they retired.

He was doing his push-ups in the guest room when he heard the phone ring again. Betty Karman called for him, and he heard the Offutt Base operator say: "I'm to inform you, sir, that the deputy commander has gone to red alert. All aircraft are being launched to the fail-safe line."

"Give me the deputy."

In seconds he was connected to the Command Post. The deputy's gruff voice was on the phone. "Yes, Hub?"

"What cooks?"

"NORAD, mostly. Somebody's jamming the North Atlantic Barrier Line, and now the DEW-line's getting it, and there's no indication of number or intent."

"An exercise by the 4713th?"

"4713th, hell! It looks more like a ferry-hop to Cuba!"

Hub Younger's heart began to beat. Damn it! Damn the Senate, damn the Secretary of Defense, damn Washington, damn politicians! His post was where the other man was, in the giant amphitheater at Omaha, not here as a house guest.

"I'm going to the Pentagon War Room," he said. "Carry on. I'll be back to you in twenty minutes."

He tore into the guest room, put on his shirt, stuffed his socks into his pockets, jammed feet into shoes, and loped down the stairs. Betty Karman stuck her head from the kitchen.

He paused. "I got to get to the Pentagon! Where's Alf?"

"He left for the blockhouse!"

"Why in hell didn't he wake me?"

"For a yellow alert?"

"It's red now! Call the airstrip for a helicopter for me. Did he leave a car?"

"There's Porky's," she said. Porky was a plebe at Annapolis . . . "Can you drive an M.G.?"

"I can drive anything," Younger said bitterly. "If it'll get me to the War Room."

Yesterday a flight of Soviet long-range bombers approached to within a few miles of the north coast of Alaska, then flew parallel to the coast more than one hour before returning to the Russian mainland.
—UPI PRESS RELEASE

Chapter Thirteen

MALCOLM SCOTT at at 30,000 feet, bouncing in the heaving turbulence of the front ahead. The refueling northeast of Newfoundland had gone beautifully; rendezvous had been precisely on schedule. Twenty minutes ago he had heard Kiwi Barcus say cheerfully in his Australian cockney: "Thank you, Life-Blood Two. Disconnect!"

There would be no more interplane messages until after the attack except in case of emergency. The nine aircraft were dispersed. None were any longer in sight. Fifty miles on either side of him Live Oak Two and Three were jamming. He looked at the second hand jerking around the panel clock before him. In two minutes he was to start his descent.

He settled back and stretched his arms. It was the last chance he would have to relax until the mission was virtually completed and they were joining again with the tankers south of Newfoundland for the long trip home. Ahead of him, barely out of sight behind the line of thick, black cumulus clouds under which he would skim when the time came, the great nation lay, defenses doubtless awakened and groping, though the man in the street would know nothing.

In Washington, D.C., two hundred miles beyond his nose, those who cared to brave the weather forecast would be motoring toward picnics in the spring countryside or strolling the Potomac.

He remembered suddenly that it was Armed Forces Day in the U. S. He had been in Washington for the parade the year before and he could imagine the ruler-straight lines of West Point cadets, all gold and gray, and the easier, swinging stride of the Annapolis midshipmen sweeping past the White House in advance of the spectacle that would grind by, doubtless in rain, for hours.

In the Midwest, Lennie would be sleeping late; the vision of her lying in bed stirred him, but the flare of jealousy he had known against the man who would marry her had cooled. It was better this way.

At NORAD Headquarters under Cheyenne Mountain in Colorado, the sun would be low in the sky, well down the peaks, but the excitement would be high. They would be feeling blindly for the aircraft jamming their tentacles; unable, as long as all the aircraft kept up the screen, to single out any one.

But now they would know. They would know from Canada to Mexico, from the Atlantic to the Pacific Coast, where it was only 8 A.M. and the storybook towers of San Francisco would only just now be gleaming in the morning sun and Los Angeles would be stirring under its brown blanket of smog. But knowing that something was coming, and stopping it, were two different things.

The second hand jerked past the minute. It was time to begin the gentle, half-hour dive to wave level. He eased the throttles back so as not to outdistance his screening craft, gently shoved the yoke forward, looked over at Mike O'Moore.

The Irishman was grinning widely. There was a light of battle in his eyes.

Secretary of Defense Charles Van Ness was standing to the right of the President as the Marine band from Quantico swung by. The weather was a shame, he thought: a line of fat-bellied rain clouds was sliding in from the north, and the moist breeze off the Potomac hinted that soon they would be standing in rain.

Van Ness had watched the regiment of midshipment parade past with some amusement. Had it not been for his eyes he would undoubtedly have been the braid-laden Chief of Naval Operations standing half a dozen men away from the President, gold flashing in the shifting sun. His father, who had died a bitter graveyard admiral, would probably have preferred him to be. The hell with him. Power was more interesting than bangles. He felt an arm on his sleeve. It was his military aide.

"Yes, Jim," he said, hating to turn from the spectacle.

"Red alert, sir. SAC's scrambled."

The Secretary felt a tug of irritation. He was all for the endless drills with which SAC and NORAD tested their metal, but today was a day to relax. The aide went on, his voice low, "Somebody's jamming the Atlantic Barrier Connies. We can't seem to triangulate. It's more than one aircraft."

The sun broke through the clouds for a brief moment, and then disappeared. The Secretary felt a chill. He looked at the grave man beside him, who was smiling tiredly down on a Maryland National Guard unit. He hated to bother him. But during a red alert he should be in the White House shelter, and not outside watching a parade.

He mentioned the alert. "Sir, I think you'd better go inside."

"Oh now, Van . . . How can I go inside? It's nothing, and I can't have thirty thousand troops march by in what looks like is going to be the rain of the month and not be here."

"Whatever's jamming is already south of Newfoundland," Charles Van Ness reminded him. "We may want to shoot it down, you should be where you can keep up on it."

"Operation One-Two?" grunted the President. "I don't believe it!"

"They said that at Pearl."

The President hesitated for a moment, looked down at the troops, and reluctantly left the stand.

General Alf Karman sat in the midst of his battle-staff behind the glassed-in balcony, wishing he had a target toward which to scramble his fighters. The giant iconorama screen flashed lights from across the pit in which his duty controllers and Communications officers worked. His hands were as wet as if he had been sitting in one of the F-106 alert craft waiting on a runway, indicated here by a colored light. To the right and left sat the men on whom he depended for help.

He had had, on entering, a weather briefing. Nothing was good. The jamming which had brought NORAD from readiness condition three to two and now to one was still continuing. He tried to think of anything he might have forgotten. He had called Hub Younger; Hub had been already on his way to a helicopter for the Pentagon. He looked across at the screen before him. Yellow arrows for SAC aircraft filled it: SAC was on its way to the points at which it would return if no "go code" were received. A few green arrows for other non-hostile flights of special interest were scattered about. There were no more than the usual number of orange arrows for unknown aircraft, and these would only mean aircraft pending identification. There were no red aircraft for hostiles, because no one had yet picked one out from the radar screen, cluttered with weather and the damnable jamming.

Each arrow on the screen carried a number. It was the track identification number. If he or one of his battle staff wanted details of an arrow, he had only to punch in the number on the individual consoles before him. Then, on a scope like a small TV, would appear altitude, speed, and course. But before the hostile arrow would appear, an old-fashioned radar must pick it from the mess.

He glanced at the iconorama again. A few stars indicated friendly aircraft carriers off the Atlantic; there was a circle within a square near Newfoundland—an unidentified submarine. Off Alaska was a triangle, base up—a fleet of Soviet trawlers—nothing unusual about that. A few circles on DEW-Line and the mid-Canada Line indicated radar "outages" or breakdown: no indiction of sabotage for there were no more than usual.

It was the row of red pulsing circles along the Atlantic Barrier Line and the Pine Tree Line, indicating active jamming, that was causing the scare. As he watched, the easternmost mid-Canada Line radar went to a red circle as well. As if it were too much for NORAD, readiness condition changed from one to zero.

Alf Karman shifted uncomfortably. It was time to make sure that the skies were cleared for action, in case they ever got a target. At the end of the line of consoles occupied by his battle-staff, a phone rang. The SAC liasion officer picked it up. The young man listened for a moment, called to the general: "SAC reports no SAC planes in the jammed area."

"Check the 4713th again," General Karman demanded. "And tell them no games!" The "Friendly Enemy" Squadron was a fast and sneaky antagonist, perfectly capable of turning his sector into a shambles if it had perfected some new jamming technique.

"No 4713th aircraft in the area, either, sir. They say honest. And they're shook."

"Okay." Now, at least, he was certain that they were dealing with something Russian. He flicked on a microphone.

"Ops briefer?"

From a separate Romeo and Juliet balcony overlooking the lower level, the operations briefer looked across at the battle-staff row. "Yes, sir?"

"Give us the picture," Alf Karman said.

He had never noticed before how much the silvery-haired light colonel enjoyed his job. He seldom was called but he was ready now. He got to his feet with ponderous dignity, like an ancient oracle summoned before his Emperor. "A slight increase in operational activity was noted during the past twenty-four hours. A total of forty-seven tracks were detected in the Siberian complex. Cuban activity consisted of twenty-four tracks which flew definite patrol patterns. Ballistic Missile Early Warning System computers at Thule reported nineteen known U.S. satellites and Clear, Alaska, reported fifteen known U.S. satellites—"

"Skip the space age crap," Alf Karman broke in unkindly. This was no time for compliance with forms. "Give me the unknowns!"

The ops briefer looked hurt. "Unknown aircraft activity consisted of six unknowns in the Early Warning System and four unknowns in the Continental Radar Coverage. Naval activity include eighty-five Soviet trawlers off Alaska—"

"But we're an Atlantic sector," Alf Karman said impatiently. "Since we're rushed, let's stick to our own backyard."

"And ninety-seven off Newfoundland—about normal. Unknown subs Echo Two and Bravo Five are still active and being tracked and being reported by the Navy. The duty controller at the Twenty-Six Region NORAD reports jamming of picket ship No. Four, four hundred miles east of Boston."

"What condition jamming?" Alf Karman wanted to know.

"Condition three."

The ops briefing continued, giving details of what already showed on the iconorama. Karman cut the colonel short as reports began to flow into the complex. "Emergency readiness alert," a battle-staff officer reported.

"Reclassify all unknowns as hostile or friendly," Alf Karman said.

A hollow voice came over the intercom, and Alf Karman recognized it as that of General Hub Younger's deputy in Omaha. "This is SAC in Omaha. Airborne alert aircraft are approaching their Positive Control Points. Follow-up wave will be launched immediately. We are standing by for countdown on our missiles."

"Jesus Christ," Alf Karman heard his deputy breathe. "When it happens, it happens but fast!"

Alf Karman flicked a switch on his mike. "Duty controller, this is General Karman. Transmit Commander in Chief NORAD's declaration of emergency readiness. Let me know verbally when we have one hundred percent readiness on the runways. I want a verbal report from the Bomarc batteries, Nike-Ajax, and Hercules, too. *Verbally*. Okay?"

These ships would show on the iconorama, but now that the chips were down, he found that he really did not trust the screen. He wanted the comfort of the human voice. There was nothing more he could do until the radars which were supposed to pinpoint his adversaries somehow peered through the fog of jamming and weather and told him where the enemies were. He looked at the iconorama. A whole series of little red circles told him that he was reduced to a World War 1 general awaiting a blow he could not see.

In a distant room under blue light, the little teams of men were standing around their consoles, electronic light-guns bright in their hands. In another chamber the huge computers squatted dumbly, crammed with the knowledge of men. The sleek, arrowhead interceptors crouched on the runways of Maryland and Virginia and Washington and the Carolinas, lethal and ready.

But until his radars could find them a target they might as well have been sitting in Spads.

He shivered slightly and sat back to wait.

General Hub Younger flashed across Fort Lee in the M.G. roadster, heading for the airstrip. He tried again on his pocket transmitter to reach the War Room, or even Alf Karman's blockhouse. He heard nothing. The car had a steel roof: perhaps that was cutting down the signal strength. He pulled to the side of the road, got out. He spoke into his transmitter.

"Communications Central, Communications Central! This is Hub Younger. Do you read me?"

The tiny black pocket set, hardly bigger than a pack of cigarettes, was dead in his hands. He shook it angrily; it spat static back at him. He was cut off from SAC and he had not been cut off for ten minutes in the last two years.

Cut off. All the gadgets, and he was cut off as thoroughly as the girl in Omaha from Zach Chandler this morning. "Scott's taking a Vulcan," she had said. He stood thinking.

Scott's taking a Vulcan. Nine Vulcans, apparently. But where? To Nairobi, really? Or could it be, could he possibly be, at the bottom of the jamming? Could he be bringing a group of Vulcans west? It was impossible, incredible, for no one would risk it, and yet, they had dared so much before, this island breed, when he served with them in the wild wave-top rides across the North Sea and the Lowlands. They did not think as we did; they were insular, dogged, sometimes tricky. He wondered if Malcolm Scott with his magnetism and Kimball with his rank could somehow have collected around themselves enough suicidal airmen to try to prove their point.

He made a screaming U-turn and started back for Alf Karman's blockhouse.

Any attack by manned bombers could be met with
volleys of atomic rockets and missiles—certainly a
thought to deter any nation from striking at all.
—AIR DEFENSE COMMAND
April, 1963

Chapter Fourteen

MALCOLM SCOTT, hands firm on the yoke, lurched blindly
through scud and clouds at eight hundred feet, seventy-five
miles from the New Jersey coast and heading for Fort Lee.
His mind had become in these last minutes extraordinarily
acute. He could see the overall picture, himself as a part of it,
and yet his giant's-eye view did not in the least interfere with
the most minute detail of his flying.

"Captain from nav-plotter," Pilot Officer Latham said on
the intercom. "Distance seventy miles to Atlantic City. Your
course is good."

"Very well," Malcolm Scott said. His voice sounded firm
in his ears. He glanced at his radar altimeter: "Seven . . . six
hundred feet, descending at one hundred feet per minute." He
was well past the Atlantic Barrier Line. The first of the obsta-
cles under which he must crawl were behind him. David Ricardo by now would be 600 miles north of him, sweeping past
the Pine Tree Radar Line, heading for the site on the photo on
his lap, the ICBM silo on the hill near Bangor, Maine. Kiwi
Barcus would be 1,000 miles northwest, streaking toward the
south shore of Lake Michigan.

He craned back for a moment to look at Zach Chandler. Zach was sitting behind the copilot seat, staring straight aft, jaw outthrust, lips tight. He really believes, Scott thought, that we won't survive it. He had a great desire to reassure the young man, promise him that he would see Pixie and Skipper and Jennie again. But nothing he could do would erase the anger in his friend's eyes, so he did not even try.

He was at 500 feet, still descending toward the invisible, scud-shrouded Atlantic below, when it happened. He heard an exclamation from Kraft.

"Captain! Scotty, for Christ's sake! Come starboard! Come starboard, *now!*"

Instinctively Malcolm Scott hauled back on the yoke, put the aircraft into a violent right bank. He left it there, pressed the button for his lip-mike. "What is it?"

"I have a target dead ahead! A surface target! And I'm getting radar pulses from it!"

Damn, damn, damn! A stray U. S. warship, on its way to Norfolk or up the coast? Perhaps even a radar picket ship on its way home, or on its way to take its station. Whatever it was, stumbling directly over it was a chance in a million; his screening planes were too far aft to have given him protection, and if it was straight below, he was well over its radar horizon.

If he tried to jam it himself, he would give his position away to contiguous radar on the Eastern Seaboard. His only chance was to hope that if he had been "painted" by the warship's radar at all, he had not been caught by its fire-control system.

"Commencing evasive tactics," he grunted into the mike.

"Very well, sir," Kraft said. "I get pulses from it. It's fire-control radar! God, Scotty, I think they're locked onto us!"

Quickly, instinctively, Malcolm Scott reversed the controls. He felt the blood drain from his face as the G-forces crushed him into his seat. He heard Zach Chandler, unrestrained by harness, crash against the back of O'Moore's seat. He held the left turn until he was heading north, then leveled his wings.

"Did we break his lock?" he asked Kraft.

"I hope so, I bloody well hope so," Kraft said fervently.

"We're drawing away. He's two point six miles, three, three point five . . . Oh, God!"

"What?"

"He's launched something! It's big! A Terrier! Or something! Oh my God!"

Malcolm Scott, shrouded in the clouds, entirely on instruments in a gray-white vacuum, glanced outside. Off his port bow was a dark peak of clouds that meant a thunderstorm. Instinctively he headed for it as a mole might burrow deeper underground. As he pulled the shuddering aircraft into a climbing left turn he caught out of the corner of his eye, low and to the left, a bright meteor curving toward him. His hands clenched on the controls. If it was a Terrier ship-to-air missile, and if it was locked on, and if he could not break the lock, then this is how he would go, in a split second, in a blinding flash. Suddenly he found that he was ready; his regret was not for himself but for the men on his crew, though they had volunteered, but mostly for Zach, who had not; for Zach, and Pixie, and Skipper, and Jennie.

"It's locked on!" Kraft yelled, his voice muffled by the hood of his radar. Beside him Malcolm Scott sensed O'Moore tensing for the blow. And then, miraculously, the comet streaked past below the window. It seemed for a moment to waver. There was a sudden flash, a mighty blow in the cockpit, and the aircraft was thrown on one of its great bat-wings.

Without thought, as acrid smoke filled the cockpit and the cabin behind him, Malcolm Scott fought for mastery against the laws of physics: the unforgiving concrete facts of thrust and lift and drag and sheer, ponderous weight. When he won he was at 200 feet by his altimeter, praying that if there was an electrical fire it would all be over quickly, that the ship would not launch another such demon from hell, that no one had been killed by the nearby explosion, of what must have been a devilish proximity fuse, the last blind blow of a monster that had been outwitted.

He looked around the cockpit. Smoke was swirling about: there was a tear in the plane's structure not three feet above Kraft's head. Kraft was staring at him fixedly, his eyelids blinking in surprise. Shock. . . .

They had to bring Kraft to his senses. Wherever the electrical fire was, it was in Kraft's special and mysterious province. O'Moore plunged across the plane, slapped Kraft twice, and whirled him aft. "You have a fire, you idiot! Put it out!"

Stiffly, mechanically, Kraft reached for an electrical cable, braced his foot on the panel, and yanked. Immediately the smell of smoke stopped. For almost three minutes Malcolm Scott sat tensely awaiting the second missile from whatever warship they had passed. There was none. O'Moore returned to his seat.

"What's up next, Doc?" he asked brightly, like the Bugs Bunny character, but there was a question in his eyes, too.

"Nav-plotter from captain," Malcolm Scott said. "Can you give me a course to Washington?"

O'Moore looked happier, as if he had thought Scott would abort. The hell with that, thought Scott. We've gone too far. He was waiting for an answer from Latham, and when it did not come, he turned in his seat. "Is our ICS out?"

Mike O'Moore nodded. Malcolm Scott's heart sank.

"Our radio's out too, then."

Mike O'Moore shrugged. "We're on radio silence anyway."

Malcolm Scott stared at him. "Yes, but how the hell, if we got a fighter on our tail, could we identify ourselves? How could we get him off before he shot us down?"

"It's no matter, Scotty," Mike O'Moore said. "If our radar's out, which it is for sure, that being a radar cable he pulled, we'd never know if we had him on our tail anyway. Right?"

Malcolm Scott nodded. Well, this *was* the end, then. They would have to abort. There was only one thing to do—to head north for the rendezvous point, hope that the other aircraft had had beter luck, refuel, and return to Tarrington. There was no other choice. To attack the Atlantic Seaboard unable in the ultimate extreme to save himself or his crew would be a piece of foolishness beyond comprehension. There were still two other aircraft to succeed. Air Marshal Kimball himself would not have gone in.

Or would he? You didn't quit. You went on, and pressed home the attack, regardless. He tried to turn back to the north, away from the coast, throat tight and heart heavy. All of the work, all of the plans, were dead. The camera hung heavy around his neck. He found that he could not make the turn. Something deep inside forced him to go on. He sensed Zach Chandler, suddenly, scrambling to his feet, staring over his shoulder.

"You're not going in?" Zach murmured.

"Of course I am." He looked up at Zach, and found himself smiling. "You didn't think I brought you all this way for nothing?"

Zach Chandler looked into his eyes, shook his head, and retreated to his nook behind O'Moore. He looked to Malcolm Scott like a very sick young man.

In the War Room under the Pentagon, Secretary of Defense Charles Van Ness put down the message that told him that a diplomatic source in Moscow, pressed hurriedly, had validated the CIA's information. Red China and Russia were one again, for practical purposes. The world would know it tomorrow, if it survived today. He studied the dispatch that told him that a U. S. warship on the high seas had launched a missile. He watched as the red circles of jammed radar spread like a cancer across the face of the Northeast United Sates. The Joint Chiefs of Staff were at their stations. General Hal Norwood turned to him, stolid and stocky.

"I think that fix the *Canberra* got before she fired is going to be the only one you get until the weather breaks."

Charles Van Ness found himself reevaluating the general. The Old Man was as calm as if he were engaged in an exercise; the rest of them were simply trying to seem calm. Of course, it was not the Old Man who had to inform the President. He picked up the gold phone. Immediately, he was talking to his chief. The President had authorized an inquiry over the hot-line to Moscow. There was only delay there: no one was ever authorized in Moscow to say anything. Or were they deliberately stalling? Van Ness told him of the *Canberra*.

The President's voice was very quiet. "Why did she launch without authorization?"

"The authorization exists," Van Ness reminded him, "in the case of a naval ship that thinks she's being attacked. It has ever since the Tonkin Straits. Ever since the Egyptians at Salamis, to be precise."

"That's right," agreed the President. "If it thinks it's being attacked."

"Apparently she thought she was being attacked. Sir, this raid is an act of war. I think it's the first phase of Operation One-Two!"

"How many hostile aircraft are involved?"

Van Ness could not answer.

"See?" the President said. "You don't know. So how do we know it's an act of war?"

"One aircraft is an act of war, if it's heading for Washington!"

"We don't know that any are heading for Washington."

"The aircraft being tracked by the *Canberra*," Van Ness announced, "is on almost a direct course for Washington, D.C."

"All right," the President said reluctantly. "Shoot it down."

"And the rest?"

There was a pause. "Yes. Is SAC launched?"

"Yes sir."

"I have a message," said the President suddenly, "that Fidel's under house arrest and Raúl's taken over. It fits, doesn't it?"

"It sure does. What about the ICBMs?"

The President did not answer for a long while. "Start the countdown," he said finally. "We have no choice."

The Secretary replaced the phone. His tapered fingers were trembling so badly that it took him two tries to get it on the cradle.

> "Assume the perfect missile. I still say you are in a muscle-bound position. You are either off the button and at peace, or you are on the button at war."
> —GENERAL CURTIS LeMay

Chapter Fifteen

DEEP in the soil of Nebraska, Captain Morris Epstein brushed the breakfast crumbs off his console and tried to concentrate on his Statistics Text. But Dan Frost, just behind him, was punching the buttons on the VSRA system, checking out the individual missiles in their silos. Gravel Gertie's electronic voice came back, "Kilo One, no apparent malfunctions. Kilo Two, auxiliary pressure below normal, but correcting. Kilo Three—"

Morris Epstein was awaiting the end of the check when the high-pitched warble drowned out Gravel Gertie. "This is Hangdog," announced SAC Headquarters, "with a message for the Primary Alert System."

Quickly both men began to copy the code: "Tango Yoke Alfa November, Break . . . Alfa Yankee Mike Zulu."

Epstein was decoding it, racing Danny Frost to be through, when he heard Frost gasp. "Morrie?"

"Yeah?"

"Finished?"

"No," Morrie said brusquely. His deputy always beat him and it irritated him. He finished and stared at the decoded message. His mouth felt dry. He ran swiftly through the letters again. He sensed Danny Frost looking over his shoulder. He looked up. Danny was gazing at the paper, his eyes strangely alive.

"That's what I read, Morrie. Goddamn it, that's what I read!"

Morris Epstein looked at him for a moment. He was slipping into rapids from which there was no escape. Then Dan Frost had lunged back to his seat, was strapping himself in, flicking off the arming switches at the same time: "One armed, two, three . . ."

Morris Epstein stared at the plastic cover over the key-slot on his Launch Control panel. He had never lifted it. His arms were leaden as he removed the key from around his neck. Then he raised the cover. "Oh, Christ," he moaned. For the first time in his life, he was going to have to insert the key.

In the Washington Air Defense Direction Center, General Alf Karman stared fixedly at the one pulsing red arrow on the iconorama approaching Washington, D.C. There were undoubtedly other hostiles along the Eastern Seaboard. As an Air Force officer it hurt him to think that had not the U.S. Navy picked up a clear return on this one, it would not be on the screen at all. But something was better than nothing, and all thoughts of a Soviet ferry formation to Cuba were dispelled when one looked at the unerring direction that this particular hostile, after its close miss, was taking. This aircraft was going to destroy Washington.

For the fourth time in two minutes he punched the arrow's four-digit number into his console. On the scope before him he saw that its altitude was 300 feet, its ground speed 500 knots, its course zero-seven-five. It was still in a weather front. The Navy ship had lost it and now its position was intermittently doubtful as contiguous radars along the New Jersey coast picked it up and lost it in the "grass" of the storm.

Alf Karman flicked a switch on his console. He noticed that the throttle-jockey was talking, plain-language, to his intercept director, apparently reluctant to trust the automatic system now that the whistle had blown.

"I.D., this is Alfa Lima Two Four. I am at my stop point now."

"Roger, Alfa Lima Two Four, this is your intercept director. Your target is *not* a faker. Repeat *not* a faker! He is a stranger. He is now at one o'clock range three-zero heading west. Altitude unknown. Starboard. Alfa Lima Two Four, we've got contact with him. Give me your own range and bearing from Atlantic City. Lost contact with *you*. Weather."

Impatiently, Alf Karman snapped off the switch. He sat back. He knew that the President of the United States was in his concrete bomb shelter, that in the Pentagon, Joint Chiefs of Staff were in the underground War Room. His own blockhouse was not hardened, but he could not have cared less. He hoped that word was going to the troops in the Armed Forces Day parade to get somehow under cover, but he doubted it. It had all happened too quickly.

If the hostile got through, and if it was nuclear, it would not matter anyway.

General Hub Younger drove to the entrance of the Direction Center, jammed on his brakes, and shot from the little M.G. At a full gallop he headed for the door, still sockless and acutely conscious of his yellow sport shirt. As he ran, he grabbed for his wallet. Thank God he had not forgotten that!

He stopped at the sentry by the high wire fence, jammed his card under his nose. The air-policeman looked at him strangely. There was an old Air Force fable that General Curt LeMay, fired on for not stopping at an Air Force sentry box, had returned to chew out the sentry for missing him. It was one of the stories that seemed to follow LeMay. Had Hub Younger not recalled it at this moment he would simply have ignored the sentry and rushed for the door.

Instead, he waited, seething, while the guard called his sergeant. The sentry drew himself up and saluted, "He says you can go in, sir. But you got to go to the Security Office, inside. First door to your right, after the second corridor."

Hub Younger glared at the young man and sprinted for the building.

• • •

Malcolm Scott burst momentarily from clouds over the
Virginia countryside. For a moment he thought that Pilot
Officer Latham had miscalculated. Then he caught a
glimpse of the wooded area he had seen from the lightplane, went into a steep left bank, and nodded to O'Moore.
O'Moore put his hands on the controls, nodded, and took
over. Ahead, in a shaft of sunlight through the churning
cumulus, Scott saw the Fort Lee complex amid the trees.
O'Moore dove for it wildly, popped their dive brakes,
dropped their gear, and slowed the aircraft, as Malcolm
Scott put his camera to his eye. O'Moore managed to circle
it once before they were in clouds again, fumbling through
impenetrable vapor. Scott had had hardly a glimpse of the
blockhouse through the viewfinder, but it would have to do.
"Head for the Potomac," he told O'Moore.

So much for Fort Lee. He doubted, in this weather, if he
would be able to photograph the Capital, but he had another
idea, a spur-of-the-moment idea, a mad idea. "Climb, you
Irishman," he said exultantly. "Head for the sun."

He turned to Zach Chandler as the ponderous aircraft
began to gain altitude. The young man had been standing behind O'Moore's seat as they made their run on Fort Lee. He
was looking rather green.

"What do you think?" Malcolm Scott yelled exuberantly.
"What do you think now?"

"I think," Zach Chandler said, "you're going to screw
around until you get killed."

General Hub Younger raced along the brightly lighted corridor. He had ignored the sentry's order to go to the Security
Office; he had no time. And he had thought he had visited
enough direction centers to know the way to the Battle-Staff.
There was no one in the corridor. He was lost.

He turned into a cavernous room full of electronic equipment. Seventy-five feet away across bays of electronics racks,
a lone Air Force technician worked. Hub Younger dashed between the rows of whirring tapes and caught the young man
by the arm.

"Where's the Command Post?"

The young man looked up from the pollywag trace of an oscilloscope, as pained as if he were a scientist interrupted in an experiment.

"Up one flight—"

"Show me, for Christ's sake," Hub Younger blurted.

The boy stared at him blankly. "It's condition zero! I can't leave!"

Hub Younger glared at him and started up the stairs. He found himself in another deserted bay, with squat dynamo-like machines lined on either side. Green scopes stared at him. Not a soul was in sight. My God, he thought suddenly, the ICBMs! Suppose the countdown had started? In frustration he banged on the solid gray shell of a dynamo. It purred gently back. "Anybody here?" he howled down the bay. There was no answer.

After his climb to 10,000 feet, approaching Washington from Fort Lee, Malcolm Scott tightened his seat belt and shoulder straps, put away his camera. They passed down a narrow cloud canyon, gaudy with golden sunlight and purple cumulus. He warned his crew to hang on. Then he eased the nose into a gentle dive, whisking faster and faster down the heaving white gulch while its sides closed in on him. He watched the airspeed build: Mach .6, Mach .7, Mach .8 . . . They were all at once at the snow-white floor of the canyon and into a gray limbo. The controls grew rigid under his hand. The cockpit was very quiet. Suddenly O'Moore understood what he was doing. He let loose with a wild Celtic yell, slapped Scott on the back of his shoulder, and burst into laughter.

"A bit of a thump?" He turned excitedly to the rest of the crew. "He's going to break every window in town!"

There was a quiver throughout the craft as it touched the sonic barrier, and all at once, in the thick, turgid air, they had burst through the speed of sound. Eyes on his instruments, he eased forward on the yoke even further. Suddenly they broke from the low scud. The Capitol shone for an instant in the dull light, there was a glimpse of the Washington Monument, and then the city was lost beneath them.

But there was no question of it: whether they had been seen or not, they had left their mark.

The young British air attaché picked himself up. He had been sitting in the reviewing stand, gazing trancelike at too many bands, too many massed colors, too many ragtag veterans' drum-and-bugle corps. Five minutes before, he had noticed a flurry of activity in the Presidential box; for some reason word was going out to cancel the parade. Just before the blast had tipped him over in his seat, a clerk from the Embassy had squirmed through the seats and handed him a note: *Return to Embassy at once. Apparent Soviet probe at U. S.*

He had been getting up to go when a tremendous explosion staggered him. He had tangled his feet in the rickety folding chair, and taken a most undignified pratfall to the wooden platform. He was the only one who fell, but he went unnoticed in the shock.

It had been a sonic boom to end all sonic booms. The troops swinging by fell into momentary confusion. A few real veterans among them looked as if they would dive for the gutter. A bass drummer looked at his torn drumhead. The attaché was sure he heard glass shatter in a nearby office building.

He looked up swiftly, and glimpsed a great white batwing flashing between cloud bellies. His first thought was that some Air Force idiot had simply allowed his Mach meter to climb too high. He had had a momentary feeling of sympathy for the man, whoever it was. When he landed, they would simply hang him on a hook.

And yet, dusting himself off, he had second thoughts. His visual acuity was good; his retention of image was excellent. He could study the shape of the fuselage better in memory than in reality.

With the bat-shaped wing, the aircraft could easily have been a U. S. Navy Skyray. It must have been, undoubtedly, a

Skyray from the Naval Air Test Center at Patuxent River. He felt better. He put the other thought from mind. He would have known of any RAF planes on a good-will trip to the U. S.

For a moment, he thought he had seen a Vulcan bomber.

The Air Defense Command has long had a priority
requirement for an Improved Manned Interceptor.
It would have a minimum of dependence upon control from the ground.
       —AIR DEFENSE COMMAND NEWS RELEASE
          1 September 1963

Chapter Sixteen

MALCOLM SCOTT climbed through thick clouds. The Vulcan
shuddered as it went back through the portal of sound-speed.
He had made his presence felt, if only for a fraction of a
second; more effectively, too, than any number of matching
photographs side-by-side in the newspapers. Let the press experts of the Defense Department try to explain away a foreign
bomber penetrating to the capital. And on Armed Forces
Day. . . .

Now, if he could only somehow evade the angry wasps
sure by now to be following him. Now that the climax was
over, he shuddered at the crazy impulse that had sent him in.
For if the fire-control radar on the ship had tracked him successfully enough to have launched, there had been clues to his
whereabouts ever since.

He turned to Kraft. "Any chance at all?"

Kraft turned, shaking his head. "No chance of transmit-
ting, sir. I have our receiver working intermittently."

Malcolm Scott sagged in his seat. It would be luck, all
luck, from here on unless Live Oak Four or Live Oak Seven
had identified themselves. Then whatever NORAD Direction

Center—presumably Washington Air Defense Sector at Fort Lee—was directing his own pursuit, could surely put two and two together and decide that if one attacking aircraft was British so were the rest.

And yet . . . He could not really bring himself to hope that the other aircraft had had to cry for quarter.

"Fighter chatter," Kraft announced. "Channel Two."

Swiftly, Malcolm Scott shifted frequencies. Static crackled in his earphone. "Alfa Lima Two Four . . . Alfa Lima Two Four, I'm giving you to another weapons team. I'm giving you to the Senior Weapons Team. Acknowledge."

"Roger."

And then: "Alfa Lima Two Four, I have your hostile at two o'clock from you. New range Nine . . . Course northeast . . . Measuring angels two . . ."

"Angels Two" was fighter talk for 2,000 feet. Malcolm Scott glanced at his altimeter. They were climbing through 2,000 feet. And they were heading northeast.

"Captain from AE," Kraft yelled. "They're damn near locked onto us!"

"I know it," muttered Malcolm Scott. "Drop chaff."

Tinfoil strips began to pour from the bomb bay. "Launch decoys," he yelled. He felt a bump as a decoy dropped clear. Suddenly Zach Chandler was hanging over him. "Christ, Scotty, squawk *emergency* on your IFF!"

"Our IFF," Scott said gently, "is out! Any other bright ideas?"

Zach Chandler turned white. He shook his head, retired miserably to his nook behind the copilot's seat. The fighter-pilot's voice snapped into Scott's earphones. It was a very young voice, and highly excited. "Intercept director from Alfa Lima Two Four! I.D. from Alfa Lima Two Four! I'm locked on! I have him at twelve o'clock, range seven! Closing!"

The I.D.'s voice was calm and very mature. "Roger, Alfa Lima Two Four. Close in to identify visually."

Malcolm Scott's heart jumped. If he could get into sunlight, give the fighter a look at him . . . He must reach a clear area, and soon. The only answer was to climb.

"Visually?" he heard the pilot say. "It's clobbered up here!"

"Roger, Two Four," the I.D. said. "I'll try to get you permission for weapons release."

Behind him Malcolm Scott heard Kraft let out his breath. "Oh, God! He wants weapons release!"

Knowing it useless, Malcolm Scott pressed his mike switch. "Pursuing aircraft! Pursuing aircraft! Lima Alfa Two Four, from your target! Please break off! We are an RAF Vulcan! We have no IFF! We are an RAF Vulcan!"

He listened for a moment, tapped his mike, and tried again. There was no answer.

Malcolm Scott pushed the throttles, already in full-forward position, against the stop. The sea of cloud which had protected them on their way was drowning them on their way out. He bored upward toward sunlight and life somewhere above.

General Hub Younger stood before the lens of a TV camera in the corridor outside Alf Karman's combat operations center. He displayed to the lens his I.D. card and spoke to the anonymous voice which had queried him: "I'm General Younger, damn it! I have to see General Karman!"

Almost instantly, the nebulous, hidden intelligence behind the door recognized him. The door swung open, Hub Younger stood in the glassed-in balcony, trying to adjust his eyes to the dim light. He saw Alf Karman's birdlike profile silhouetted against the lighted iconorama on the opposite wall and stumbled down the line of staff officers like a late arrival in a dark movie house.

"Alf!"

Karman was intent on the screen, his body tense. Quickly he punched four buttons on his console. His head bent over the green TV tube before him, and he studied the numbers. He turned and called to a naval officer sitting three consoles to his right. "No Navy planes, Commander?"

"Not a one. Clear all the way to Quonset Point."

"Alf . . ." began Hub Younger. "Listen to me."

Karman shook as if annoyed by a mosquito. "Tactical Air Command?"

"None sir!"

"SAC?"

"No SAC planes, sir."

"FAA?"

"No commercial flights," answered a civilian.

Alf Karman took a deep breath. "Permission granted," he said into his microphone.

"Alf!"

Alf Karman looked at Hub Younger as if he had never seen him before. "For God's sake, Hub! I thought you'd go to the War Room."

"Alf, what's the situation?"

Alf Karman pointed to the iconorama. "Everything's jammed. Apparently by high-flying Soviet aircraft we can't triangulate because they're working in pairs. They're screening very low-level flights, sporadic in nature."

"Where's SAC?" Hub Younger demanded.

"SAC's cocked. Your missile countdown's started."

"Christ!"

"We've had a low-level run directly over this center, over Washington, D. C., over Boston, and over your shop—"

"What?"

Alf Karman nodded. "Smack over SAC Headquarters! At two hundred feet. In and out of clouds—nobody even saw him!"

"How are they doing it?"

"From about six inches off the ground," Alf Karman said bitterly. "In and out of weather. With more damn jamming than I've ever seen! And nobody's got a shot off yet, except one picket ship on its way back to Norfolk! But that'll be changed in about three seconds flat."

"What do you mean?" Hub Younger demanded, his heart thumping.

Alf Karman smiled grimly. "There's a young man about sixty miles north of here in the middle of a big cloud layer with an airplane strapped on his back." Alf Karman's eyes took on a distant look, as if he were riding in the plane himself. "And on the panel in front of him, he has a great big meat ball. He's locked on solid, I've just given him permission to fire."

"Wait a minute, Alf—"

Karman flicked a switch, and Hub Younger heard an excited voice: "One o'clock, Range Four. Now my *weapon's* locked on."

"You got an eyeball?"

"Negative. Range Four... Range Three... Weapon release clear?"

"Affirmative!"

"Roger... Range Two. My weapon is tracking. Range..."

Hub Younger grabbed Alf Karman's arm. "Listen, Alf! Have they dropped anything?"

"Just chaff. And a decoy."

"Well, then, what the hell's the evaluation? What do we *think* it is?"

"A diversionary attack, maybe, while they sneak a big batch of fighters into Cuba on a ferry hop. Maybe the start of the whole show. We don't know *what* it is, but it's hostile."

"I don't think it is!"

Alf Karman stared at him. "What do you mean?"

"I had a message... I had a call from London! I think it's the RAF!"

Alf Karman stared at him for a split second, grabbed the microphone. "I.D. from General Karman! Hold his weapon!"

There was a brief silence. "Sir?"

"Hold his goddamn weapon!"

"Alf Lima Two Four, this is your I.D.—"

"Roger, I.D. *Weapon released!* Breakaway, breakaway, breakaway!"

Alf Karman turned to Hub Younger, his face blank. He shook his head. Hub Younger felt the room reel around him. He moved to a chair and sat down.

"God," he breathed. "Oh my God...."

> "Full-scale nuclear war is the form of aggression we are least likely to encounter in the forseeable future."
>
> —ROBERT S. McNAMARA
> November, 1964

Chapter Seventeen

CAPTAIN MORRIS EPSTEIN sat in the shrieking vault and stared blearily at the console before him. In his hand lay the key; the plastic cover over the Launch Control panel lay open, the slot ready for it.

"Cooperative Launch Switch cover 'off,'" announced Danny Frost, a strange, excited note cutting through the electrical whine. Now both slots were ready for the keys which, if turned precisely together, would loose the ten Minutemen in their complex.

Morris Epstein licked his lips. Suppose the code was wrong? Suppose it were all some kind of high-level plot to test, to *really* test the officers in the capsules. Perhaps it was a way of separating the men from the boys.

"Morrie? I said my cover's off," urged Danny Frost.

"Insert your key," Morrie Epstein said thickly. He thought of Alice and his daughter Debbie in the little home in Omaha. In an hour or a day or a week he might emerge from his vault to find it all gone: Alice, Debbie, house, the world. He had a crazy urge to break out and join them; or drag them back here where they would be safe.

"My key is in," chanted Danny Frost. "No-shit in."

Morris Epstein fumbled with his own. He placed it in the slot, closed his eyes, and pushed. The mechanism clicked; now the key was irretrievable. If this was a drill, some kind of headquarters trick, they would know he had inserted it, perhaps court-martial him if he was wrong. He tried wildly to think if he had missed a step in authentication. He had not. The key was in, and legally so; he had had no choice.

"My key is in," he reported.

"No-shit in?" Frost checked.

"No-shit in."

"Conference call?" urged Danny Frost.

Morris Epstein came back to life. "Conference call," he croaked. Reports came in from the silos. "Kilo One, ready. Kilo Two, ready. Kilo three in the red . . ."

"Hold Kilo Three," Epstein said automatically. "Go on."

"Kilo Four ready, Kilo Five ready . . ."

He reported to Wing when all were ready for launch; despite his reluctance, their complex was as usual the first one ready. A few more like today, he thought, and he and Danny would be trading their blue scarves in for gold ones; the carrot SAC held before the donkey. Then he remembered that after today, if the countdown progressed another two minutes, there would be no scarves, blue or gold.

"Launch on your count," the Wing said. Morrie Epstein had a wide desire to check with them once more. Damn it, if the world were to go out in a cataclysmic roar because Morrie Epstein, the little fat Jewish boy from Boyle Heights, turned a key in a lock, it should go with more ceremony than the bare everyday drill-words *Launch on your count*.

"Didn't you hear him?" asked Danny Frost.

"I heard him," Morris Epstein said dully. He felt the key between his fingers. It was cold and still damp with his body sweat. "Rotate key on two, release on six."

"Roger," said Danny Frost.

In a comfortable shelter sixty feet below ground level under the White House, the President turned to his coding officer. The officer had just been on the hot-line to Moscow.

"They're checking, sir. They say they're checking again."

It was Saturday in Moscow. It could be a trick, or there might genuinely be no one quickly available. But what was the use, anyway? If the Soviet planes presaged all-out attack, the Russians would deny it. If they believed that the U. S. ICBMs were in the final stages of countdown, it would still not change their plans, because they had already accepted this risk when they sent the planes.

A few seconds before, he had felt a slight jolt. For a moment he was sure that the attacking plane had bombed. But they had told him that it was only a sonic boom; perhaps the enemy's bomb release had failed. And seconds later he had been informed that an interceptor had fired successfully, that the Washington hostile was hit and gliding blindly to a crash landing somewhere in the weather.

There were still the other strikes: one, apparently, on the Midwest and one on the Northeast. But was it enough to release ICBMs? Or would he be sending the world into conflagration for what might still be a diversionary attack? Suppose he released his ICBMs in anticipation of a threat that would never really come. Not one American had yet been hurt . . .

Angrily he thought of the beautiful Omaha plans, the "SIOPs." Each had assumed a massive ICBM attack from over the rim of the northern world; great waves of Bison bombers, too, instead of this nebulous thing. They had told him that there would be not the slightest doubt that all-out nuclear war was on. No decision to make, really: his duty would be simply to transmit the word and let the chips fall where they may.

Some of the old dogs had had doubts: "I want all the flexibility in the world so that I can do something in case I am surprised, which I am sure I will be," Curt LeMay had once said in defense of the manned bomber. Well, we still had the manned bombers; the B-52s and B-58s were streaking toward their positive control points now, and LeMay was right: they were no problem.

If they received no "go-code" they would return. They were retrievable. The missiles straining in the holes, once the awful instant arrived, were no more to be swayed from their course than the sun or the stars.

What in the hell, he thought, are we doing?

He grabbed for the golden phone.

Morrie Epstein sat strapped in his seat beneath the Nebraska sod. He licked his lips. He could not find the words. Danny Frost's voice cut through the whine of the generators. "What the hell, Morrie?"

Epstein took a deep breath. "Rotate key on two, release on six," he began again. "One, *two* . . ." he turned the key to the right, as if starting his Chevy. He heard Frost's key click simultaneously in the lock on the other console. He hesitated, looking desperately up at the line of lights on his panel, praying for a red one. They were all green, including the one which indicated that across the prairie two other men in an identical capsule had reached a similar stage in the launch procedure. It was real, it was no nightmare, the "go-code" was valid. And still he sat silent, holding the key against its tension.

"Are you counting?" demanded Frost behind him. "Christ, sound off!"

"Three," Epstein croaked. "Four, five . . ." His voice failed.

"Six?" yelled Frost. "Are you releasing?"

Morris Epstein sat frozen, holding the key against its tension. He could hear Frost cursing. Frost could not leave his console, because the keys had to be released simultaneously. A precaution, Epstein thought sardonically, against madness or overeagerness by one of the partners; no one had thought, apparently, of cowardice. So long as he clung to the key neither their complex nor their twin would be first to launch.

He heard Danny Frost swivel his chair. "Epstein, release that key!"

Epstein turned. Frost had his .38 leveled at him across three feet of space, holding it in his left hand, his right still on his key. "Release it, you fat bastard!"

"No," said Morris Epstein dully. "No, I won't."

"What the hell's the matter with you?"

"I want to check ... I want to make sure ... I just don't want to make a mistake ..."

"Mistake? You stupid son of a bitch, the only mistake you can make is to hang onto that key another three seconds!"

There was a click as Danny Frost cocked the revolver. Morris Epstein tensed, closed his eyes. Suddenly the speaker on the wall of their capsule warbled: "All stations, Primary Alert System! Do not launch! Do not launch! Hold your fire!"

He opened his eyes slowly. Danny Frost's face was a comical, terrible mixture of surprise and something Morrie Epstein would not soon forget no matter how he tried. Epstein shivered. "Put your gun down," he said mildly. "And hang onto that key!"

Danny Frost nodded dumbly. He looked at the green eager eyes on the console. "What the hell are we going to do now?"

"Now," said Morris Epstein, "very, very carefully, we are going to sit here and uncock these birds."

Chapter Eighteen

ZACH CHANDLER survived the impact of the interceptor's Falcon missile because he was crouched riding backward behind
the copilot's seat and the real force of the blow passed through
the fuselage two feet over his head. He looked at the three
men facing aft. Almost at his feet lay the young bombardier,
his face shattered. The stocky nav-plotter sat slumped in his
seat, a gaping wound in his neck spurting blood in ever-de-
creasing jets until finally as Zach struggled to his feet there
was nothing but a trickle around the jagged laceration. Kraft,
the radar officer, was crushed against the far bulkhead, eyes
on infinity.

The slipstream through the hole in the fuselage rose in
pitch from a howl to a scream. They were diving. He heard a
groan behind him. In the copilot's seat O'Moore sat lolling,
his head moving with every yaw. In his hard-hat a jagged hole
oozed matter. Zach was suddenly nauseated, but he must not
quit. Malcolm Scott sat, hand on the yoke, face pallid. Zach
lunged vaguely for the controls. He felt Scott's hand on his
wrist.

"I've got it, lad." Scott grinned. There was a trickle of

blood from the right corner of his mouth; Zach had a crazy desire to wipe it away.

"You can't land it!"

Scott's face was dead white in the sudden sunlight. "Don't be an ass. I'll get her down all right."

Zach Chandler stared at him incredulously. The lean Scottish face was drawn, the eyes were those of a man struck from behind, but he seemed to be functioning perfectly. In his lap a pool of blood was growing, growing, growing . . .

"Scotty! I'll try." He begged, "Let me move O'Moore."

"Won't have time," Scott blurted. "Look, Zach, get back . . . Get back to your nest. I'll either get her down, or I won't. Too bloody late . . . too late to change seats. Can't get him out of there anyway."

Zach looked at the altimeter. It read a thousand feet, eight hundred, six . . . Scott was right, there was no time. He glanced out the window. They were diving through clouds. This, then, was the end. The end of all the dreams of trailering with Pixie across the country when Skipper and Jennie were grown, the end of the trips to Mexico and the end of their dream of the great Northwest. This was how it would end, on some peak in western Maryland or Pennsylvania or Virginia or wherever the hell they were.

He could not accept it. He scrambled aft and surveyed the shambles. He eased the dead navigator from his seat, swung his chute into the corner behind O'Moore's seat. He tore a pair of flight jackets from an aluminum bulkhead, bundled them into pillows, pulled the hard-hat from the dead man, jammed it on his own head. Then he dropped, facing backwards, spine against the back of O'Moore's seat, bracing himself as best he could.

"Ready, lad!" he heard Scott shout. He found himself counting the seconds, and he would never know why, and he had counted to twelve, with his eyes closed and his hands gripping the fuselage frames and his shoulders jammed tightly against the back-rest, tightening his stomach muscles and waiting for the last second of his life, when there was the grinding, sliding crash and a rip of tearing metal and an interminable wail of some protesting part, as if the craft protested its dismemberment.

And then only silence. He found himself unable to move. He wondered if the shock had painlessly broken his back. Now he heard a steady drip, drip, drip, and felt rain on the top of his head. He tried to move again. He was powerless. Very faintly he could smell smoke. He looked helplessly through the jagged hole at the leaden sky.

"Hey!" he yelled at the top of his lungs. His voice sounded hoarse in his ears. "Hey! Anybody!" Now the smell was heavier, the sickening, heavy odor of a fuel fire. He heard metal expanding in the heat, and a crackle of flame. He heard a moan, too, from the pilot's seat. Scott was still alive. With a tremendous effort he lurched to his feet. Thank God, he had not broken his back. He whirled to face Scott.

The features were drawn, the skin green, the eyes half shut and glazed. He began to fumble with Scott's blood-soaked seat belt. Scott's eyes snapped open. He shook his head. "Get out of here, Zach," he said weakly. "Get out, you idiot."

Zach Chandler continued with the seat belt and felt steely fingers on his wrist. "Let go!"

Scott shook his head. "It's no use, Zach. I've bought it, can't you see? Christ, man, I'm dying! My stomach . . . Now, Zach, get out."

Zach Chandler loosed the belt, grabbed Scott's shoulders. Scott shook his head.

"No. The camera . . . Now listen! Get the film to Geoffrey Flynn, London *Express* . . . Press Building in Washington. You understand?"

There was a moment of silence, and the smell was headier, and in the distance, in the far distance, Zach Chandler could hear excited voices. Scott tore the camera from his neck, shoved it at Zach. "Take it! Zach? Deliver the films?"

"The hell with the films!"

Malcolm Scott's eyes closed and his head fell forward. Blood trickled from his chin. Zach threw off the safety belt, had him half out of the seat, when there was a muffled explosion in the rear portion of the plane. Now he could smell not only the jet fuel, but a worse smell as well; he had never experienced it, but it was burning flesh, from the rear of the flight deck. Heat seared his back. Scott's eyes were empty; he was dead. Zach found himself sobbing, struggling with the body. But he could stand the heat no longer. In a moment he was crashing through the exit hatch.

Three men in farm overalls were racing across the field as he slid down the mammoth bat-wing. He ran toward them, afraid to look back. There was an explosion behind him. He pitched forward on his face.

When he got up he turned around. The plane was an inferno. In the distance he could hear a siren. He was watching when in five minutes, there was a *chunk . . . chunk . . . chunk* above him. He looked past a clump of trees. Approaching was an Air Force helicopter. It hovered for a moment, rotors gesticulating wildly, and settled fifty yards away.

In fifteen minutes the Vulcan was in embers and the field was under guard of the Maryland State Police. Zach Chandler, shaking uncontrollably, was thrashing south to Washington.

> "I think that any people will support their govern-
> ment in not putting out information that is going to
> help the enemy. And, if necessary, misleading
> them."
>
> —ARTHUR SYLVESTER
> Dept. of Defense
> Before Senate
> Investigating
> Subcommittee on
> TFX.

Chapter Nineteen

ZACH CHANDLER stood in the War Room in the basement of
the Pentagon. He was having another fit of shivers; he had
been having them for an hour, off and on, in full view of Hub
Younger, General Hal Norwood, a NORAD general he had
never seen, and the Secretary of Defense himself.

The Secretary of Defense, necktie loose, coat off, was sitting at the gold phone talking to the President.

"It's all wrapped up, sir. It was definitely an RAF raid.
Mission was photographic, to prove they'd penetrated. The
other eight are apparently over international waters now, refueling south of Newfoundland. The Air Ministry's said they
will disavow it completely. I told them *we* were going to release it to the press, and *they* could explain why they lost five
officers on an unauthorized flight. So they ended up asking us
to keep the lid on. This never really had their blessing, anyway. Frankly, I think when those planes get home, they'll find
more RAF policemen around than they ever saw."

The Secretary paused as the President spoke. "We *have* to
hush it up," he said once, and finally: "I think we can, sir. I
know we can. And I want to try."

He replaced the phone. He faced his officers. "I can't say, gentlemen, that this has been the best Armed Forces Day we've ever had." He waited for a laugh. None came. His eyes grew hard. "But I think we can depend on the British not to publicize this. All right. Are we clear on what happened? General Karman?"

General Karman nodded. General Younger and General Norwood simply stared at them. The Secretary went on. "One: For our own military consumption, the Stewart Air Force Base 'Friendly Enemy' squadron penetrated our defenses with more success than usual. They made a run on an ICBM site near Omaha, and SAC Headquarters, Omaha. They succeeded in a simultaneous run on an ICBM base near Bangor, Maine, and the city of Boston."

He waited for assent. When one was forthcoming, he said firmly, "We are entitled to spread a smoke-screen when the defenses of the country are in question. Two: a Navy F-4D Sky Ray, with the bat-wing configuration we all know so well, on a routine test flight from Naval Air Test Center, Patuxent River, inadvertently exceeded the speed of sound over Washington, D.C., in a dive, causing a sonic boom. There was no life or property endangered, but flying personnel at NATC are being cautioned to avoid the area, which is a restricted one."

The military men regarded him impassively. The Secretary took a deep breath. "Three: a Vulcan of the RAF Bomber Command, on a goodwill Armed Forces Day mission with a U. S. Air Force officer as passenger, en route from Tarrington Aerodrome in Northern England to Andrews Air Force Base near Washington, became lost, crashed, and burned in bad weather in eastern Maryland. There was one survivor, Major Chandler, the U. S. Air Force officer. Names of the British personnel are being withheld pending notification of next of kin."

The generals neither agreed nor dissented. The Secretary looked at General Norwood. "Does this sound reasonable to you?"

The general smiled. "It sounds about normal, sir."

"What do you mean by that?"

"I have no comment," the general said. "I'm still on active duty. I'm under civilian control. But . . ."

"But what?"

"Nine RAF Vulcans, not the fastest bombers in the world, penetrated our defenses. *One* was shot down. Partly by poor luck, because he got too close to a Navy ship. Has it taught you anything?"

The Secretary glared at him for a moment, turned to General Karman. "General?"

"I'm not a Public Information Officer, sir. I don't know."

"So you'll go along?"

"Of course I'll go along."

The Secretary of Defense nodded, turned to Hub Younger. "General?"

Hub Younger looked at him for a long moment. "Scott was one of my best friends. They *did* penetrate. I'd like to think he taught us something."

"He did," the Secretary said slowly. "He did, Hub. But don't you think this administration is as capable of using what we learned as the opposition?"

"I imagine."

"Then let *us* take a shot at it."

Hub Younger took a deep breath. "I think control of news is a blind road, Mr. Secretary. Some day we'll lose our credibility."

"The Government has an inherent right to lie to protect itself," the Secretary said.

Hub Younger looked into the Secretary's eyes for a long moment. Then he sighed. "I'll go along."

The Secretary smiled at Zach Chandler. "You've had a long day, Major."

Zach nodded. He had stopped shivering, but he was empty inside, squeezed of feeling. What he wanted most of all was to climb on a SAC aircraft with Hub Younger and head for home and Pixie. "Yes sir."

"Be very careful," the Secretary said, "not to discuss this except in the terms I've outlined. With anyone. Including your wife, if you're married."

Zach Chandler nodded. He and General Younger left the War Room and traveled the long basement corridor together.

"I'm leaving from Andrews in an hour," Hub Younger said. He looked sick. "Do you want to drive there with me?"

"I'll get there, sir," Zach said. "I'd better pick up a uniform hat in the arcade and clean up a little. If it's all right."

"I'll see you at the plane," Hub Younger said. Zach watched him walk down the passageway under the steam pipes. He was heading for the ramp to the area reserved for the Joint Chiefs of Staff. He watched him for a long way. The general seemed older, not quite so trim, almost shabby.

Zach Chandler moved into the brightly lighted arcade, past the gift stores and ticket agencies and flower shops. The people were better dressed even than those in London, he noticed suddenly. The girls were prettier, the men healthier. But somehow they seemed all stamped from the same mold.

He paused outside the phone booth, thinking of calling Pixie. But when he stepped inside, he discovered that he was leafing through the Washington phone book. Finally he dialed a number. A British voice answered.

"Mr. Geoffrey Flynn, of the London *Express*?" asked Zach.

"Here."

Zach Chandler took a deep breath He saw sleek interceptors drawing pencil-straight contrails against a sapphire sky; he remembered the comradeship of the Ready Room, the fresh-scrubbed look of an Air Force base, the solid little bank account that grew month by month until one day, with retirement, it would buy him ease. Then he thought of a cheap flat by a college campus with Pixie frowning over the bills. He wondered what one did when a sick child needed care and Uncle Sam was not around to help.

He took a deep breath. "I have a roll of film here for you," he said quietly. "A roll of film and a story."

Bestselling Thrillers —
action-packed for a great read